Truth or Date

PORTIA MACINTOSH

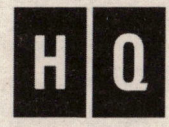

ONE PLACE. MANY STORIES

This novel is entirely a work of fiction. The names, characters and incidents portrayed in it are the work of the author's imagination. Any resemblance to actual persons, living or dead, events or localities is entirely coincidental.

HQ
An imprint of HarperCollins*Publishers* Ltd
1 London Bridge Street
London SE1 9GF

www.harpercollins.co.uk

HarperCollins*Publishers*
Macken House, 39/40 Mayor Street Upper,
Dublin 1 D01 C9W8

This paperback edition 2025

1

First published in Great Britain by
HQ, an imprint of HarperCollins*Publishers* Ltd 2016

Copyright © Portia MacIntosh 2016

Portia MacIntosh asserts the moral right to be
identified as the author of this work.
A catalogue record for this book is
available from the British Library.

ISBN: 9780008757601

This book contains FSC™ certified paper and other controlled
sources to ensure responsible forest management.

For more information visit: www.harpercollins.co.uk/green

Printed and bound in the UK using 100%
Renewable Electricity at CPI Group (UK) Ltd

All rights reserved. No part of this publication may be reproduced,
stored in a retrieval system, or transmitted, in any form or by any means,
electronic, mechanical, photocopying, recording or otherwise,
without the prior permission of the publishers.

Without limiting the author's and publisher's exclusive rights, any unauthorised use of this publication to train generative artificial intelligence (AI) technologies is expressly prohibited. HarperCollins also exercise their rights under Article 4(3) of the Digital Single Market Directive 2019/790 and expressly reserve this publication from the text and data mining exception.

PORTIA MACINTOSH is the bestselling author of over 30 romantic comedy novels. From disastrous dates to destination weddings, Portia's romcoms are the perfect way to escape from day-to-day life, visiting sunny beaches in the summer and snowy villages at Christmas time. Whether it's southern Italy or the Yorkshire coast, Portia's stories are the holiday you're craving, conveniently packed in between the pages.

Formerly a journalist, Portia has left the city, swapping the music biz for the moors, to live the (not so) quiet life with her husband and her dog in Yorkshire.

Find out more at portiamacintosh.com and follow her on Instagram: @portiamacintoshauthor

Also by Portia MacIntosh:

Between a Rockstar and a Hard Place
How Not to be Starstruck
*Always the Bridesmaid**
Drive Me Crazy

* Previously published as *Bad Bridesmaid*

Praise for Portia MacIntosh:

'Smart, funny and always brilliantly entertaining, every book from Portia becomes my new favourite romcom.'
Shari Low

'I laughed, I cried – I loved it.'
Holly Martin

'The queen of romcom!'
Rebecca Raisin

'This book made me laugh and kept me turning the pages.'
Mandy Baggot

'A fun, fabulous 5-star romcom!'
Sandy Barker

'Loved the book, it's everything you expect from the force that is Portia! A must read'
Rachel Dove

'Fun and witty. Pure escapism!'
Laura Carter

'A heartwarming, fun story, perfect for several hours of pure escapism.'
Jessica Redland

For Joe,
fist-bump

Chapter 1

'You look good in red,' Nick tells me, stifling a laugh.

Were I not so happy to have just tied the knot with the love of my life, I would've climbed the nearest palm tree, removed the biggest coconut I could find and thrown it at my darling hubby because, as much as I love him, I hate it when he's right. Last week as we shopped for the few last bits for our honeymoon, I dragged Nick into Hollister where I saw this beautiful cream sundress. I knew that it would be perfect for our trip to Hawaii, but Nick didn't seem convinced. He just doesn't buy into fashion; he's one of those guys who just doesn't get it, whereas I'm the kind of girl who would swap a kidney for an Hermès bag. It wasn't so much the price Nick took issue with (although he did say it was a lot of money for very little material), what he worried about most was the fact the dress was cream.

'You'll spill,' he told me as I admired it on its hanger.

'Fuck off,' I replied.

'You will,' he insisted. 'You're the messiest girl in the world.'

Of course, this just made me want the dress all the more, so I bought it and here we are, the first day of our honeymoon and I've spilled my Lava Flow cocktail all the way down the front. Just like Nick said I would.

Nick retrieves the chunk of pineapple that garnished my drink from my cleavage and pops it in his mouth.

'I told you you'd spill on it.' He chuckles. 'It's a miracle you didn't spill on your wedding dress.'

'That's because I *couldn't* eat in it,' I admit, although it wasn't because I didn't want to. 'If I so much as inhaled too deeply, it felt like it might burst open – and flashing my boobs on my wedding day is just the kind of *Carry On* moment you expect of me. None of the glossy wedding mags prepare you for the fact that your wedding dress will be the most uncomfortable thing you'll ever wear.'

'Yeah, they don't warn you that the first thing your new bride will do when she gets to the honeymoon suite will be hurry off her dress before pillaging the minibar either.'

I scoop some of the cocktail slush from my chest and flick it at Nick's bare stomach. He just laughs, lying back on the sand to catch some rays.

'Throw it in the sea,' he suggests. 'Back to its natural habitat. I'll bet it has missed the sound of the waves in the shop – so stupid.'

'Leave Hollister out of this,' I snap, jokily.

I peel off my dress, lie down on the sand next to Nick and rest my head gently on his bicep.

'I'll tan weird if you cuddle me.' He laughs, the sweltering heat from the Hawaiian sun beaming down on us.

'You'll get over it,' I reply.

Lying here with the man of my dreams, with nothing but the peaceful sound of the ocean filling my ears and the delicious smell of strawberries filling my nostrils, I sigh and smile to myself. I am so disgustingly happy.

Unable to resist him a second longer, I climb on top of Nick, leaning forwards to kiss him passionately. He places his hands on my hips before running them slowly up my body. I part our lips, but only so I can moan softly at his touch.

'I love you, Nick,' I tell him.

'I love you too, Ruby,' he replies. 'Ruby … Ruby … Ruby …'

Nick's voice grows louder, louder still and then more aggressive. It sounds like he's pissed off, come to think of it.

'Ruby,' he shouts. 'Wake up.'

I jolt awake suddenly, sitting upright.

'What the hell?' he asks, angrily.

I glance around for a second, taking in my surroundings … I'm not in Hawaii at all, I'm in my living room. I'm not wearing a bikini, I'm in my underwear. I'm not lying on a beach, I'm on top of Ben, a guy I've been seeing for a couple of weeks. Oh, and Nick isn't my husband, he's my flatmate. My boring, stuck-up, joyless flatmate that I can't stand. And I was just having a sex dream about him – eww! I feel my cheeks flush with shame – not because he's caught me semi-naked with a bloke, but because I was dreaming about *him*. That I was in love with him, that I'd married him … *I was about to have sex with him!*

'What time is it?' I ask him, rubbing my tired eyes, only to cover my hands in black eye make-up.

'It's 7 a.m.,' he tells me, his eyes shooting laser beams of judgement at me as he glares. Luckily for me I'm used to Nick looking down his nose at me, and anyway, the sheer volume of body glitter I'm wearing can easily deflect even the strongest laser.

'What day is it?' I ask.

Nick shakes his head and sighs. 'Friday. It's Friday, Ruby.'

'Oh fuck, I'm at work in an hour,' I reply as I massage my temples, my hangover from last night now in full force.

As Nick stands over me, eating a bowl of Weetabix like he does every morning after he gets back from the gym, about to head out to his proper serious job, I can feel him judging me. It's not my fault he doesn't know how to have fun, is it?

'So this is your online dating weirdo. How are things going?' he asks, nodding towards the heavily tattooed, muscular man that I'm using as a bed. I take a moment too long to answer. 'That badly?'

'All good,' I reply, unconvincingly. I've been dating Ben for about three weeks now, and things aren't exactly going that well. Last night was our third date, and despite every girly magazine I could get my hands on assuring me that date three was when the magic happened, the magic did not happen last night. Still, from the way Nick is looking at me right now, I doubt he believes that. In Nick's head I'm his chaotic flatmate who seemingly ploughs through internet dates, when in reality that's not the case – I wish I were getting even one per cent of the action Nick thought I was.

Nick fakes a gasp.

'Are you telling me that you hooked up with a guy you met via your phone and it's not a fairy-tale romance?' he asks sarcastically.

I cast my mind back to our date last night. As much as I don't want to give Nick the satisfaction of being right, the need to tell someone feels greater.

'Things have been going well, it's just … I met up with him yesterday and he told me he was taking me to a family party,' I start.

'Weird,' Nick chimes in. 'You've only been on a couple of dates with him, kid.'

'I know, and weirder still: what he didn't tell me was that it was a wake.'

'A wake?' Nick echoes loudly in disbelief, and in a much higher pitch than his voice usually is.

'I'm awake, I'm awake,' Ben says, panicked as he jumps to his feet. He does so without having realised I was on top of him, causing me to fall back onto the sofa. As he glances between an angry-looking Nick, and me in my underwear, he puts two and two together – coming up with wrong answer.

'Look, calm down, nothing happened, OK? I didn't sleep with your girlfriend,' Ben babbles, stressing it in such a way that makes it sound like this is an excuse he has to make often.

'Oh, charming,' I say, annoyed that Ben thinks I'm the kind of girl who would have a boyfriend and still date around, but he isn't listening.

'She's not my girlfriend, she's my roommate,' Nick corrects him. I watch as Ben expresses visible relief.

'Well, in that case, good to meet you. I'm Jonathan,' he chirps, offering Nick a hand to shake. Nick doesn't oblige.

'Your name is Jonathan? I've spent three dates calling you Ben,' I blurt out.

'Yeah, I thought that was like a cute nickname or something,' he says and laughs.

I giggle, puzzled, but what I see as a hilarious story for social media, Nick is completely unimpressed by.

'I just don't get you, Ruby Wood,' Nick says angrily, pointlessly using my full name like a pissed-off parent. 'What are you doing with your life?'

'What are you, my fucking dad? Why can't you just be cool?' I ask him, sounding like a teenager whose dad just confiscated her cigarettes – incidentally, something Nick has done with me before. In the end it was just easier to quit smoking than it was to put up with his complaints and his borderline OCD smell-removal techniques.

'I've got to get to work,' Nick tells us. He heads to the kitchen, rinses his bowl and spoon, places them in the dishwasher and then leaves without so much as a 'see you later'.

Jonathan – not Ben – and I are sitting on the sofa next to each other awkwardly.

'So your roommate seems fun,' Jonathan says sarcastically.

'He really is like my dad or my granddad or something,' I reply, irritated, still sounding like a teenager.

'You should move out,' he tells me, like maybe that hadn't crossed my mind.

'There's no way I can find a flat this central for this cheap,' I tell him honestly. 'Nick comes from a super-rich family, but he won't take any money from them, so he reckons he can't afford to move either. If either of us should move out, it should be him, don't you think?'

'Yeah, maybe,' Jonathan replies, followed by an awkward silence.

I wonder how I managed to call him by the wrong name for so long. I suppose that's app dating for you – it's like fishing with multiple lines. I guess as I reeled this one in, I mixed up his name with a different fish.

'Listen, Ruby, we've had fun right?'

I think for moment. No. No we haven't. On our first date he suggested we go to the cinema – a rookie error, because it involves sitting in silence for two hours – and on the second we went to a bar and got drunk. Oh, and then the wake date. Jonathan is a good-looking dude, but he's a bit weird. There's something almost tortured about his personality, like he's got some issues he needs to work through. Don't we all, though? Still, he does have his good qualities too, so I'm happy to see where this goes. I'm not going to ditch the guy just because he took me to a family funeral without telling me.

'We have,' I lie with a warm smile.

'Well, I think we should call it a day,' he tells me.

I feel my smile drop. 'What?'

'I just … I think we're moving in different directions.'

'Oh my God, seriously? Are you really giving me the old lines? Is it not me, is it you?'

Jonathan grabs my hand.

'It *is* me,' he assures me, giving my hand a reassuring squeeze.

'You're damn fucking right it's you,' I reply.

Jonathan drops my hand and jumps to his feet, wrestling his clothes on as he talks, his tone suddenly becoming significantly less friendly.

'OK, cards on the table, when we got back last night I thought I might get lucky, but you didn't even want to sleep with me,' he explains.

'Dude, we'd just got back from *your dad's wake* – that you didn't even tell me we were going to.'

Oh, did I not mention that it was his dad's funeral? I suppose I didn't want to give Nick too much ammunition for when he teases me about this every day until one of us moves out.

'Yeah, well don't you think I needed some comfort after that?'

'So I'm supposed to bang you out of sheer sympathy?'

'Well, it would've been nice,' he replies, like it's a fairly reasonable expectation.

'You're disgusting. Get out,' I demand.

Jonathan puts on his shoes and heads for the door, slamming it behind him.

Lying back on the sofa, I massage my temples for a moment. My head is banging, and I've got to be at work in an hour. Is getting dumped a good enough reason to call in sick?

'Awkward,' I say to myself. 'So, so awkward.' Not only what just happened with Jonathan, but my dream about Nick too. Not only do Nick and I not get on, but we're like enemies, both driving the other crazy, but neither of us is in a position to move out. The fact we're stuck with one another only makes us hate each other even more.

I glance around the floor for my outfit from last night, only to find that Nick has folded my dress and placed it neatly over the back of the sofa. I grab it, shaking my head at his anal neatness as I meaningfully and defiantly unfold it. All communal areas of the house must be neat and tidy to a military standard. Sir, yes, sir.

Tossing my clothes through my bedroom doorway, I head straight for the shower. I know that I'm running late, but after an uncomfortable night on the sofa cuddled up to a sweaty, emotional wreck of a man, there's no way I can go to work without washing some of yesterday's failed date off of me. I'm literally going to wash Jonathan out of my hair – well, his sweat and tears at least.

I turn on the shower, cranking up the hot water to make the bathroom nice and steamy while I brush my teeth. I've got that fuzzy-mouth feeling you're left with after too many sugary alcoholic drinks. Typically, I'm out of toothpaste, but that's what flatmates are for, right? Borrowing things from.

I can see from Nick's toothpaste tube that he's used approximately 1/8 so far, with the used 1/8 neatly folded over a few times, thus giving the appearance of a perfectly full, slightly smaller tool. Does he really have that much spare time on his hands? Really? In another act of defiance, I not only use his toothpaste, but I squeeze from the middle of the tube, leaving behind a big, fingertip-shaped dent in it.

Finally stepping into the hot shower feels glorious. I can feel my bad date washing off me. Sure, I'm annoyed at how he behaved, but mostly I'm just annoyed to have another bad date on my romantic CV. Hardly seems worth putting Jonathan down, for a mere three weeks, but they always say it's better to put jobs down that you didn't have for long/got fired from, rather than have big, unaccounted-for gaps in your employment, right?

I grab my delicious-smelling piña-colada-scented shower gel and rub it all over my body. I love the smell of it because it reminds me of my two favourite things: cocktails and the beach. Which reminds me, I'm not only washing away Jonathan, I need to scrub myself clean of that sex dream about Nick. Nick Hall! I can't believe it.

I think to myself as I shampoo my hair. I'll admit that the first time I met Nick here in this flat, the first thing I noticed about him was how sexy he was. A sexy doctor, no less – that's like every girl's fantasy. Sharing this small space didn't suit us though, and it's amazing how quickly you can go off a person when they start to grate on you. One thing I can definitely put on my CV is that I'm not shallow, because not even Nick's chiselled good looks, bulging biceps or romance-novel-worthy profession can sway how I feel about him.

So why the hell did I dream that about him today? It can't mean anything, can it? All that stuff about dreams meaning things has got to be a load of bollocks.

I shut off the water, and shut my dream about Nick out of

my mind.

Once in the messy confines of my bedroom – where I am free to express my unorthodox organisational skills as I see fit – I grab a dress from the large pile of clothing on my bedroom floor – the division of my floordrobe, which I have dubbed Mount Clothesmore – and search for my make-up bag because today my face is going to need everything it has to offer. If I don't get a move on, I'm going to be late for work, but it's better to be late than ugly, right?

Chapter 2

'So he took you to a wake and then dumped you? Fuck me, that's as rough as you look.' Millsy laughs as I meaningfully drain the takeaway coffee cup I filled with a double shot vanilla latte the second I arrived at work – fifteen minutes late, which isn't too bad considering.

'You don't look so hot yourself,' I reply.

'Erm, yeah I do,' he says, and he means it.

Millsy leans over and looks at himself in the reflection of the shiny silver coffee machine. He checks his eyes for dark circles before securing the topknot they make him pull his dark brown hair into for work. He makes a noise of approval – the kind that most men would usually reserve for a topless calendar or a bird they fancied. Millsy mostly just fancies Millsy.

Joe 'Millsy' Mills has been my best friend my whole life – my entire twenty-seven years on this planet. Our parents lived next door to one another, and because he's only three months older than me, we started playing together almost immediately and that was it, we became inseparable. We went to playgroup together, then school, and even now we're supposedly grown-ups, we're still best friends, still playing together – except our games have changed a little as we've become older.

I credit/blame Millsy for the way I've turned out. Despite my girly-girl appearance (because who doesn't love that girly shit? Even Millsy loves a face mask and a regular brow appointment) I'm a total tomboy on the inside. I grew up doing whatever Millsy wanted to do for fun because, as he always reminds me, he is the eldest, and so video games, football and then eventually 'lads' nights out have become my hobbies. It's funny because, to look at me, you'd think I was your typical *Sex and the City*–loving, spa-visiting, wine-drinking lady, rather than this messy, unscrupulous, coffee-addicted, sailor-mouthed hot mess you see before you.

'What's wrong with me?' I ask him.

'There's nothing wrong with you.' Millsy pauses, thinking for a second. 'Well, no, there are lots of things wrong with you, but none that dick would've thought of when he ditched you. It's because you didn't shag him, simple enough. For some lads, that's a good enough reason to give up.'

I can always count on my bestie for brutal honesty.

Sadly, all of the men playing the dating game at the moment seem to be similar in their attitude. One thing I've noticed is that I'm always willing to give men the benefit of the doubt about things. So what if they've got a bit of grey hair and they're only twenty-six? So what if they're not particularly stylish? So what if they could do with using a stronger deodorant? I give people a shot. Men, I am noticing, are not often like this. You can be too fat for them. You can be too frigid for them. You can text them too much. They don't need much of a reason to ditch you and move on to the next girl.

'What are your relationship goals?' he asks me jokily, posing like the sassy-girl emoji.

'My relationship goals are: to have one. I'm sick of being single,' I tell him.

'So are all single girls, so you're not alone,' Millsy tells me, as though it's going to be of comfort to me.

'I am literally alone, that's the point,' I joke.

'Man up. Plenty more fish in the sea.'

'Which is why I've done something stupid,' I start slowly.

'Oh God, go on.'

'I've agreed to go on a date tonight.'

Millsy laughs.

That's the thing with dating apps, you meet all these seemingly lovely dudes and then you kick yourself when you date the wrong ones. You'll be talking to a few people, and then you'll have to pick just one to date and you can just guarantee I'll pick the wrong one. I wind up with guys like Jonathan, who will leave me feeling annoyed I wasted so much time shaving my legs for dates that never worked out. It's not like the men I meet in real life are much better; my last real-world boyfriend cheated on me, so it's obviously just my taste that is the problem.

Even in my dreams, I'm sleeping with the wrong people. I still can't get over that I was dreaming about Nick. I know I'm going on about it, but it's so weird. To dream about Millsy would be weird, because he's like a brother to me, but Nick is like my sworn enemy and that's much worse. Like, Batman and Robin getting it on would be weird, but Batman and The Joker shagging is just plain ridiculous because they hate each other so much. I consider telling Millsy about the dream, but he'll probably freak out more than I did about it.

Maybe it was stupid of me to make a date for this evening as I was walking to work, but I can't think of a better way to get Jonathan and Nick out of my head. And no matter how bad things go with one guy, I'm always full of hope that the next one will be the one for me.

Millsy glances towards the door. 'Ruby would/Ruby wouldn't?' he asks.

'Ruby wouldn't,' I tell him with certainty. He's talking about the rocker-looking dude who just left the coffee shop. What it is, we play this game called Ruby would/Ruby wouldn't – an obvious pun on my name: Ruby Wood. Whenever a man walks past us,

Millsy poses the question and I reply with one or the other. It's daft, but it keeps us amused during long shifts. Obviously Ruby has no intention of sleeping with any of these people – it's rare I meet a bloke I don't want to punch within minutes of meeting him (which is why I'm so annoyed things have fallen flat with Jonathan, but I'm trying not to go on about it).

I think one of the best and worst things about growing up with a bloke for a best mate is that it has made me wise. I know all the moves men make to try and get girls into bed ('oh, but I love you/I've never met anyone like you/my dad just died' et cetera), and as such I don't credit men with an ounce of sincerity when they try to chat me up. There's no equivalent game where I ask Millsy who he fancies, because Millsy can't let a pretty girl walk past him without essentially announcing that he 'would' anyway – usually loud enough for them to hear. It makes me laugh because he says it, but he rarely pursues the girls he announces it to, so even though he 'would', he often isn't going to.

'Well, I was out last night, and I don't look half as bad as you, Rubes,' Millsy brags. 'And I was on time for work.'

'For once,' I reply.

Sally, our manager here at Has Beans coffee shop, is pretty laid-back, especially now that she's pregnant. She's going on maternity leave any day, so we're maybe pushing our luck a little more than usual in the hope she won't care.

I like working here. Well, no one likes working anywhere, do they? But there are worse gigs to have. I mean, it's pretty easy work, I get to spend my days messing around with my best friend and I'm allowed as much free coffee as my nervous system can handle, but it's more than that. I just like the vibe in coffee shops. You've got places like Starbucks with their contemporary artwork and their jazz music playing in the background, or Costa with their comfortable seating and family-friendly environment.

Has Beans is by no means as huge as either company, but of all the branches in Yorkshire, the one I work at in central Leeds is the busiest. During the week, lunchtime is dominated by office workers and shop employees looking for a caffeine fix and something to eat to break up their day and spur them on until the evening, but by the afternoon the place is more peaceful, with writers and students all face-down in their laptops. The thing I love is how the vibe can change depending on the customers. When it's quiet, it's quite relaxing. I can sip my latte and listen to the latest James Bay album playing on the stereo – my hangover likes this. Similarly, when we've got a gaggle of mums with screaming babies in, I often consider trying to tie my own tubes with the tongs we use with the panini press.

'So when is your audition?'

'Monday morning,' he replies, his usual confidence waning slightly.

'So I guess you'll be taking it easy the next few nights then?'

'Mate, I won't be out at all – anyway, don't you have a date?'

'But it's Friday night,' I protest. Going out is what Friday nights were made for.

Millsy, like me, is a bit of a pleasure seeker and as such, I don't think I've ever seen him take anything seriously other than trying to get away with being drunk every waking moment of his life – until recently.

At school, our grades weren't up to much, but we were outgoing, cheeky, confident and – most importantly – excellent at lying. Naturally we gravitated towards the arts, and soon found that acting might just be one thing that we were good at. The thing is, it's not a realistic career goal, is it? Which is why I gave up trying to 'make it', but recently Millsy seems to think he's got a real shot.

If I'm being honest, I think he's wasting his time – I mean, if he were on track to be Leonardo DiCaprio-famous I would happily be his Kate Winslet. Let's face it though, hardly anyone makes it in the acting business. And he's not going up for a role in the new *Star Wars* flick, it's a local production of *Macbeth*. I forget which part he's auditioning for, but it's all very weird and last-minute. The guy they had for it originally got hit by a bus on the way to the first rehearsal. He wasn't life-threateningly injured or anything, but he wound up in hospital. His understudy went to visit him and fell down a manhole in the hospital car park – you couldn't make this shit up. So, sucks for those guys but great news for Millsy. Sucks for me too, because it's going to cut into our drinking time.

'So, which *Macbeth* character are you auditioning for?' I ask, not really all that interested, but willing to pretend I am for my mate.

Millsy throws a chunk of his brownie at me with frustration, which I realise quickly enough to attempt to catch it in my mouth, but not so quick I actually succeed. Man, I want a brownie now.

'You're not supposed to say the title, it's "The Scottish Play" in theatre circles,' he reminds me. 'You know that.'

'Ooh, sorry,' I say sarcastically. 'So, go on, then I can stop pretending I give a shit. Who are you auditioning for?'

'Banquo.'

'Cool,' I reply, holding the word on for longer than seems even a little sincere. We were in an end-of-year production of *Macbeth* when we were at school, and I wasn't mad about it then either. I liked it when we did *Bugsy Malone* and *Grease*, when I got to dress up in pretty clothes and sing – Shakespeare didn't write nearly enough musical numbers.

Sally shuffles out from her office and hovers around the counter.

'I can't sit at that desk a second longer; the baby wants me to move. There's just so much admin to do though.'

I am in the process of simultaneously toasting a panini and making an Americano for a customer, but I'm pretty sure she's angling for Millsy to take over and give her a break.

'Yeah, well, it'll be out of you soon,' Millsy replies, oblivious to her hint. 'Why don't you come for a post-night-out vindaloo with us or bounce on one of those big balls – that brings 'em out, right?'

'Is your topknot too tight or are you stupid?' I ask him. 'You can't just "bring them out" when you feel like it. Remember that time we got in from Saturn at 4 a.m. and you were so hungry you took your burger out of the microwave when it still had half the time left? You spent the whole day at work throwing up.'

Millsy rubs his chin thoughtfully.

'I remember having to call the plumber,' Sally adds, a distant look in her eye, like a solider recalling a horrific war memory. 'Pass me a lemon muffin, please. I'll get back to work.'

Millsy laughs to himself as he obliges. 'Wasn't that also the night you pulled a teenager?' he asks me.

'You mean the night I kissed a student. And he was twenty – hardly makes me a cougar, does it?'

'Yeah, but that dodgy beard made him look fifteen.'

'He was in a nightclub, Millsy, so he had to be at least eighteen.'

'You were in nightclubs when you were fifteen.'

He's got me there.

'Dude, you've got to stop going on about this.'

'But it's funny,' he insists.

'Well, I think the real reason you blocked the work toilet is funny, but I don't tell people, do I?'

Millsy laughs, but his cheeks flush a little. 'OK, we take these stories to our graves, deal?'

'Deal.'

We bump fists, like we always do. It can be to seal a deal like today, to celebrate some sort of victory or even just to say hello.

Millsy begins the much-hated task of cleaning the panini press while I rearrange the pastries and cakes to make them look neater – an excuse, of course, to stealthily eat a brownie, because if it's stealthy, it's healthy. Everyone knows the calories don't count if no one sees you eat it. Seizing my opportunity, I stuff a rather large chunk into my mouth just as a customer approaches the counter.

'Ruby would/Ruby wouldn't?' Millsy asks under his breath as

the man crosses the shop.

'Oh shit,' I whisper back. 'Ruby nearly did!'

I watch Millsy's face light up, like he might be about to witness something hilariously awkward. Little does he know, this is a fella I've told him about that I met via a dating app recently, and our final date was a nightmare.

'Ruby,' he says as he approaches the desk.

'Michael,' I reply. 'Hello. What can I get you?'

I see a glimmer of recognition on Millsy's face. He's heard of Michael.

His amusement quickly turns to anger.

'Medium cappuccino and a slice of coffee cake, please.'

'You want to be careful with all that caffeine,' Millsy warns him. 'You won't be able to sleep at night.'

Michael laughs and turns his attention back to me.

'So, you said you worked here, I thought I'd check it out. And here you are.'

'Yep, here I am …' … at my place of work, you creepy weirdo.

Michael seemed like the most charming man in the world, but after a whirlwind amazing three dates, at the end of the third date he ended up coming back to mine. As we started kissing and fell back onto the sofa, it quickly became apparent that Michael wasn't very good at this stuff, but worse than that, he went from nought to *Fifty Shades* before he'd even got my clothes off me. The second I felt him giving me a love bite on my chest I did what any mature young woman would do: I smashed a vase by kicking it off the coffee table.

Nick came running in and went mad – like I knew he would – so I told Michael it was probably best if he left. I mean, if that was his foreplay, the main event would've left me unable to sit. Once he was gone, I looked at myself in the mirror and I was covered in scratches and love bites. I looked like I'd been in an accident. And, you know, each to their own and all that, I get it, people are kinkier now, but you don't just go for it during your first time, and you don't do anything that leaves a mark without permission. Probably – this has never happened before. Needless to say, I didn't want to go on another date with him so I slowly stopped replying to his messages. I guess that's why he's turned up at my work a few months later.

'Are you doing anything tonight?' he asks.

'Erm, yeah, I'm going out for dinner,' I tell him honestly. I don't mention that I have a date with another guy I met through the very same dating app.

'Time for a quick drink after you finish here though, surely?' he persists.

'I don't, sorry, I need to go home and make some adjustments to my new dress. Do you ever just look at a dress and think: that would look great, if only it were shorter?'

Michael immediately says no while Millsy says yes.

Millsy stops him before he can say anything else. 'Take a seat, pal. I'll bring your drink over.'

Michael thankfully senses that he's not getting anywhere and goes to sit down.

'That the prick who covered you in hickies?' Millsy asks.

'It is indeed – wouldn't think it to look at him, would you?'

'Want me to do something disgusting to his cake – I think the loo is free,' he suggests, completely straight-faced.

I laugh and kiss my friend on the cheek. I assume he's joking. 'It's fine. Looks like he's got the message.'

I glance over at Michael, who is glumly looking at his phone. I can tell from his frantic hand actions that he's doing the instantly recognisable left and right swiping people do on dating apps. Because that's what you do, you swipe one away and move on to the next one.

'Aww, doesn't he look miserable,' I say sarcastically.

'Yeah,' Millsy replies, rummaging around in his nose before plating up Michael's cake. 'Sucks to be him.'

Chapter 3

Getting ready for a first date requires as much mental preparation as it does physical prep work. Sure, it's important to look and feel your best, and for that you've got to wash, shave, wax, pluck, dry and moisturise every last inch of your body before caking yourself in make-up, dousing yourself in perfume and slipping on something skimpy. Said skimpy outfit will be carefully selected, and you can guarantee it will be the first outfit you pick out – which would be great if you didn't put it on, take it off, and then proceed to pull out everything else you own, trying various combinations of different outfits on before deciding you actually had it right with the first one. By which point, of course, you'll be running late.

So the whole time you're whizzing around your room doing all of the above like a sparkly Tasmanian devil, you'll be alternating talking yourself out of going with persuading yourself you absolutely should go, because you're single and you have to give men a chance, lest you die alone – isn't dating fun?!

The mental preparation is possibly even trickier than trying to wing your eyeliner without winding up looking like Amy Winehouse or searching for an outfit that makes your bum half the size it is – and mine is pretty big, so that's quite the task. First of all, you need to constantly talk yourself into it. It will be at the forefront of your mind to cancel because you are gross, and boys don't like you, and you're incapable of sustaining a relationship with anyone other than your mobile network provider and the platonic ones you have with barmen all over town to get service quickly. You know none of these things are true (except the last one) but it's easy to convince yourself that you can put it off today and meet the love of your life the next ~~day week~~ month …

It's nice to know as much as possible about who you're dealing with, and Facebook is great for that, but I'm yet to friend the guy I'm meeting tonight and he's got his privacy settings spot on, which sucks for me stalking him. I did have a quick flick through his profile pictures, careful not to knock 'like' on any from six years ago like I did with someone once before – nothing says cray-cray like 'liking' an old photo. After flicking through this guy's photos, I've got to say, he's so far out of my league, we're playing different sports. There's only one thing for it: control tights. The illusion of a flat stomach might level the playing field, at least a little.

I lie back on my bed and begin gently rolling the tights up my legs one at a time, careful not to ladder them because this is my only pair. It's a new pair, and as such, the tights are super tight. I sometimes struggle to keep them up high enough at the back, causing them to roll down and give me this weird back podge that I could have an anxiety attack about if I thought too much about it … no, I *don't* have a fat back, it's just the way control tights kind of round everything up, and God forbid my date puts his hand on my back and figures out where my control tights are hiding my stomach. The solution to this problem that many people probably weren't even aware was even a thing, is to tuck my tights into my bra, but that's really difficult to do on your own. Luckily, I have a solution to this problem too.

'Nick,' I call out at the top of my voice.

'What, what's wrong?' he asks, bursting through my bedroom door. He's wearing an apron, causing me to giggle at him. Then again, I probably don't look so cool right now either.

'Shit, Ruby, I thought maybe one of your online dating weirdos was hacking you up in here.'

'You wish,' I reply.

'You want me to pull your tights up again, don't you?'

'What are roommates for?' I say with a sweet smile.

Nick shakes his head as he walks over to me, knowing that sometimes the easiest option is to just humour me.

'You know, I struggle to recall a single thing you've ever done for me,' he starts as he yanks up my tights, wrestling them under my bra at the back.

'Erm, I helped you glue that vase Heather made you back together,' I remind him.

'Yeah, because you smashed it having sex on the sofa.'

'I wasn't having sex – foreplay, if that.'

'Too much information.'

The process of pulling my tights up isn't pretty for anyone involved, so I think the fact that Nick and I dislike each other makes him perfect for the job – I don't care about how unsexy I look in front of him.

'So, where is Heather tonight?' I ask – not that I care.

'She's on her way over, so can you hold your breath or something to speed this up? I don't want her to see us like this; she might get the wrong idea.'

I roll my eyes, even though Nick can't see my face.

'Dude, you're literally wrestling me *into* my clothes. That's as unsuspicious as you can get.'

'Whatever, Ruby. Look, I don't even know why you wear these things – you're not fat.'

'I ain't thin, doll,' I reply in a very matter-of-fact manner.

'If you're not happy with how you look – for some wild reason – then go on a diet, go to the gym – anything that means I don't have to do *this*.'

Nick goes to the gym at least once a day, he eats clean and

he is in excellent shape. My cardio involves running for trains, the only lifting I do is food to my mouth, and as such I am a comfortable size twelve ... occasionally a ten, if I don't eat salt for a few days, or a fourteen if we've just had a major holiday like Christmas or Valentine's Day, the latter of which is best enjoyed alone, eating chocolate and watching films starring Hugh Grant.

'The gym sounds awesome, but have you ever thought about punching yourself in the face?' I ask, straight-faced. 'That sounds much more fun.'

'Hey, I'm not saying you need to go, I'm just all for whatever gets me out of being the person who has to pull your tights up. Just out of interest, how do you cope when you need the bathroom?'

'I drink light and thank God for my excellent bladder control,' I reply.

'Wish I hadn't asked,' he replies as he heads for the door. He hovers in the doorway for a second. 'Date tonight?'

'How did you guess?' I ask, fully expecting him to give me a lecture on how I go on too many dates.

'The scary tights, Beyoncé playing – it's like you're simultaneously making yourself feel sexy enough to pull someone, whilst reminding yourself that you don't need a man.' I think for a second, considering whether or not this is possibly a compliment, until he adds: 'You know, in case he scarpers like the rest.'

'You can leave now,' I tell him. 'Your girlfriend will be here soon. We don't want her catching you in my room, while I'm in my lingerie.'

'You were right before,' he calls back. 'No one would suspect a bloke of sleeping with a girl in those things – you're locked in them, like a suit of armour.'

I look in the mirror, examining my slightly smaller-looking, tights-clad body and sigh. Dating is horrible, isn't it? Just a ridiculous nightmare that's absolutely impossible, with all these rules of what you're supposed to do, what you're not supposed to do, how you're expected to behave – and most people stick to them.

And even though we have bad ones, we suck it up, we have our grumpy flatmate pull us into our tight-tights and we get right back on the horse, ready to give someone else a chance.

Does my optimism for finding someone deplete every time I go on a bad date? Maybe, just a little, but it also hardens me to it. I don't take it personally anymore. I don't wonder what's wrong with me if someone tries to cover me in love bites, I wonder what's wrong with other people, and while that may be a depressing thought, it doesn't hurt or damage my self-esteem, and I don't feel bad about myself in the slightest. In my control tights, I am untouchable – literally, apparently.

With every first date there is always this thought at the back of your mind that if you just get it right this time, it might be your last ever first date, and wouldn't that be wonderful?

I grab a dress from the top of Mount Clothesmore. It's a short black number with a mesh panel down the front. With a little bit of extra weight comes a great pair of boobs, so I may as well work them to my advantage. The truth is that I probably could stand to lose a few pounds. If I went on a diet, my nearest and dearest wouldn't be hurrying me off to The Priory to talk to someone, you know? I'm just normal, I guess. Not skinny, not fat – but most importantly, not bothered. I'm happy in my skin. I know how to dress to make the most of what I've got and I love eating and drinking way too much to become the girl who only orders a salad in restaurants. I certainly have no intention of ordering a salad tonight. I imagine I should, according to the rules of the dating game. Even if I don't plan on keeping it up forever, I could order a salad the first few times we go out to make him think that I'm this dainty little thing who doesn't stuff her face and then, once he's suitably charmed by me – boom – that's when I reveal my secret appetite for red meat and dessert.

Hair – check. Make-up – check. Tights – check. Dress – check. Heels – check. That's me ready to go. I grab my handbag to make sure I have the necessities: purse, extra make-up, rape alarm – all the things you need for a successful date with a man you've never met before.

I make my way into the living room, grabbing my keys from the bowl on the coffee table where Nick insists we keep the keys, ready to make a dash for it before his girlfriend arrives, because if there's one person I like even less than Nick, it's Heather, Nick's current girlfriend.

'How do I look?' I ask Nick, who is stirring something over the cooker.

'Not like you've got terrifying tights on, kid,' he tells me, which I think is a compliment.

Nick has called me kid since pretty much the day we met. At first I thought it was just one of your typical terms of endearment used by Yorkshire folk, but then as we realised we were never going to get along, and he started comparing me to an immature child, I realised that he probably calls me kid because he thinks I am one. I call him much worse, so it's fine.

'How does the food smell?' he asks.

I walk over and peer into the pan, but its contents are not recognisable to me, not by sight or smell.

'Erm, what is it?' I ask.

'It's vegan stew. Will you taste it for me?'

'I'd rather close the fridge door on my head,' I reply.

I watch as Nick takes a spoon from the drawer, scooping a little out of the pan and tasting it. As he does, a little drops down and it lands on his apron, which he promptly begins cleaning. It's only now that I'm looking at his apron that I notice the slogan: *meat is murder*.

'Taste good?' I ask him.

'Yeah, I mean, it's not the same as meat, but as long as Heather likes it.'

'Boy, she's got you whipped.'

Nick pulls a face.

'No she doesn't.'

'So I suppose you've made yourself a meat version, then ...'

'Look, I don't expect you to understand, but this is what you do when you're in a relationship: you make sacrifices. If Heather doesn't want me to eat meat in front of her, I won't. She's happy for me to do it when she's not around.'

'What kind of vegan that?' I dare to joke. 'That's like a policeman who is OK with murdering people, so long as you don't do it in front of him.'

'So you acknowledge it *is* murder,' I hear Heather say victoriously from behind me.

I jump out of my skin. I'd no idea she was here. 'How did you get in?' I ask, accusingly.

'Nick left the door open for me.' She gets back to the subject at hand. 'So you acknowledge that they're both murder?'

'That is not the comparison I was drawing and you know it,' I tell her.

Heather shrugs, walking over to Nick and kissing him lightly on the lips. 'Looks delicious,' she tells him.

'I know I do.' I laugh. 'Shame about the food though.' Neither of them laugh.

As I head for the door, a notification comes through on my phone. It's from my date, asking if we can meet an hour later because he's run over at work.

'Ah, crap,' I say out loud, to no one in particular.

'Language,' Heather scolds me, before backtracking. 'Sorry, teacher reflex. Although you probably shouldn't swear; it's not very becoming of a lady. You'll do better on dates if you're more ladylike.'

I plonk myself down on the sofa. No point leaving yet, I'll be far too early.

'Thank you, Cilla Black, I forgot you were the expert – remind me how you two met again?'

'Nick was my sister's obstetrician,' she tells me, giving me the refresher I didn't actually need.

'Oh yeah, how romantic,' I say sarcastically. 'That means he saw your sister naked before he saw you naked – and they say romance is dead.'

'Don't tell me you're not going,' Nick interrupts before Heather has a chance to reply. 'We've planned a night that doesn't involve you.'

'Mate, as much as I'd love to stick around for a Friday night of cardboard stew and the missionary position, I'm still going. I'll just be too early if I leave now. But you know what that means.' I adopt a faux-enthusiastic tone to my voice. 'I get to make small talk with you guys for even longer.'

'Oh joy,' Heather says, with an equal amount of sarcasm.

Heather Johnson is exactly the kind of girl I would have expected Nick to wind up with; in fact, she's perfect for him. They both have sensible jobs (Heather is a primary school teacher), they both watch what they eat and, most importantly, they're both so, so incredibly boring.

Heather takes a seat on the sofa next to me. Nick, whose crap stew clearly doesn't require any attention at the moment, wanders over and sits in the chair next to us.

'So you're going out like that?' Heather asks me.

'I am,' I reply, all smiles. Heather likes me about as much as I like her, which is not at all. She never really gave me a chance. I think she just dislikes me because Nick dislikes me – but she's also a total mean girl, which has an effect on her people skills. Still, if she thinks she can upset me, she's wrong. 'What's wrong with it?'

'I can see your bra,' she tells me.

'Good,' I reply. 'It was expensive.'

We sit quietly for a moment before I decide on a silence-breaker.

'I actually heard a vegan joke the other day. Would you like to hear it?' I ask her.

'Oh, go on then,' Heather replies, scooting to the edge of her seat, ready to laugh.

I mean, it was a vegan who told me it, and he found it funny, so it's worth a try.

'How do know if someone is vegan?' I ask.

'I don't know, how?'

'They tell you,' I reply, slapping my thigh. 'Funny, right?'

'So what you meant is that you heard a joke about vegans, not a vegan joke,' she corrects me.

'Same diff, right, miss?'

'Well, I won't be telling that one at Vegan Club,' she says with a frown.

'Vegan Club?' I repeat back to her in disbelief.

'Yes,' she replies. 'We meet every Sunday at Baa Bar Black's. All welcome.'

'Wow. So I'm going to guess the first rule of Vegan Club is the opposite of the first rule of Fight Club,' I joke.

I'm not sure if Heather doesn't get the reference or just doesn't find me funny, but she ignores me, turning to Nick.

'Darling, what do vegan zombies eat?'

'What?' he asks, without much enthusiasm. I can tell he's just enduring the seconds until I leave, so they can get on with their boring night.

'Graaaaaains,' she replies, laughing her head off. 'And you thought vegans didn't have a sense of humour, Ruby.'

'I did say that,' I reply, pulling myself to my feet. 'But it was still nice to have you confirm it to be true. I'm going to get going; enjoy your night, you crazy kids.'

Neither of them say goodbye to me, but as I head out through the door, in the seconds before I close it, I overhear a snippet of their conversation.

'How long do you think this bloke will stick around?' Heather asks Nick.

'Not long,' he replies. 'They never stick around for long.'

Chapter 4

'Hey, babe,' the large, muscular blond-haired dude towering in front of me says as he pulls me close, planting a kiss on either side of my face.

'Hello,' I reply, my voice sounding funny thanks to his exceptionally tight embrace. He's got that sort of Lennie from *Of Mice and Men* strength going on, where I don't think he realises just how tightly he's hugging me. One of my many Matcher rules (Matcher is my dating app of choice/force because I'm oh-so single) is to never go on dates with dudes who look like they could/would strangle me, and Lennie here could choke the life out of me with ease if he so chose. I'm hoping that he won't though, because this guy is kind of a celebrity around here. His real name is Deano Gamble, and he plays for the Leeds Lions rugby team. He's a hooker, apparently. No idea what that means but I laughed for way longer than was cute when he told me during our first phone call.

I started talking to Deano on Matcher and we've been twenty-first-century flirting ever since; WhatsApping, Snapchatting and FaceTiming. That was until three weeks ago when I started dating Jonathan and went cold on him. Luckily when I reached out to him again, he still wanted to go on that date we'd been talking about.

Satisfied we were both who we said we were, we've arranged to go for dinner – tonight is our first date. Our conversations haven't really been too in-depth and I think he was drunk during our brief FaceTime, but if I have learned anything during my Matcher-ing, it's that if you spend too long chatting beforehand, you have nothing to talk about on your first date and it's super awkward.

I didn't know what Matcher was until I discovered that my boyfriend was on there. It's weird, because he kept making comments to me about online dating, joking around with me about seeing what was out there … I assumed he was kidding as he chatted about it with me on the walk back to his after a night out. I was listening, of course I was, but I didn't really care because I had a boyfriend, what did I need to know about dating apps for? David, my then boyfriend, was perfect on paper. He had a good job, his own flat, a nice car, a handsome face – all the things you're supposed to look for in a partner if you're shallow, but I didn't care about any of that stuff. I felt so safe with him and when he would lie in bed with me at night, cuddled up in the dark, he would tell me how all he wanted was for us to get our own place.

That night we got back to his and had sex, but that's about all I could tell you about it: that we did it. It wasn't special or memorable in any way, and when he was done he rolled over, checked his phone and then went to sleep. I climbed over him to go to the bathroom, sat down on the loo and thought about things. About how cold he was, about his new fixation with dating apps – did he tilt his phone away from me when he checked it? I was sure he did. And when I started really thinking about it, he'd changed the passcode on his phone a matter of days ago, because 'someone at work' had learned it, and was on a one-man quest to get into his Facebook account and post something embarrassing on his behalf. He never did tell me the new code … Alarm bells were ringing so loud they were deafening, and it was making me dizzy.

I walked back to the bedroom where David was fast asleep, his phone on the bed next to him. That's when I realised he'd fallen asleep with it unlocked and then I did something I've never done before and I've never done since – I looked on his phone. I felt sick with myself for looking but that's nothing compared with how I felt when I looked through his apps and saw Matcher. Still willing to give David the benefit of the doubt, I considered whether or not this might just be curiosity and, with my heart banging hard against my chest, I ventured inside the app.

Once in there, I got lost, drowning in a sea of matches and messages from more girls than I probably have in my phone contacts. I still felt like I was reaching, looking for something to grab onto to save me, but all I was seeing was conversations *my* boyfriend was having with single girls, telling them how he'd been single for a while, how he'd never met any girl who was worth the effort, how he'd love to go on a date with some red-headed girl, a veterinary nurse, some chick over from Australia on holiday for two weeks, a bird looking for 'no strings' fun, a single mum all the way in Doncaster – *my* boyfriend was putting out all kinds of bait and reeling in any fish he could get his hook into.

I locked his phone, placed it down next to him and climbed back into bed. I woke him up and gave him a handful of opportunities to come clean, but he didn't. It was lie after lie. Even though it was 3 a.m., I packed up my things and I left, because without trust, what's the point?

David was my first proper grown-up relationship, and I thought we were going to be together forever. We were together just over a year, but we got so serious so quickly, we'd been talking about moving in together. Getting a place with David in Leeds was all I wanted. When the shit hit the fan, I thought to myself: who says I need a man to move out of my parents' place and into the city? That's probably why I was so quick to move in with Nick, despite not knowing him all that well. He was a means to getting what I wanted, even though it turned out that I *did* need a man to move out: Nick. I probably would've been happier living with my lying, cheating bastard of an ex.

One of the things I've learned about Matcher is that it makes people greedy. Because you can't just chat to one person, you wind up chatting to a whole bunch of different people. Say you pick just one to go on a date with and wind up having a blast – you don't think maybe something could go somewhere with this person, you realise just how easy it is to get more dates. Why date one person when you can feasibly date at least four people a week? It's horrible really. But that's the world we're living in now.

When I first started using Matcher I was very cautious about who I spoke to and I certainly didn't plan on meeting up with anyone. I knew that Millsy was never off it, and that it allowed him a different girl to date every night, but I didn't fancy it for myself. 'Single AF' as Millsy described me, because the bulk of his vocabulary is internet slang these days, he told me to sign up 'for the banter' last year, so I did, and I was surprised when I got talking to one dude who seemed pretty cool called Jack. I chatted with him for two months before I met him – which is ages in the online dating world. He had his own place in the centre, he was gorgeous and he seemed really kind and funny – until I met him.

Well, when Jack turned up, he looked nothing like his photos at all. He was significantly bigger than he appeared in his pictures, and shorter than I imagined too, which didn't help. He wore these little rimless glasses which – and I feel bad for thinking this at the time – made him look a bit like he needed his hard drive checking, but I can honestly say that I didn't care, because he was nice, and sweet and kind and funny – except he wasn't. He didn't just look different in person, he acted it too. Our chats were friendly and flirtatious, but we'd never really got onto the subject of getting it on, which is why I was surprised when – fifteen minutes into our date – Jack pinned me up against a wall and kissed me like a porno director had just shouted 'action'. And right in the city centre, on a Tuesday lunchtime too. I wiggled free of his grasp awkwardly, steering him into the nearest shop in an attempt to halt his horses a little. I thought I was being a bit of a prude – which is unlike me – but Jack only got worse. He was like a horny teenager who had been granted unlimited access to boobs for the first time – except he hadn't. When he wasn't grabbing me, he was going behind me to try and unzip my dress. I let this go on for fifty minutes – forty-nine minutes longer than this excuse of a date should've lasted.

Needless to say, this knocked my Matcher confidence and it took me nine months before I even dared to meet anyone again, but I did, and I have continued to meet fellas since, but no one has ever dazzled me. Everyone has been weird or, worse, boring. It's full of vapid, topknot wankers who bang on about 'cheeky Nando's' and how much they lift at the gym, and are on a one-man quest to shag as many girls as possible by any means necessary.

These days, I don't really give meeting up with dudes a second thought, and I'd rather do it sooner than later, get it out of the way, see if they're weird or boring and then move on to the next one if they are. I breeze through it like it's dull, mindless admin work. This one is no good, on to the next. Unlike Millsy, I'm not sleeping with my dates – I rarely find Matcher dudes tolerable enough to sleep with. Millsy teases me and says I'm weird, but I just can't fancy someone if I think they're a bit of a dickhead, no matter how hot they are. This is why Millsy tells me I'm 'doing Matcher wrong' because I'm not 'making the most of it'.

So, back to Deano. It sounds strange, but I'm instantly more trusting of 'known' people because I feel like they have too much to lose to murder girls they meet on Matcher. Another reason Deano seemed safe was because Millsy could vouch for him – well, the opposite of vouch for him, it turns out. When Millsy was a teenager he had a choice, he could pursue rugby or acting and he chose acting, much to his dad's disappointment – and his own, to be honest, because he's really struggled to find work. That's why he's so psyched about this *Macbeth* gig. In an attempt to sort of feel like he was acting and still be a part of the team his dad so wanted him to play for, Millsy took on the job of team mascot, which basically means he dresses in a big, stupid lion costume and roars on the side-lines during games. I often remind him that this particular job neither counts as acting nor being a sportsman, and I think he did feel a little daft to start with until he realised he'd get all the chicks that the real players didn't want, so he's quite happy with it now. Millsy has lots of silly little jobs, it's surprising he's found time to seemingly sleep with the entire female population of Leeds.

When I found out Deano played for the Lions the first thing I did was ask *my* lion what he was like.

'He's a monumental bellend,' Millsy told me.

'So are you,' I reminded him playfully.

'He just shags his way through Matcher.'

'Again – are you talking about you or him?' I laughed.

'I'm serious, Rubes, most of the team have Matcher and we just use it to plough through girls.'

'You say "we" like you're one of the team and not the glorified stuffed animal who twerks to "Sexy and I Know It" at halftime,' I persisted with my teasing, unwilling to take his advice.

'Fine, go out with him, but he isn't your type. You heard it here first: Ruby wouldn't.'

So here I am, with Deano the hooker, and I have to say he scrubs up well. He's wearing black trousers with a black shirt that his muscles look fit to burst out of. He's clean-shaven, something that seems to be a rarity amongst the menfolk of Leeds these days, and his short blond hair is perfectly messy.

A waiter shows us to a quiet corner of Vici, an Italian restaurant. Deano's choice and one that scores him major brownie points (or tries, if we're sticking with the rugby theme) because I love Italian food.

It's such a romantic setting, with its rustic feel, twinkling fairy lights and soft music – the perfect environment for a date.

'So have you had a good day?' I ask, making small talk as we wait for our food. I don't know what it is, but the conversation feels forced and difficult. Deano is quiet, but in a strange way. He's clearly not shy, he just seems to have nothing to say.

'Good, cheers,' he replies in his thick Yorkshire accent. 'I had physio this morning, chilled this afternoon.'

'Cool,' I reply, giving him a few seconds to ask how my day was, but he doesn't. 'Well, mine has sucked. I had a hangover this morning, I was late for work and then a customer was absolutely horrible to me.'

'You should've told them to "piss off".' He laughs.

'Well, I would've liked to, but you know what they say: the customer is always right. Except when they're wrong, like today.'

'What do you mean?' he asks.

'What do I mean?' I echo.

'The customer is always right except when they're wrong,' he repeats back to me.

I can't help but cock my head and furrow my brow in confusion.

'It's a joke,' I tell him. I mean, I know it's not my best material, but even so.

'I don't get it,' he tells me.

'Never mind.' I smile as the waiter sets a steak down in front of Deano and a pizza in front of me.

As the smell of the food fills my nostrils I feel my mood lift. It looks incredible too. I can't wait to tuck in, except …

'Come on, what do you mean?' he persists, clearly annoyed he's not getting it.

'It's just a saying – it doesn't matter. You know what they say: explaining a joke is a bit like dissecting a frog; you learn a lot but the frog dies in the process.'

Deano thinks for a second. 'What do you mean?' he asks again.

Are you fucking kidding me?

'It doesn't matter,' I laugh, taking the pizza slicer and resisting the urge to use it on myself instead of my food. I've just realised something: Deano is dumb. Maybe it's come from years of getting his head stomped on out on the rugby field, I don't know, but that's why he's so quiet – he has nothing to say, and I instantly don't like anyone who doesn't get my jokes because personally I think I'm hilarious.

We eat our food in near-perfect silence, with the exception of "That's Amore" playing in the background, the quiet buzz of everyone else's conversations, and the sound of Deano chomping on his steak loudly. His steak is so rare I'm surprised I can't hear it mooing – not that it would have a chance to open its mouth at the rate he's shovelling it down.

As the waiter heads over to clear our plates, he asks us if we'd like to see the dessert menu. To be honest, I'm bored out of my mind and I want this date to be over, but my pizza was so delicious and I know they have amazing desserts here, and something yummy and sweet would mean the night wasn't a complete washout.

'Yes please,' I reply. He promptly brings me a menu, so I start scanning the list.

'They do bomboloni,' I say excitedly out loud.

'What do you mean?' Deano asks – his catchphrase it seems.

'They're Italian doughnuts,' I reply.

'If it fits your macros,' he replies, and it's my turn to be confused.

'What do you mean?' I ask, followed by a little chuckle because I just inadvertently did a Deano.

'Heavy on the carbs, high in fat – is it really worth it?'

'Dude, they're doughnuts,' I remind him. Everyone knows doughnuts are bad for you but we still eat them because *they're doughnuts*. And these are Italian, cream-filled doughnuts with chocolate sauce, so they're super impossible to resist.

'So, what can I get you?' our very enthusiastic waiter asks.

'Nothing for me, cheers,' Deano replies.

'Yeah, I think I'll give it a miss too, thanks,' I tell him, handing my menu back.

The enthusiastic waiter's face falls, like a kid who just found out there's no Santa Claus. I feel similar inside.

'I'll get you the bill,' he tells us.

It's not that I'm taking this muscly moron's advice, but I don't really want to spend any more time with him. He's not a bad person, but he's boring and his priorities are all wrong. Doughnuts above everything.

'I'll be back,' he tells me, wandering off in the direction of the toilets.

The only thing stopping me leaving right now is my manners, so I sit and wait until he returns.

Moments later Deano is back as promised and I am happy because it means I can go home.

'The men's room was out of order. I had to use the disabled toilet,' he tells me.

'Good for you,' I reply, confused as to why he thought I'd be interested, although I wouldn't be surprised if he did have some kind of brain damage courtesy of his job.

'Anyway, while I was in there, I was just thinking about how much I want to take you in there and fuck you right now.'

I stare at him blankly, blinking my eyes in disbelief once or twice. Not only is that a pretty gross request anyway, but it's not like we've been getting on. We have zero chemistry and he said no to doughnuts – so why would I want to have sex with him?

'So, shall we?'

Oh shit, he's serious. 'Erm, no!' I squeak.

Should I be flattered right now? Also, why does it need to be the disabled loo? Why can't it be the regular loo? What does he need all that extra space for?

'Well, I had to ask,' Deano says. 'Want to go somewhere and grab a drink?'

Yes, but not with you. Soon as I get out of here I'm going to swing by one of my favourite bars (because it's a pretty safe bet one of my friends will be there) and drink until I forget this date happened.

'No, I'm pretty tired. But thank you, it's been, erm …' Nope, can't even lie.

'Yeah, maybe see you again soon?'

Not a chance, mister.

'Maybe.'

Chapter 5

I gaze down at my half-eaten birthday cake. It's a big, pink thing. Like a cupcake for a giant or a drunk twenty-seven-year-old woman hoping for diabetes ASAP, covered in a heap of pink frosting, littered with dolly mixtures and jellybeans, reminiscent of something fresh out of a Willy Wonka novel. The box it came in said that it was intended to serve twenty, but by the time Millsy and I cut ourselves a piece the other night, there was much less than eighteen slices of a similar size left. It seemed like a reasonable portion size at the time, but as we munched our way through it whilst watching old episodes of *South Park*, we started feeling increasingly sick. Millsy, whose motto is "work out more to eat more" was the first to bow out, but I wouldn't be beaten.

It was the middle of the night, but we were still a little tipsy and when Millsy is drunk, he regresses to being a stroppy toddler. He threw the remainder of his cake in the bin, but he was so sickened with it that he couldn't stand to watch me eat mine either, so he took my cake from me and threw it away too. I'd have been angry, were it not so funny. He denied all knowledge of it the following morning.

It's 1 a.m., and I've just got in from a Matcher date from hell with Deano – but, aren't they all? It was so bad, I had to go to a bar and chain-drink cocktails to try and forget that it happened, but now I'm home, starving and in need of something to soak up all the booze, and I finally feel strong enough to tackle the cake again.

I pop the kettle on and grab myself a big, sharp knife from the drawer. I cut myself a generous wedge and pick at it with my hands, eating it straight from the box. Well, Nick likes me to keep the kitchen tidy, so it's one less plate to wash. I am raining cake down on the kitchen table as I shovel handfuls into my mouth, but it's so sweet and glorious my only qualm is that I'm technically not getting as much cake in me as I potentially could. My God, cake is wonderful.

I observe that one side of the cake is not quite even, and shave some off with the knife, like a sculptor perfecting a piece of art – a piece of art I'm eating by the slice whilst simultaneously picking jellybeans from the top with my other hand.

'Jesus Christ,' I hear Nick's voice behind me. 'Look at you.'

'Fuck off,' I tell him through a mouthful of cake. 'It's my birthday cake.'

'It's not even been your birthday,' he reminds me, as though I might not be aware of when my birthday is (or isn't).

'I'd had a bad day, so Millsy bought me it,' I tell him. 'Isn't it past your bedtime, Granddad?'

Nick rolls his eyes as he heads for the cupboard and removes a glass, before filling it with water from his lame little filter jug that he keeps in the fridge.

'Just getting a glass of water,' he tells me.

Watching him drink makes me suddenly thirsty, so I turn on the tap and lean over the sink to drink from the stream of water.

'You're like an animal,' he observes. 'And I thought better of Joe, eating cake. He'll struggle to keep his body like it is, if he puts junk in it.'

'He's always eaten shit, and he's always been a babe, so he's fine,' I reply snippily, straight to the defence of my friend. 'Anyway, he's a sweetheart. I'd had a rough day at work, so he bought me a birthday cake, because birthday cake is my favourite,' I inform him, shovelling another handful into my mouth, as if my point needed proving.

'First of all, birthday cake can't be your favourite, because a birthday cake is any cake that is eaten on a birthday. Second of all, how bad can your workday be in a coffee shop, seriously? You want to try spending a day in my shoes – people's lives are literally in my hands.'

'Mate, you're a gynaecologist. The only things literally in your hands are vaginas.'

'Only a few more weeks of obstetrics and gynaecology for me,' he reminds me. He's doing that rotation thing new doctors do where they sample a bit of each area of medicine. Judging by the few stories he's told me, this won't be the area of medicine he chooses to practise, I'll bet.

'So why was your day so bad? Did you give someone decaf by mistake?' he teases.

Annoyingly, he's not far off the mark. We had the grumpiest woman come in, asking for a skinny mocha with an extra shot. I was working on the till and Millsy was making the drinks. He prepared her coffee while I placed the granola bar she'd requested in a takeaway bag – something people hardly ever buy because they look like all the loose bits that have broken off from all the other cakes, swept up and glued together. It didn't take us long at all, still, she tapped her perfectly manicured nails on the counter impatiently.

I handed her order to her and watched as she headed for the door, but as she reached for the handle with one hand, she raised her takeaway cup to her mouth to take a sip before turning on her heels and marching back up to me.

'Is everything all right, madam?' I asked in the friendly manner they insist we adopt when speaking to customers. Even the ones we want to hit over the head with a milk jug.

'I asked for a double shot and this is not a double shot,' she says angrily, slamming the cup down in front of me.

I glanced over at Millsy.

'It is, ma'am,' he replied. 'I definitely put two shots in there.'

'Are you two saying I can't tell?' she snapped. 'Don't you need any training at all to do a job like this? My God, they could train monkeys to do better. At least they'd acknowledge that the customer is always right.'

I took a deep breath and gritted my teeth, because although every fibre of my being was telling me to grab the panini press and throw it at her, I knew that my actions might by frowned upon in the eyes of my employers/the law.

'Not to worry, we'll make you another one,' I told her, but it wasn't enough.

'I want to watch him pour each shot in, because clearly he needs someone to count for him. Honestly, if he spent less time at the gym and you spent less time drawing your eyebrows on, you could maybe find jobs you were competent in.'

I glanced over at Millsy, smiled sweetly and said: 'When you've made this lady's drink, there are some boxes of coffee that need moving from the back door, please.'

Millsy nodded, knowing exactly what he needed to do. The truth is, we don't even have a back door; that's just our secret code for teaching a lesson to horrible customers – the ones who truly deserve punishing. Never mess with the people who are serving you food and drinks.

I watched Millsy switch from using regular to decaf coffee with the sleight-of-hand skills of a seasoned magician. As he poured the two shots of fuck all into the customer's cup, she applauded him sarcastically.

'There, that wasn't too difficult for the two of you, was it?' she asked rhetorically before taking a sip. 'Much better.'

OK, so maybe we shouldn't be playing coffee god, but she asked for it, and by the afternoon when the caffeine withdrawal headache hit her like a ton of bricks, I hope it made her realise that she needs to be nicer to people, because if karma doesn't get you, vigilante baristas will.

Nick, clearly irritated by the fact I'm not rising to the bait, carries on talking to me.

'I thought Joe was never setting foot in here again?' he says. I find it weird that Nick calls Millsy by his first name, rather than his preferred name.

'You were away for the night,' I remind him. 'He won't come over when you're here because you're the reason he has to climb out of the skylight for a cig.'

'I told him he can't do that either.'

'Yeah, and that's why he won't come over when you're here. You've got so many rules: don't smoke in the flat, don't climb onto the roof – you're a drag, man,' I ramble, occasionally glancing at the cake as I wonder if I can manage any more without throwing up. Nope, no more.

Nick heads back towards his room. Well, it is way past his bedtime.

I scoop my hair up with my hand and let it fall down around one side of my face, sighing heavily. This catches his attention and he stops before he opens his door.

'Are you OK?' he asks, almost begrudgingly.

'I'm fine,' I assure him, heading for the sofa and plonking myself down.

I tip my head back and rest my eyes for a second. I don't know if I'm exhausted from all the late nights and early starts, or if I'm maybe slipping into a diabetic coma from that slab of cake I just effortlessly devoured, but I can't keep my eyes open.

I give myself five minutes before forcing my eyes open again, only to see Nick standing in front of me, except now he's got his nerdy plaid dressing gown on – untied, showing off the body he's spent hours in the gym perfecting.

I stare for a moment longer than I should, stopping only when

Nick takes a seat next to me.

'Want to talk about it?' he asks.

His moment of concern takes me aback. 'What do you care?' I snap.

Nick places his hand on my bare knee and gives it a gentle squeeze.

'Look, I know we don't get on, but I'm allowed to care about you, right? I mean, you must care about me a little – what would you do if you found out I left for work one morning and got hit by a car?'

'I guess I'd care,' I reply. 'But, like, about the stress of finding another roommate so I could afford to stay here – I could wind up with someone even worse than *you*.'

Nick laughs at the joke I didn't realise I'd made. That's when I realise his hand isn't on my knee anymore, it's on my thigh, and the gentle squeezing he was doing before has turned into more of a caressing motion.

I shift my gaze from Nick's hand to his eyes. He's looking at me in a way I've never noticed him do before.

'What are you thinking?' he asks.

'I'm trying to work out why you're being so nice to me,' I reply. 'It's out of character.'

'If you think that's out of character,' he starts slowly, as he runs his hand up my thigh, 'then try this.'

Before I know what's happening, Nick is pushing me back on the sofa, pressing his body down on top of me. He grabs a fistful of my long wavy locks firmly with one hand as he pulls off his dressing gown with the other. As much as I dislike Nick as a person, I have never been able to deny that he has one hell of a body – in fact, it's one of the first things I noticed about him when we first met. All that eating clean and exercising near-constantly is really paying off for him, I admit it, but I never imagined I'd wind up in a situation like this with him, and now I'm not just looking at him, I'm really looking at him, and I want him more than anything.

He kisses me keenly, like he's been waiting all these months to do it and now he finally can, he can't control himself – least of all his hands.

When I came home tonight I figured Nick would be in bed because it was late and he always gets nice early nights. That's why I felt safe kicking off my heels, slipping off my dress and putting on one of Nick's gym vests that I grabbed from the dryer, so I didn't have to make the long trip to my room to find something comfortable to wear while I devoured my birthday cake.

Usually that's two offences that would land me in Nick's bad books. My first offence is strolling around inappropriately dressed, the second is wearing Nick's clothes. He hates that. He says I leave them covered in glitter and stinking like a mid-range stripper. Perhaps that's why he's so keenly pulling the vest over my head, throwing it to one side before running his hands up my body, slipping my bra straps off my shoulders, kissing my collarbone, gently flicking his tongue against my skin.

Just when I think it can't feel any better, Nick slips his hand into my knickers and I can't help but moan wildly. My moans of pleasure get louder before quickly changing. As I raise my hand to my aching head and grumble in pain, I slowly open my eyes, only for the sunlight to burn them. That's when I realise it's morning, and that I must have fallen asleep on the sofa. I'm still wearing Nick's vest, which means I dreamt the whole thing. Shit, another sex dream about Nick!

'Why does this keep happening to me?' I ask myself.

'Because you make bad choices,' Nick replies, startling me. I glance towards the kitchen and see him standing there, smartly dressed, eating cereal as always.

I quickly break eye contact with him, absolutely mortified. I mean there's no way on earth he could know what I'd been dreaming but I feel like he's looking straight through me, like he can see it written all over my face.

'What happened last night?' I ask him, concerned.

'Not much, you went on a date with one of your Matcher psychopaths, came back steaming drunk, ate enough cake to kill you and then fell asleep.'

'Oh. So I didn't say or do anything bad?'

Nick stares at me for a moment.

'Erm, no, only all of those things I just listed to you.'

'That's OK then,' I say, exhaling a deep sigh of relief.

'Well, I've got to go shopping and then get to work. Another day of fucking around, is it?'

'I hope something really gross happens to you at work,' I reply, massaging my temples.

'You could use your free time to do something good,' he suggests.

'Good?' I reply, saying the word slowly as I cock my head. 'What is … good?'

Nick laughs.

'I'm serious,' he insists. 'Do something to change the world.'

'Like?'

'Like give blood, that's such a little thing to do to make such a huge amount of difference.'

I frown.

'Needles,' I tell him. 'Nope.'

'You'll only feel a little prick – stop it,' he snaps at me, before I have the chance to reply with a 'that's what she said'.

'So is that how you spend your free time?' I ask him.

'I wouldn't call it a hobby,' he replies. 'But blood donation, platelet donation – what's twenty minutes or a couple of hours to make a difference?'

I feel my eyes widen with horror. 'Mate, do you want me bleeding dry or something?'

'Mate,' he replies mockingly. 'It looks like someone beat me to it. You're looking very pale this morning.'

"Mate" is one of those words that has crept into my vocabulary

– something that happens to me all the time with slang words. At first I'll use words sarcastically, then as in-jokes, then suddenly, that's it, words like "mate" and "BAE" and "on fleek" are in my day-to-day vocab.

"Mate" is definitely something I have picked up from Millsy, who calls everyone from me to his mum to his doctor mate.

Hanging out with Millsy and my brother Woody growing up, I do worry that I've turned out "more boy" than I should have. Maybe that's why I don't have too many female friends. It's like when a kitten gets in with a litter of puppies and thinks it's one of them. It will act just like its adopted siblings, play like a dog, eat like a dog, truly think like a dog and feel like a dog ... but at the end of the day, it's still a cat. I'm a cat amongst the dogs. I find stupid gross-out comedies funny. I swear like a sailor who keeps stubbing his toe on the same bunk bed. I get riled up over football and borderline homicidal when I play video games.

Sometimes I think it would be nice to have female friends, but I just don't seem to get on all that well with girls. Sometimes I think they're ridiculous creatures, especially when it comes to the opposite sex. They have no chill. They'll text a guy a million times and wonder why he isn't texting back. Worse still, they'll sleep with a guy on the first date, thinking it will win him over, only for him to ghost. And what do they do when he ghosts? They decide not to text him for a few days. Because that will teach him, and if he replies, he must be really interested, right? Surely if you're trying to figure out a guy, it makes more sense to withhold sex instead of text messages? Then again, it's not exactly like I have it all figured out, is it?

'It's just my hangover,' I tell him.

'It's not taking care of yourself,' he corrects me. 'It's drinking too much, not sleeping enough, thinking you can eat Coco Pops for three meals a day and survive.'

Hmm. Perhaps he has a point there – not that I'm willing to admit that to him.

Chapter 6

As I hover around outside Millsy's flat, I take in the stunning view he has, but does not appreciate. Well, I say it's his flat, but it's actually his uncle's. What Uncle Mills actually does, I've never quite understood. He travels around the world, teaching doctors a procedure they need for the company's weird clinical trials. To me, this sounds a little sketchy, but Millsy assures me his uncle is going to "save humanity, or something". This may or may not be true, but it affords my best friend a gorgeous one-bedroom bachelor pad in a prime location with a stunning view of the River Aire and the Royal Armouries, rent-free.

Sometimes, when Nick is stressing me out, Millsy offers me his (technically his uncle's) sofa to sleep on, but with the possibility his semi-nomadic uncle could return at any point, he'll want his bed back, Millsy will get the sofa, and I'll wind up homeless. Giving up the flat to Nick would be letting him win, and that's just not on either – also, with the amount of Matcher girls Millsy has slept with in there, I deem his sofa a legitimate pregnancy risk.

I lean on the wooden fence outside his building and glance around. It's busy, yet weirdly peaceful – you don't feel like you're in a city centre. There are people hanging out on the grass because it's surprisingly warm for October today, having picnics, fishing

– it's a picturesque Saturday lunchtime.

The reason I'm hanging around outside, admiring the Aire & Calder navigational canal (which I know to be its name now, because I just heard a tour guide telling a flock of tourists that's what it's called) is because Millsy has a girl in there with him. We're supposed to be catching the train home to Outwood to visit our parents, but he needs to 'finish up'– whatever that means.

Bored, I decide to amuse myself. I take a gold wedding band from my handbag and stand it on its side on the fence in front of me. I use a finger to gently twirl it around in circles before channelling every sad thought I've ever had: the fact I've lost a charm off the Juicy Couture bracelet my parents bought me for my birthday, the end of that film where the dog dies, the fact *I'm* probably going to die single and alone – shit, that one was a bit real. Anyway, it only takes a few seconds before my sorrowful frown catches the attention of two twenty-somethings walking past.

'Are you OK?' the first girl asks. She's got her long, bright purple hair up in a bun on top of her head, the structure supported by a hair doughnut so big it looks like a burden. Her naturally red-headed friend, who appears equally concerned, looks like she could've been an extra in *Pretty In Pink*, her hairstyle and outfit positively Eighties, even though she was probably only alive for a year or two of the decade.

'I'm fine,' I tell them. 'It's just … I've just found out my husband has been cheating on me.'

'Oh my God, that's proper rough,' the first girl says. 'Totally,' the second echoes. 'What are you going to do?'

'That's what I'm trying to figure out. We've only been married a few months – together for ten years though. I don't think I can live without him.'

The girls stare at me for a moment, fascinated by the seeming collapse of a stranger's life.

'You can't take him back,' the purple-haired girl tells me. 'You just can't. He'll do it again and again if you do.'

'You've just got to be strong and start again,' Molly Ringwald wannabe adds.

I think for a second, my expression dominated by a look of faux anguish. 'You know what,' I start, my confidence slowly coming back to me. 'You're right.'

I pick up the ring from in front of me and examine it for a second before meaningfully throwing it into the river. I watch as the ripples disappear before exhaling deeply.

'You go, girl,' the first girl says as they wander off, the show over. I turn around and watch them head up the steps, noticing that Millsy is standing behind me. He gives me a slow clap as he approaches me.

'Bravo,' he praises me. 'It's nice to see you've still got it in you.'

'I act for fun, not work,' I remind him. 'Anyway, that was too easy.'

'Great improv with that ring though,' he says, leaning on the fence next to me. 'I would've gone all Andy Serkis, giving it the precious thing and all that.'

'Oh I'm sure that would've had those two girls eating out of your hand – speaking of girls, where's yours?'

Millsy wiggles his eyebrows.

'I got rid when I came out, during your matinee. I reckon I could handle seeing this one maybe one more time, don't want her meeting you, do I?'

I furrow my brow.

'Don't give me that face, Miss Wood,' he says and laughs. 'You know you're a cock-block. girls see that I'm close with you and run a mile – God knows why. But most blokes seem to find you fit, so we've got to keep you out of the way. You know the score.'

The fact Millsy doesn't want to sleep with me is actually the highest compliment he can pay me, because Millsy only sleeps with girls he doesn't plan on keeping in his life for very long.

'They have no need to be jealous,' I tell him. 'I know where you've been, I won't even share drinks with you – herpes is for life.'

'Fuck you! So I had a cold sore last year. One, once. It's not the same as herpes.'

I laugh as he passionately defends his cold sore, like he always does when I tease him about it. It's just too easy.

'OK, sorry.'

'Right, we going for this train?' he asks as he zhooshes his messy brown hair.

'Sure, right after you jump in and get my ring back for me,' I inform him, staring at him expectantly.

'What?'

'My ring. I saw where it landed. That was a real gold one, I threw it by mistake.'

Millsy looks worried sick, the reflex to help his best friend without question doing battle with his aversion to jumping in dirty water and getting his hair wet.

I watch as he appears to reach for his T-shirt, as though he were going to take it off, before I put him out of his misery.

'Don't worry, Tom Daley, I'm just kidding. It was a cheap one, from a Primark set. Plenty more at home.'

'You monster.' He laughs. 'You're lucky I don't care enough about you, or I would've just jumped in.'

I grab him and hug him.

'I love you too.' I laugh. 'Even though you're dumb enough to think you can retrieve a tiny ring from a huge river.'

'They'll be retrieving you from a river when I strangle you and dump you in the Aire,' he warns me.

'And there's me thinking you weren't going to give me the same treatment you give all your Matcher girls.'

'Come on, trouble. Train,' he insists with a chuckle.

Considering it is October – and we're up north – it's not that cold today, perfect for a stroll through my favourite part of Leeds. The Calls area is a mixture of offices, flats and bars/restaurants. Along with Call Lane and Lower Briggate, it makes up the heart of the gay scene in Leeds, so it's great for peaceful walks during the day, before it comes alive at night.

This is the part of Leeds where I wish I lived, instead of my flat-share hell above a bar on New Briggate, further up the hill. I mean, it's not awful where I live. It's in the city centre, and it's right next to Merion Street, which has some pretty cool bars, but I want to be down by the river where it's pretty. Situated midway between where I live and where Millsy lives is the Trinity Centre, full of all my favourite shops as well as a whole host of bars and restaurants, so naturally when we hang out, that's where we go. Yes, it's awesome, but it doesn't hurt that we can both easily crawl home after. It just sucks more for me because I'm headed up the hill, whereas Millsy heads down.

When I put this argument to Millsy once to try and blag a night on his sofa, he countered it with: 'at least you're not at risk of getting mugged like I am' – he quickly added that he meant because he walks along the edge of the river in the dark, and not because I don't look like I can afford anything worth stealing. Neither place is anywhere like where we lived for most of our lives.

Finch Avenue, that's the street Millsy and I grew up on. In cute red-brick detached houses, down a quiet little cul-de-sac in Outwood, a town near Wakefield that no one has heard of.

Millsy didn't just grow up on the same street as me, he lived in the house next door. Our mothers have been best friends since before we were born and, as a side effect, our dads are best friends too. Except, now that I think about it, I don't think our dads have ever liked each other all that much. One thing I remember about growing up here was how they were always competing with one another. It was all about who had the neatest lawn or the most impressive tool – I know, that sounds like an extension of *something*, but in the suburbs having a large strimmer is exactly that.

I guess our dads are quite different people, too – opposites, in fact. Millsy's dad is a big, tall, broad, bald-headed rugby-loving dude whereas my short, skinny, curly-haired dad would much rather watch the football – or "girls' rugby" as Daddy Mills would put it.

Our mums are both your typical suburban housewives who quit their jobs the second they fell pregnant. They both moved on to the street at the same time, both had two kids – and they even managed to give birth in the same years. Our mothers were already pregnant with their first two kids when they met, but whenever it is mentioned that Millsy and I were conceived around the same time, Millsy's dad assures us that it wasn't a keys-in-a-bowl-on-the-table kind of thing – something that had never crossed my mind until he brought it up.

Millsy's older sister and my brother Paul, or Woody as he's more commonly known, are both thirty years old and both model children. They're both married to sensible partners, they both have kids and they're both doing all the shit you're supposed to in the name of making your parents proud. Sadly – although at least we're keeping things symmetrical – Millsy and I have really let the side down. We'll often synchronise our visits home together, catching the train before going our separate ways at the bottom of our drives, before clocking a little family time and then heading back into Leeds to hit up our favourite bar together – where we'll swap accounts of the ridiculous things our parents just said to us, because we're both such let-downs, apparently. So we're both headed for thirty, both single and both working jobs that aren't that impressive for our parents to tell their friends about – but so what? We're both happy. That's all that matters, right?

Despite the trains being every thirty minutes, we always seem to successfully just miss one, giving us near half an hour to wait for the next – not that long, but just long enough to annoy me. I hate just missing trains, it makes that thirty-minute gap seem like a lifetime. That's why we popped to Starbucks to grab a coffee, except now we're about to miss the next. Carefully running along the platform with our hot drinks in our hands, we dive through the train doors with only thirty seconds to spare. We made it, but the train is rammed.

As we walk along the train it isn't until we reach the final carriage that we notice two free seats. It's an arrangement of four, with one person on each seat. This means either Millsy or I are going to have to take the seat next to a little old lady, which faces in the wrong direction, which we both hate. I'm expecting an argument on my hands, or at least a thumb war or something to settle who gets to sit in the good seat, but as we approach it, Millsy dashes to sit down next to the old lady.

This is confusing to me, because if it were a hot, young thing he'd secured himself a seat next to, I'd know exactly what Millsy was playing at; he'd be angling for a date or admission to the train equivalent of the mile-high club – wait, scratch that, he's already a member. I remember him telling me a story about the time he had sex on a train. In fact, he reminds me every time he sees a train CCTV camera, telling me that they've ruined his fun now – not because they prevent him from doing it, just because he feels the pressure of the audience.

Hmm, maybe Millsy really has banged his way through every young girl in the West Yorkshire area and his resolve – rather than just staying on this train to Doncaster – is to start on the older ladies.

As I follow his lead and take the only remaining seat on this busy train, I realise what his game is: Nick is in the next seat. Crap, he must be on his way to Wakefield for work.

'Hello, Doctor, fancy seeing you here,' I say, taking a seat next to him reluctantly, but trying not to make it awkward. I often see him on the train, but I can't really ignore him when I'm sitting next to him, so I may as well be pleasant.

'Ooh, are you a doctor?' the little old lady asks. Nick looks embarrassed.

'He is,' I reply, for some reason feeling the need to help him out.

'Well, your mum must be so proud of you,' she says sincerely, a huge smile plastered across her face. 'So, when they put out messages on public transport saying, "Is there a doctor on the train?" you can run forwards and save the day?'

Nick opens his mouth to speak but Millsy gets in there first.

'Yeah, well, only if the person who needs help has, like, a pulled vagina or something.'

'He's working in gynaecology,' I add, not only to explain to this lovely old lady why Millsy just said that to her but, again, in Nick's defence.

Millsy absolutely hates Nick. He didn't really take to him the first time they met, but as Nick started imposing more and more rules in the flat, and being less and less nice to me, Millsy's hatred for him grew and grew.

The last time Millsy and Nick spoke, they had an explosive argument over Millsy smoking in the flat. Well, not even in the flat – Nick was being a grump about Millsy climbing out of the skylight to smoke on the roof. In the heat of the moment Millsy swore he'd never be in the same room as Nick ever again, and he hasn't – this doesn't count, obviously. It's only a nine-minute journey and Millsy can't very well jump off a moving train, can he?

'Well, I think that's great,' the old lady starts. 'There's no shame in that. When I had my prolapse—'

'OK!' Millsy says awkwardly. 'Tell you what, if you wait for us to get off the train at the next stop, the two of you can talk properly, in detail. Doctor/patient confidentiality and all that.'

Nick shoots me a glance, as though to say 'control your child' but Millsy is a grown man and I can't make him behave.

'So my date went well last night,' I tell Millsy in an attempt to defuse the situation. Of course, this is a lie, and I'll set my friend straight once we're alone.

'Did it?' Millsy asks. 'I'm surprised to hear that.'

'I'm surprised to hear that too,' Nick interrupts, raising his eyebrows. 'Considering you came home alone and put your face in a cake. That's not really a good sign, is it?'

The old lady, clearly sensing some tension, starts rummaging around in her handbag.

'Would anyone like a sweetie?' she asks, offering the bag around. Nick and I decline, but Millsy takes two.

The lady pops one in her mouth, smiling widely at Nick as she does so. It's only a matter of seconds before her smile turns to a look of panic, then she starts coughing.

'Is she OK?' I ask Nick.

'No,' he tells me, jumping to his feet. He very calmly and quickly examines her.

'Are you choking?' he asks her.

'Mate, of course she is,' Millsy interrupts.

'Thank you, Dr Mills. I'm asking to determine if she can speak or not.' The old lady nods as best she can.

'Her airway is obstructed, can you two give me a bit of room please?' he asks Millsy and me.

'Yeah, sure,' I reply, moving out of the way.

'I'm going to help you, don't worry,' Nick tells her, still completely calm.

Supporting her chest with one hand, Nick leans the lady forwards and begins hitting her back with the other but it's not working.

Everyone is crowded around Nick, watching the scene play out. It's horrible, watching this poor, sweet lady suffer like this. I so hope he can help her.

'OK, I'm going to perform the Heimlich manoeuvre. Ready?' he asks her, not expecting an answer, obviously just using his soothing tones to keep her as calm as possible.

He helps her to her feet before standing behind her, placing his arms around her, locking his hands just above her stomach before thrusting them towards himself. It only takes two thrusts before the lady coughs, the guilty sweet flying out of her mouth, landing on the floor in front of me. She coughs and gasps for breath as Nick helps her sit down.

'Can you speak?' he asks her.

'Yes,' she says weakly. 'Thank you, thank you so much.'

'No thanks needed,' Nick assures her. 'We'll get you off the train at the next stop, make sure you're OK.'

'Thank you,' she says again, sitting back in her seat as she continues to find her breath.

'You saved her life,' I say to him quietly as he uses his phone to call for an ambulance.

'Just doing my job,' he tells me.

Chapter 7

We hop off the train at Outwood Station. I watch as Nick escorts the old lady to the ambulance to get checked over.

'Just doing my job,' Millsy says, mimicking Nick's voice. Having grown up in Ilkley, Nick is very well spoken and his Yorkshire accent is weak, unlike Millsy who is a consonant-dropping Wakey lad that no amount of elocution lessons could help.

'Millsy, he saved her life. She would've died right in front of us if he hadn't been there.'

'Yeah, OK, that was impressive for a doctor who usually spends his days swabbing for chlamydia, but why are you defending him all of a sudden?'

'I'm not, I …' My voice trails off. 'How do you know that swabbing is how they check for chlamydia?'

'Don't change the subject,' he replies quickly. 'Now you have to tell me what's up.'

'You have to promise not to laugh,' I insist. My friend nods. 'I've been having sex dreams about Nick.'

Millsy, unsurprisingly, bursts into laughter.

'Oh my God, that's disgusting.' He cackles as we walk the short journey to the street where our parents live. Then he looks at me, and I don't know what he sees in my eyes, but it cuts short his laughter.

'You're not enjoying them, are you?'

'No,' I say quickly. 'Of course not. I just don't understand why they're happening.'

'Something must have triggered them,' he reasons, reluctant to believe such a thing could happen without some kind of traumatic inciting incident.

'Oh shit, actually, last week I walked in on him in the bathroom,' I recall. 'It was so awkward.'

'What, like on the toilet? You filthy girl.'

I roll my eyes. 'No, not on the toilet, you moron. He was shaving, standing in front of the mirror wearing nothing but a towel, water running down his face, dripping down onto his body before rolling down his abs …'

Millsy pours a little water from the bottle he's been drinking from into his hand and splashes some in my face.

'Kind of like that?' he asks.

'Millsy, what the fuck?' I shriek. 'What did you do that for?'

'Erm, because you were about five seconds off coming,' he tells me, very matter-of-factly.

I feel my cheeks flush with embarrassment.

Millsy thinks for a moment before his eureka moment.

'I've figured it out! You're so horny because you haven't had sex in so long, and you're dreaming about the man you spend the most time with – who isn't like a brother to you,' he adds quickly. 'Otherwise I'd be offended you weren't dreaming about me.'

'I mean, obviously,' I reply sarcastically as we arrive at our destination. 'Well, see you on the flipside,' I tell Millsy, bumping the fist he offers me before we go our separate ways.

As I stand outside the red-brick house where I grew up, I take a moment to admire the garden that my dad works tirelessly to keep looking good – no, not good, great, perfect even. His lawn is always perfectly short and neat, the flowerbeds always look beautiful no matter what the season, and there isn't so much as a weed in sight. My parents are pretty much perfect generally, actually. The house is as flawless on the inside as it is on the outside, their marriage is perfect – well, about as perfect as one can be in the twenty-first century. They also have the perfect offspring in the form of my brother. And then there's me, the only black mark on the Wood family's perfect suburban life.

That's why I dread these visits, because my parents want nothing more than to help make me perfect too. They think that if they follow the cliché child cookbook, that they can whip me up into something edible, or shape me like one of the bushes in the garden, just hacking away at the rough, undesirable bits that give it character and make it stand out from all the other bushes on the street. They don't want a stand-out shrub, they want a bland, basic bush that they can brag about.

I know that as soon as I walk through the front door, they will pounce on me. They'll grill me about my life – have I found a proper job? Do I have a boyfriend? Have I thought about getting on the property ladder? The truth is that I'm happy with my 'not proper' job, I could get *a* boyfriend if I just wanted *a* boyfriend but I'd rather wait for one I can actually stand to be around, and the only sort of ladder I feel overly concerned with are the ones I'm constantly putting in my tights.

Still, I know that my parents care about me, and that's why they're so concerned. All of this is because they love me, and to be honest I could do with a little family TLC right now.

I stroll up the driveway and open the front door. Both of my parents' cars are parked in the drive, so I mentally prepare myself for a double dose of affection, as always presented in their non-traditional format.

The house is quiet – too quiet. My mum should be in the kitchen cooking something – anything – and my dad should be in the living room, watching a quiz show, shouting the answers back at the screen. There's no sign of life anywhere downstairs, but it's weird that their cars are outside – and the door was unlocked, so they must be in. I glance out of the kitchen window into the back garden but there's no sign of them there either.

The floorboard above my head creaks slowly and quietly, as though someone is moving around up there. Should I go up? I suppose I could get Millsy first, but what if my parents are in trouble? Am I over-reacting here, or is this weird? Maybe I've seen a few too many horror films.

I'd hate to over-react, but there's only one thing for it. I take a large knife from the kitchen drawer and slowly tiptoe upstairs with it. The room above the kitchen is my parents' bedroom, so I creep across the landing towards their closed bedroom door. I hover for a second, unsure how to play this. Do I creep in slowly and quietly, or do I burst through the door like a knife-wielding maniac? Slowly and calmly seems like my best course of action; after all, I don't know what I'm going to walk in on.

I push the door open gently, conscious of that familiar creaking noise it makes that reminds me of my childhood. When I used to have nightmares I would be too scared to go into my parents' room in the night in case the creaking of the door alerted the ghosts and monsters of the house to the fact I was walking around in the dark at night. I remember how loud it seemed then, but it seems even louder now.

I poke my head around the door. It's very dark because the curtains are shut, but I can see that the room looks perfectly tidy, with a made bed and nothing out of place. Most importantly, the room is empty, so what was that noise I heard? And where the hell are my parents?

I am just about to head back downstairs when I hear a noise. I tilt my head, putting my ear to the air to listen closely. A chill washes over me and I get that ghostly feeling like someone has just poured ice-cold water down my back. I've never been one to believe in ghosts, but that creepy, breathy sound I can hear in this room is like nothing I've heard before … or is it? Wait, is that giggling I hear? I take a deep breath and hold it, fear paralysing me. What do I do? Who do I call? Does Derek Acorah have a FAQ section on his website? How do you even spell Acorah? I'm not even sure autocorrect can save me with this one.

Before I can do anything, I notice the curtain move slightly – there's someone behind it. Thankfully, before I start blindly stabbing whoever or whatever is behind there, I realise that the person is kneeling down, looking out of the window, and lucky for them I'd recognise those battered Batman Converse anywhere.

I whip open the curtains to see my brother. He looks startled for a second before he jumps to his feet and rugby-tackles me onto my parents' bed.

'What the fuck are you doing?' I ask him.

My brother quickly rolls off me – because despite this being an assault, I imagine it's way too much like a hug for his liking.

'Hey, sis, nice to see you too,' he says sarcastically.

'Woody, seriously, what are you doing? I nearly stabbed you! Where are Mum and Dad?'

'Well, it wouldn't be the first time.' He laughs. 'And didn't they tell you? They went on a cruise with Millsy's parents. They'll be gone for a month.'

'Erm, no, they neglected to mention this to me,' I tell him, unable to hide my offence. 'And you're here because?'

'I'm housesitting,' he announces proudly, lying back with his head on his hands.

I can't help but pull a face.

'They know I hate where I live and would jump at the chance to move out for a month – why would they ask you and not me?'

'Erm, because you'd throw a house party,' he tells me, which is in fact the only reason I wish they'd given me the job. Well, that's what you're supposed to do when your parents are away, isn't it? No matter how old you are. 'Also we're having an extension built on the house, so Mum and Dad said we could stay here. It was too noisy for the baby, and Dani found it difficult too, being at home all day with all the noise going on.'

'How is the little monster?' I ask.

'Robbie? He's great. He's grown loads since you saw him last.'

'I wasn't talking about my adorable little nephew,' I reply. 'But I can't wait to see him.'

'Oi,' Woody snaps. 'Don't talk about my wife that way.'

'Why not? You do.'

Woody and Dani have been together since they were thirteen years old, when they wound up sat next to one another in physics. They quickly became boyfriend and girlfriend, and here we are, seventeen years later and they're married with a baby.

My brother was always the coolest kid in his year and as such he could've had any girl he wanted, but getting with Dani so young meant that he never made the most of his popularity and so he's only ever known what it's like to be with Dani. My brother is tall – six-foot-three – and Dani is a tiny, five-foot-two (when she was pregnant with Robbie, there was a running joke that he was bigger than she was) but despite her tiny frame, she is definitely the one who wears the trousers in their relationship. She's always seemed way too keen on flying through the motions of their relationship and, now that my brother is thirty, I think he's starting to wish he'd dedicated more time to having fun.

'Yeah, well, she's my wife, I'm allowed.' He laughs. 'She should be here any minute; she's popped back to the house for some things. She and Robbie are going to Scotland for a couple of weeks to stay with her grandparents. Which means I have this place to myself.'

'Woo, party!' I chirp.

'Erm, no. Mum and Dad left me in charge because I am the responsible one. Anyway, you don't even have any fit female friends to bring, only big, muscular dudes. Hardly seems worth it.'

'Yeah, but my big, muscular dude friends have tons of fit female friends – think about it.'

My brother does think about it for a moment.

'So, go on, what were you looking at out of the window?' I ask.

'I thought something scary was in here. Did you see something outside?'

'Nothing,' he says sheepishly, sitting upright on the bed. 'Let's go downstairs. Dani and Robbie will be back soon.'

Now I know something dodgy is going on. I jump to my feet and look out of the side window my brother was peeping out of. I only need to glance for a second before I realise that our next-door neighbour is doing aerobics in her underwear. Her name is Carol and she's lived next door to us for as long as I can remember. She must be well into her fifties now and she's had a couple of kids but she's got a cracking body. If I looked like that, I'd be exercising in my underwear next to the window with the blinds open too. She's always been a bit of a cougar, has Carol. Preying on the young men of the street, finding excuses to get them to go over and help unclog her toilet or hammer a nail or some other problem that I always imagined she'd cause herself whenever she felt lonely.

Millsy and Woody have had crushes on her since they were teenagers, referring to her as 'Barbie' so our parents never knew who they were talking about. In fact, if Millsy knew Woody was doing this, I imagine he'd show up with popcorn.

'Oh, you dirty bastard,' I tell my brother. 'I was scared shitless when I walked in here. I thought I was going to find a burglar or a ghost standing over the dead bodies of my parents, not my brother having a wank out of the widow.'

Woody laughs. 'You actors are so dramatic.'

'Hello,' I hear a voice call upstairs. It's Millsy.

'We're up here,' I call back.

Millsy pops his head around the door. Woody salutes him from the comfort of our parents' bed.

'All right, mate,' Millsy starts. 'Dani and Robbie are downstairs. She asked me to hold him while she uses the loo. Can one of you two do it? Babies.'

Millsy shudders.

'Be right down,' Woody says with a sigh.

'So we're abandoned for the month, huh?' Millsy says to me. 'Parents left me a note on the fridge. Can you believe that?'

'It's more than I got,' I tell him.

'I'm better than a note,' Woody says as he reluctantly pulls himself up. 'You're a peeping Tom,' I tease him.

'Barbie next door?' Millsy asks him.

'Yep,' Woody replies.

'God, she's like the perfect woman,' Millsy says with a sigh. 'Let's see.'

'Ergh, you boys are gross,' I tell them – in case they didn't already know.

'Come on, she works out next to a big open window; she'd close the blinds if she didn't want an audience.'

'Gross,' I repeat myself. 'Come on, downstairs.'

The side curtains are open now so I go to open the curtains on the back window too.

Millsy and Woody are shuffling out of the room. I turn to follow them but then I do a double take, glancing out of the window and into the house behind us.

'Shit,' I exclaim as I duck down. What did I just see? I pop my head back up just enough to peep over.

'Well, I know there's no eye candy out that window,' Woody jokes. 'Just Weird Ian. What's he up to? Trying to catch squirrels in his back garden with nothing but a cauliflower and a kid's fishing net again?'

Millsy laughs, but I don't. I'm too creeped out. I sit on the floor, trying to process what I just saw.

'Like I'm going to fall for that.' Woody laughs, shuffling Millsy out of the doorway so they can head downstairs.

'No,' I snap in a whisper. 'Quick, come here.'

Millsy and my brother, realising I'm serious, do as they're told and crouch down on the floor next to me.

'Right, what?' Woody asks.

'It's Weird Ian.'

'Yeah, Weird Ian our back neighbour, the one who probably strangles women.' He laughs. 'What about him?'

'I think I just saw him strangling a woman,' I reply.

The house behind my parents' belongs to Weird Ian, a forty-something-year-old supposed artist who still lives with his mum. I vaguely recall his mum from when we were younger, but as the years went by she stopped going out, and we'll only occasionally see a glimpse of her through an upstairs window every now and then. That, combined with the taxidermy animals he has in glass boxes showcased in all of his windows, is how the joke started amongst the kids on the street that Weird Ian was a Norman Bates type, whose mother probably passed away years ago, but because she's all he has in the world he's hung on to her body for company. Kids are horrible; that's just what they do, right? Come up with stories about their neighbours to make them seem more interesting.

The difference today is that, rather than just picking up on creepy vibes, I swear to God I just saw Ian wrapping something around the neck of a woman. Weirder still, the woman was in her underwear. I tell this to my brother and my best friend.

'Come off it,' Millsy replies, standing up to look out of the window.

'No, don't,' I reply quickly, but it's too late. Millsy whips open the curtains and both he and Woody stare across.

'There's no one there,' Millsy tells me. 'Are you still drunk?'

I get up and look out, checking all of the windows of Weird Ian's house, but there's nothing to see.

I frown, confused. I definitely saw something.

'Come on, I'll put the kettle on,' my brother says, lifting me up and carrying me downstairs over his shoulder. 'You're making the drinks though.'

As soon as we're in the living room my brother dumps my body down on the sofa and heads towards the kitchen to put the kettle on, as promised.

Dani, my sister-in-law, is standing there, holding the baby, an angry look plastered across her face.

'When he needs to go, he can just go, when I need to go, you have to hold the baby,' she says impatiently. Dani is every inch the nagging wife you see in the movies, and my brother is every inch the downbeat husband who wishes he'd made different choices. When we were younger we all used to hang out together, along with all the other kids from the street, so my brother and Millsy have always got on well, but these days, despite Millsy being younger, I think my brother looks up to him, like he's his hero. I think Woody not-so-secretly wishes he had Millsy's life instead of his own – heck, even I wish I were Millsy sometimes. He's young, free and single, and having the time of his life – everything my brother wishes he still had going for him.

'Ruby told me I have to put the kettle on,' he lies to his wife. 'But she'll hold the baby.'

'No, I—'

Dani hands me Robbie and dashes off to the bathroom.

Millsy laughs at me. 'You look like an office cleaner from the police station who's been asked to defuse a bomb, on her first day – blindfolded,' he adds dramatically.

'Dude, I've seen this one explode before. Don't joke,' I reply.

I am a little uncomfortable handling children, but only because I'm never sure if I'm doing it right, and also because that maternal instinct is yet to kick in for me. I couldn't think of anything worse than having a child right now, but I'm only young, right? It's perfectly normal for me to reject people on dating apps who say they have kids, because I'm terrified of guys if I know their sperms works …

Still, I absolutely adore my nephew, and even though he's only young, I'm doing my best to make sure he turns out cool like his auntie and not a dull nerd like his parents.

'Hey, dude, how's it hanging?' I ask him.

'Who taught you how to talk to babies?' Millsy laughs.

'Oh, because you're the expert are you?' I reply. 'Your only experience with babies is that panic you go through between a girl telling you she's late and then the follow-up call that you're in the clear.'

'Come on, that only happened once,' he says, pulling himself to his feet. 'And I knew I was in the clear because she was so angry – her period was definitely coming.'

'Yes, that's why she was angry,' I start. 'And not because you were googling how to change your identity.'

Millsy, who is standing next to me now, laughs. He knows I'm just teasing.

'Go on then,' I demand. 'How would you speak to him?'

Millsy takes both of his hands and places them over his mouth, his fingers pointing towards his ears. He blows hard, making a loud farting noise, which makes my adorable little nephew giggle like crazy. So it turns out all men are the same, they all love toilet humour.

Millsy does this a few more times, until Dani comes back.

'Really? I leave the two of you alone with him for two minutes and you're already being bad influences. I hope that you two never have a kid.'

'Erm, just friends,' I remind her, sounding almost repulsed. It might seem like an extreme reaction, but Millsy is like a brother to me and we get this a lot – people assuming we're a couple.

'I know that – don't be so defensive,' she replies. 'I thought you might have one of those pity deals for when you're older and still alone.'

I frown. Dani sounds like she's pretty sure that's how things are going to play out for us – and I thought we were such catches.

My brother joins us again and gestures for me to go and make the tea, so I pass my nephew to him and head for the kitchen.

I grab some mugs – including my favourite from when I was a kid: a Smarties mug that I got with an Easter egg. It's brown, with

Smarties all over it; however the colours have faded from years of milky cups of tea when I was a kid, strong cups of coffee when I thought I was a cool teenager and sneaky vodka and oranges to endure family parties throughout my twenties. I've been through a lot with this mug, and it shows.

As I make the drinks I stare out of the back window, over towards Weird Ian's house. Is it just my imagination getting the better of me? Weird Ian's house isn't the first one we gave a backstory to. When we were quite young there was a house at the end of the street that was empty for a while, but we all used to play in the huge oak tree in the garden until one day when someone new moved into it. A tall fence was built around the garden with barbed wire running along the top, there were metal shutters on all of the windows and big security lights that lit up every inch of the property.

Well, my friends and I found this so intriguing, that when our parents instructed us to stay away, we knew something was going on. Convinced it was a movie star, we hatched a plan to break into the garden by scaling the fence, snipping the barbed wire with a tool we took from Millsy's dad's tool kit, before hopping over and hiding in the tree until we saw who it was. The plan was perfect, obviously, until Millsy got his arm caught on the barbed wire. He screamed so loudly we didn't even need to tell our parents; they all heard the noise from inside their houses. They came running over, carefully freeing Millsy before taking him to hospital for stitches.

When he came back, that was when they sat us all down and explained that a registered sex offender had moved onto the street. I imagine the moral of the story is that you should never assume what's going on behind closed doors, but all I took from this was that everyone is probably a criminal and that no one should be trusted. Maybe that's why I struggle to trust guys on Matcher? Because I go in thinking I'm getting a movie star, and wind up with a sex offender instead.

I place the cups on a tray and carry them through to the living room. The first thing I notice is that Dani and Robbie have left.

'Hey, where did they go?' I ask.

'Scotland, I told you,' Woody reminds me.

'No, I knew that's where they were going, but have they left already? I figured Dani would say goodbye because, you know, just basic manners.'

'She wanted to beat the traffic.'

I shrug my shoulders.

'So, that's you a free man for a while,' Millsy reminds him. 'I hope you're going to make the most of it.'

'I've just signed up to Netflix,' he tells us.

'Oh, I see. Netflix and chill,' Millsy replies with a wink. My brother is oblivious.

'Erm, yeah. I thought I might watch *House of Cards*.'

'That's great for it,' Millsy tells him.

'It isn't Netflix and chill if *House of Cards* is on,' I correct my friend. 'It's Netflix and don't you dare lay a finger on me because *House of Cards* is on.'

Millsy laughs, but my brother looks so confused by all of our pop culture references it hurts.

'You two have lost me,' he admits.

'Netflix and chill,' Millsy starts. 'When you invite a chick over to watch TV and then shag while it plays in the background.'

'I've been married for so long,' he says with a sigh. 'I don't even know the euphemisms anymore.'

'The perks of the dating game are way more fun than marriage,' Millsy tells him, attempting to copy the 'but that's none of my business' meme with his tea, but burning his tongue because it's still too hot.

'Well, I'll be watching Netflix and chilling on my own. Might take myself out for dinner – I probably won't even put out for myself, because why would I change what I'm used to?' He laughs.

'Least you won't go blind, pal. Hey, you should come out with us.'

'Really?' My brother and I both ask at the same time.

'Yes, really,' Millsy says. 'It'll be like old times.'

I look over at my brother and I see something in his eyes that I haven't seen in a long time: a glimmer of excitement.

'We're going to a bar in Leeds, come with us,' I insist.

'Yeah, see what the cool kids do with their free time,' Millsy adds.

'Well, if you're sure you don't mind,' Woody says.

'Of course not,' I tell him. And I mean it.

'Fuck yeah!' my brother shouts excitedly, before his voice drops a little. 'Just, promise not to check me in on Facebook. Dani would kill me.'

Chapter 8

'Welcome to Thin Aire,' I tell my brother as we step out of the lift and into the dimly lit bar.

'So this is where my sister spends all her time,' he says as he looks around.

Of all the bars I frequent in Leeds – and believe me, there's a few – Thin Aire is my favourite. My local. I have put in lots of time, charm and money to become a regular here and it's finally paying off. I am on first-name terms with most of the staff. They let me jump the queue at the bar and they'll often throw freebies my way. But, like I said, this is my local, even though it's by no means the bar closest to where I live. The thing I like most about Leeds is that there are several areas all populated with bars, and each area will have a different vibe and different clientele.

With my penchant for expensive cocktails and handsome men in suits, the many rooftop bars overlooking the River Aire are where I like to be, but Thin Aire is my favourite by a mile. It's situated at the top of an eighty-metre-tall office block, and it's almost entirely made of glass. The floor-to-ceiling, wrap-around glass windows provide a stunning view across Leeds from all angles, and the coolest part is that to get up here, you take the glass lift that runs up the side of the building. Something my brother did not know, that made him feel a little green around the gills when he first stepped into the lift five minutes ago.

'I don't spend that much time here,' I reply.

'Your Facebook check-ins beg to differ,' he replies.

Right on cue, Ella, one of the hostesses walks past, spots me, and kisses both my cheeks.

'Ruby, good to see you again,' she tells me before dashing off, back to work.

'Also, that.' Woody laughs.

'We're their favourite customers,' Millsy says. 'Admit it.'

'Maybe I am,' I reply. 'You not so much. It was only last week they had to talk that crying girl who locked herself in the toilets into coming out again so they could close up.'

Millsy laughs, grabbing a menu and handing it to Woody. 'What can I say? The ladies love me.'

'Man, I want your life,' Woody says.

'Ah, it's not all it's cracked up to be,' I lie, with a sigh.

'I was talking to Millsy,' he clarifies.

After glancing at the menu, Woody offers it to both of us. We both stare at him blankly.

'Of course you guys don't need to see it,' he says.

Jimmy, my favourite barman, makes his way across the bar to us. 'Usual, guys?' he asks.

'Yes please,' I reply, much to Woody's amusement. 'And for your date?' he asks.

I watch my brother's eyes widen with horror.

'Wow, how many blokes does she bring in here if that was your first thought?' he asks Jimmy. 'I'm her brother.'

'Can't you see the family resemblance?' I ask Jimmy.

'Around the eyebrow,' Millsy jokes.

I elbow him semi-playfully.

'Jimmy, this is my brother, Woody. Woody, this is Jimmy, the assistant manager here.'

They shake hands. Jimmy fixes our drinks for us before freeing us up a table by the window, overlooking the Trinity Centre. We're high above it, but the view of the glass atrium, covered with its colourful, twinkling lights, is stunning. The best thing is that the more you drink, the more kaleidoscopic and captivating it looks.

'So, this is your life?' Woody asks as he glances around the busy bar, packed full of beautiful people with their expensive drinks. 'You just work in the café all day, dress up, come here and drink until you crawl home?'

'You say that like it's a bad thing,' I joke.

'No, I'm jealous,' he replies. 'It beats going door to door selling double glazing all day before going home to your wife, who you annoy, and your child, who you only seem to see when he's screaming or sleeping.'

'Mate, I'm definitely going to buy so many condoms on my way home,' Millsy jokes, an unimpressed look plastered across his face.

'That'll be a first,' I tease.

'So, what makes this bar different from all the other rooftop bars?' Woody asks. Right on cue, the manager steps out of the lift.

'Ask your sister,' Millsy chuckles, noticing me staring at Tom. Tom is not the manager's name; in fact, I have no idea what his name is, but the first time I laid eyes on him, I fell head over heels in lust. Tall, dark and handsome, with his sexy brown eyes and his slicked-back brown hair, Tom is built in a way that my mum would describe as 'chunky' – that sort of rugby player big build that's neither fat nor overly muscular. I made the mistake of saying he looked like Tom Hardy to Millsy once so he started referring to him as Tom to tease me – the name just stuck.

'Does Ruby have a crush?' Woody asks patronisingly.

I feel my cheeks flush. I like to think I'm a pretty cool customer, but Tom is the one person on this earth I have an uncontrollable, schoolgirl-style crush on. When I'm around him, all of my charm and wit goes out of the window.

'She does,' Millsy tells him on my behalf. 'Luckily for her, she never has to speak to him because he doesn't work behind the bar. I don't think she could speak to him if she tried.'

'Come on, I'm not that bad,' I protest.

'Erm, I beg to differ. Last week when he said goodbye to you, you babbled something that sounded a bit like "goodbye" mixed with "sweet dreams" and then you damn-near came in the lift.'

My brother chokes on his drink a little, a combination of shock and amusement, just as Tom walks past. Recognising us as regulars, he gives us a nod of acknowledgement before heading off into the kitchen.

I puff air out of my cheeks once he is past us and out of earshot.

'He's just so perfect,' I explain to the two men, who are obviously immune to his charm. 'Those big, strong arms! There's a rumour that a guy once came in wearing a snapback cap and refused to leave, so Tom dangled him over the terrace.'

'They take the dress code seriously,' Millsy jokes.

'Mate, he can dangle me over the terrace any time,' I say, biting my lip for effect.

'Mate, you've been single for too long,' Millsy reminds me. 'The only action you get is in your dreams.'

I shoot him a filthy look, which my brother notices. 'Oh shit, who are you dreaming about?' Woody asks.

'Her flatmate, Dr Dick,' Millsy tells him.

'Nick? Really?' my brother asks, shocked. He knows that we don't exactly get on.

'Really,' I admit. 'And it keeps happening.'

'Which is weird, because he's a waste of space,' Millsy adds.

'That's not exactly fair, he saved a woman's life on the train today.' I start telling Woody the full story. 'It was incredible, honestly. I've never seen anything like it. I can't stop thinking about it.' I think for a second before confessing: 'I can't stop thinking about *him*. What the fuck is wrong with me?'

It's the first time I've been able to say it out loud, to admit it to anyone (myself included), and I'm just hoping the two most important men in my life will know what I need to do to stop this.

'Do you have feelings for him?' Woody asks.

'I can't,' I squeak. 'Can I?'

'OK, hold that thought.' Millsy thinks for a moment. 'Right, the sex dreams, we've established, are because you're not getting any. And today has made this worse. You only fancy him because you saw him save that old lady. It's a thing, to be attracted to heroes. That's why nurses are so hot.'

My brother and I laugh at his reasoning. 'I'm sure it'll pass,' I tell them.

As we drink and joke together, I'm having so much fun I don't even notice a bloke walk over and stand beside us.

'Ruby?' he says, catching my attention.

I glance at him for a second and eventually realise who he is.

'Greg?' I start slowly, momentarily uncertain if I'm getting his name right or not because, I mean, I have previous with getting names muddled up. 'Hello, how are you?'

Instinctively, I stand up and hug him, as though I would an old friend, except I don't really know Greg that well at all; he's just someone I've been chatting to on Matcher. Yes, another one, but that's how these things work – you have to chat to a bunch of people at once. We've been messaging on and off for a month now, but for some reason we've never really spoken about meeting up. Still, he seems nice, so I've happily chatted to him whenever he has messaged me.

'I'm good, thanks. Had a few drinks with some of the fellas from the office. I was just leaving when I spotted you.'

'Oh, cool,' I start. 'I was just—'

'Are you from Matcher too?' Millsy interrupts.

Greg nods awkwardly.

'Us too – you're welcome to make it a foursome?'

As I see the look of horror consume Greg's face, I quickly set him straight.

'That's Millsy, my soon to be former best friend. And Woody, my brother.'

'Nice to meet you both,' Greg says awkwardly, before turning back to me. 'Do you want to grab a quick drink before I go?'

'Oh, erm, I'd love to,' I start. I actually would kind of like to hang out with him; he seems pretty cool in person. 'But I can't ditch my friends.'

'Sure you can,' Millsy insists.

'Well, there you go,' Greg says with a smile. 'I'll wait for you over by the bar.'

'OK, sure.'

Once Greg is out of earshot, I double-check with Millsy and Woody that they actually don't mind.

'What happened to bros before hoes?' my brother jokes.

'Mate, seriously, if your sister doesn't get some action soon her theme park is going to close for business for good, not just the winter. You know what I mean?'

'I do,' Woody replies solemnly. 'Cheers for that wonderfully vivid explanation.'

'I'm not going to sleep with some guy I just met, am I?' I ask rhetorically. I don't say that because I'm above it, more because sleeping with someone for the first time takes a lot of preparation. First of all, my waxing game has been a little lax recently. Well, I begrudge every single hair I remove for men who just aren't worth it and, also, it's winter and it acts as a sort of layer of insulation between my skin and my clothes – do you know how many weeks/days/hours it would take for me to grow that hair back? Also, I'm wearing my terrifying, boner-killing, stomach-holding-in tights that men neither can – nor ultimately want to – wrestle me out of. Nope, not tonight, love.

'Well, you should. You've got the fear, you just need to get back in the saddle,' he insists.

'Don't tell me, it's like riding a horse,' I say, rolling my eyes.

'It is if you do it the way I like it,' he says with a wink. 'Now get over there. This is the only way to prove to yourself that you feel nothing for Nick – it'll break the spell. Tell her, Woody.'

I glance at my brother, amused, ready for him to make a case to persuade his little sister to have sex with a man she's technically just met.

'Whatever ends this conversation the quickest,' he replies.

'One drink,' I assure them. 'I'll be back.'

'I've heard that one before.' Millsy laughs.

Chapter 9

There must be something in the air tonight – or something in the drinks at Thin Aire, because everyone is pairing up.

I've been sitting, chatting and drinking with Greg for a while now, and I have to admit, he's pretty awesome for a Matcher bloke. We're all capable of being fun, witty and interesting when we are conversing via carefully constructed messages, where we are paying extra attention to how we're coming across. In person, people aren't always as cool as they seem, but not Greg; Greg is a blast.

We've been talking a lot and drinking even more, but I couldn't help noticing that Millsy and my brother acquired the company of two twenty-something females at some point in the evening. I'm not worried about that; I know that my brother would never cheat on his wife, no matter how horrible or boring she might be, so even if they do all go back to Millsy's place, I'll bet both birds end up with Millsy while my brother takes his chances on the sofa. Still, he's missed his last train now, so he's made his sofa bed, he's got to lie on it.

Yes, there must be something in the air, because I have done something majorly out of character – I've just jumped into a taxi with Greg to go back to his. I never do this – I know, that's what they all say, but I really don't. So why the sudden change of character? Well, I hate to admit it, but maybe Millsy is right: I'm having sex dreams about Nick because I've been single for so long and because he's the male I spend the most time around who isn't like a brother to me. It's been that long since I had sex, I'm pretty sure I'm required to sit through a biology lesson before I'll be allowed to safely do it again, just in case I've forgotten all about the birds and the bees.

Millsy is horrified by my dry spell and says I'm now officially masturdating myself.

Whatever, I'm drunk, I'm having fun, I'm going to be safe – why shouldn't I let my hair down?

'Here we are,' Greg says as the Uber pulls up outside the block of flats where he lives. I don't think we're too far from the centre – far enough to need a taxi though. I'll have to get a taxi home in the morning because I'm notoriously bad with directions and getting from A to B without help is always a struggle.

Greg takes my hand and leads me through his building silently – well, it is 2 a.m. – until we're in the privacy of his flat. As soon as the door closes it's like a switch is flicked in Greg's head, like he's been waiting all this time to finally go wild.

'Bedroom,' he mutters through our kisses, leading me towards the door. I follow his lead, as instructed, ready to let my hair/guard/mother down for the first time in a long time (no, wait, I let my mother down all the time, scratch that last one) but as he releases me from his grip for a moment to whip off his shirt, I am suddenly able to properly take in my surroundings. Holy shit, his bedroom is like a *Doctor Who* museum, from pictures to gadgets to his bed sheets – Greg must be a hardcore fan. This isn't fair at all, this is the kind of thing that you should have to disclose on your dating profile. I feel more violated than I did when I was catfished, when Matt the sexy pilot turned out to be a shy, fifty-something man with no flying experience beyond his love of flight-simulation games. Yes, I stayed, and we had a nice chat about his hobbies, but needless to say there was no second date.

Now, I don't know much about *Doctor Who*, but what I do know is that I can't have sex in this room with all these monsters' eyes on me.

'Hit play on the stereo,' Greg insists. I eyeball the machine, fully convinced the *Doctor Who* theme music will start playing if I hit the play button.

'Can I use your lav, please?' I ask, stalling.

Greg nods, reluctantly. He gives me a look that tells me to hurry. It's just that I'm not into it anymore suddenly, and for some reason I can't stop thinking about what happened with Nick today, the way he jumped in to save that woman's life. He really is making a huge difference in the world, and I'm just serving coffee. Wait, why am I thinking about Nick when I'm about to have sex, or not have sex as the case may be this evening?

I look at myself in Greg's bathroom mirror and laugh.

'Ruby Wood,' I say to myself, in my head. 'How do you get yourself into these nightmare dates?'

There's only one thing for it. There's no way I can go through with it, and I'm a grown woman after all. I know what I need to do.

I walk back into Greg's room where he's waiting for me on the bed, already stripped down to his (unsurprisingly) *Doctor Who* boxer shorts.

'Do you want the good news or the bad news?' I ask, hovering around in the doorway sheepishly.

Greg's face falls. 'Erm, the bad news,' he replies, reluctantly.

'The bad news is that my "time of the month" has just kicked in,' I lie. If Greg's face had fallen before, it's so low it's in the flat below us now.

'What's the good news?' he asks hopefully.

'I'm not pregnant,' I announce brightly, complete with jazz hands.

Greg's look shifts from disappointment to horror but if the first excuse doesn't put him off, the second will for sure.

'Oh,' he replies. 'Well, never mind. Maybe next time.'

'Maybe,' I reply, and yes, that does seem to be the catchphrase I end all my Matcher dates with, and yes, it is code for "I never want to see you again".

'Well, I'll make my way home I think,' I tell him, grabbing my things.

'Don't be daft,' he insists. 'It's too late for you to be trailing out, and I would really like to see you again. Stay the night.'

It's at this point that I remember that Greg is not a bad person, just a huge, huge nerd.

'Are you sure?' I ask. That's very sweet of him, although with all these creepy eyes on me, I'm not sure I'll be able to get to sleep at all.

'I'm sure,' he says with a smile, patting the space on the bed next to him.

'OK, thank you,' I reply, hopping in beside him.

Greg leans over and kisses me on the forehead before flicking off the lamp next to his bed. Unlucky for me, the *Doctor Who* Tardis night-light in the corner of his room illuminates the place pretty well, so I can still see all the nerdy stuff around me. How does a grown man get so much passion for one thing? I mean, I know I'm passionate about things: prosecco, eyebrows, Tom Hardy – but not to the point where I'd have a room dedicated to one thing.

Why does time move so slowly when you don't want it to? When you're on a good date or having the best sex of your life or sunbathing on the beach – time goes so quickly then, doesn't it? But when you're in the doctor's surgery, waiting for your shift to end at work or spending a night trying to sleep in a *Doctor Who* shrine, time drags.

I look at my phone – 4 a.m. Three more hours and maybe I can leave without seeming rude or weird.

I wonder if Millsy is still awake, so I text him.

Ruby: Hey, you awake, mate?

I don't have to wait long for a reply.

Millsy: Sure am. I take it you're not home?
Ruby: Nope. I take it you're having a threesome …
Millsy: Nope. If I wanted to disappoint two people at the same time, I'd visit my parents.

I laugh quietly to myself, careful not to wake Greg who is fast asleep.

Ruby: Wow, you met girls in a bar and didn't pull one of them – you must be growing up.
Millsy: Oh, no, I did pull one of them. I left the other with Woody playing Mario Kart in the living room. So I guess we both got lucky tonight.
Ruby: Erm, not quite. I got very unlucky. The guy is like the world's biggest Doctor Who *fan. His bedroom is just wall-to-wall with nerdy merchandise.*
Millsy: Fuck off, you're making that up.
Ruby: I wish I were. He's got a life-sized Dalek next to his bed.
Millsy: Pics or it didn't happen.

Ah, the age-old internet rule of 'pics or it didn't happen' – standard protocol for situations where only seeing is believing.

As I sit up slowly to try and take a snap of the Dalek that stands next to Greg's bed, watching over him as he sleeps, I feel another message come through on my phone.

Millsy: Selfie!

I should've known he wouldn't make this easy for me, but I've never been one to chicken out of a dare.

The Dalek is on Greg's side of the bed, so If I angle it right, I can get myself and the Dalek in the frame whilst Greg sleeps between us, blissfully unaware of the nightmare Matcher date he's given me.

I switch to the front-facing camera and line up my shot before posing with a meaningful pout and pointing a finger towards the Dalek behind me. Just as I press the shutter button, I notice something in the digital reflection on my phone screen: Greg's eyes are open!

It's too late. As the picture takes I realise that it has captured the moment. 'What the fuck?' Greg shouts, jumping to his feet.

'I can explain,' I start. I mean, I *can* explain, but I'm not sure how well he'll take it …

'Just get out,' he yells.

I grab my things and head for the door, booking my Uber as I go. 'Weirdo,' he calls out as I close the door behind me.

Once in the safety of the quiet corridor of his building, I slip my shoes on and make my way downstairs.

And just like that I've turned my Matcher date from hell into Greg's nightmare date instead.

Chapter 10

My taxi driver drops me outside McDonald's on Briggate, where Millsy is waiting for me at a table with four cheeseburgers and two large fries sitting in front of him. You've got to love the sanctuary that a twenty-four-hour McDonald's provides, even if it is still rammed with drunk people fresh out of the clubs. You've also got to love having a best friend who will drop everything (including a bird) to meet up with you when you've had a bad night, no matter what time it is.

As I approach Millsy he spots me and starts humming a song that sounds vaguely familiar, banging his hands on the table as he does so.

I sit down in front of him and wait for him to finish. He looks so proud of himself.

'What the fuck is that?' I ask.

'Two cheeseburgers and large fries,' he replies. 'For that hangover that's pending.'

'Thank you,' I start. 'But I meant the song.'

'Oh. It's the *Doctor Who* theme music.' He laughs.

'Erm, not it isn't,' I tell him, as I struggle to peel open my sweet-and-sour sauce.

'Course it is,' he insists, taking it from the top.

'She's right,' a man on the table next to us insists. He's drunk and covered in barbecue sauce, but he's on my side so I'm not about to whip out my rape alarm.

'What is it then?' Millsy asks him, annoyed.

'It's "The Imperial March" from *Star Wars* – you know, Darth Vader's theme music,' he informs us.

'Erm, well I obviously don't know because I'm not a huge geek,' Millsy tells him, clearly irritated that someone has proven him wrong.

'Thank you,' I tell him.

'You're welcome,' the man replies, too drunk to notice that Millsy offended him. He affectionately taps me on the nose with a chip before getting back to his meal.

'I hate drunk people when I'm sober,' Millsy tells me as he takes a bite of his burger.

'You're not exactly sober,' I remind him, as I wipe chip grease from my nose with a paper napkin.

'Am I ever completely sober though?' He laughs. 'Anyway, come on, I want to see this photo.'

When I left Greg's place the first thing I did was call Millsy and the first thing he did was come to see me – although that might be because I told him all about it and he really wants to see the photo. I've been too mortified to look at it.

I unlock my phone and load up my camera roll, clicking it and turning it to show Millsy without looking for myself, instead watching his reaction.

The look on my friend's face is one of pure elation, like I was showing him the lottery numbers and that burger in his hand was the winning ticket.

'I don't think I've ever seen anything more incredible in my life,' he half speaks/half pants in a fit of laughter. 'Oh, God, look at it. Seriously.'

I take a deep breath and look. Were it a photo of anyone else, I imagine I'd find it hilarious too. It's the Dalek in the background.

It's the pout on my face. It's the look of horror in Greg's eyes.

I shake my head, smiling gently. I do see the funny side; it's just mortifying.

'I'm going to have T-shirts made with that on,' Millsy says, sipping his drink.

'I believe that,' I reply.

I unwrap my burger to see that whoever constructed it has drastically misfired with the cheese. As I scrape it from the paper and try to push it back inside the bread, I sigh.

'It's 4 a.m. and they're rammed in here, what were you expecting?' Millsy asks.

'It's not that,' I tell him. 'I couldn't sleep with Greg.'

'Damn right you couldn't, not with that thing standing next to the bed watching you.'

I give Millsy a slight smile, but I fear my friend is only trying to make me feel better.

'Are you telling me you wouldn't sleep with a girl in the same situation?'

'Mate, her best friends could be watching and I'd still be able to do it.' He laughs. 'But I don't know what else to say.'

I stare at my burger, too scared to look my friend in the eye as I say the words that are on the tip of my tongue.

'I have a crush on Nick.'

'After a couple of sex dreams and watching him save someone's life? Come on,' Millsy reasons.

'I can't stop thinking about him. I can't sleep with other people. I ... I don't know what to do.'

'Look, calm down, OK? Let's not over-react. You're drunk, you've had a rough night. Just go home, get to bed, chill out and in the morning you'll have forgotten all about it, OK?'

'OK, sure,' I reply, but I'm not convinced.

Chapter 11

After dragging my half-drunk, half-hungover butt up the hill to my flat, I struggle to find the concentration and the energy involved to unlock the door. It's not my fault though; the lock on this thing is a little temperamental. I take my key out and put it back in, I jiggle it around in the lock – nothing works. Exhausted and exasperated, I stop trying, leaning forward to rest my head against the door. In the second before my head makes contact, the door is opened from the inside, causing me to fall straight into Nick's arms.

I pause in his strong grip for a moment, until he hurriedly pushes me back onto my feet and releases me, like I'm something gross he accidentally caught as a reflex that he can't wait to put down.

'Wha … what are you doing up?' I babble.

'I'm going for a run,' he tells me.

'At this time of night?' I ask.

'Ruby, it's morning.'

'Oh.'

'No prizes for guessing what you've been doing until this time,' he says, unimpressed.

'Not *that* – honest,' I insist, worried about what he thinks of me for the first time in my life.

Nick glances down at my body briefly before making eye contact again. 'Your dress is on inside out,' he tells me.

I look down and see that he's right. Fuck.

'Goodnight,' he says as he heads downstairs, not really sounding like he means it. God, he looks good in his running gear. He's wearing tight pants and a fitted vest with a hoodie loosely over the top, probably to combat the chilly morning weather, along with a beanie hat covering his short, neat, dark hair.

'Wait,' I call after him, because for some reason I don't want him to leave. 'What are you doing today?'

Nick turns around and looks at me, visibly puzzled why I'd ask such a thing. 'Why, do you want to grab a coffee?' he asks.

I'm momentarily tongue-tied – luckily, it turns out.

'Ruby, I'm kidding, don't look so worried.' He laughs. 'I don't want to hang out with you either.'

Words we've exchanged with each other a thousand times, but now they really sting.

'No, right. Yuck,' I say, unconvincingly.

'Anyway, I've got some time off so I'm going to go stay with my family in Ilkley tonight, so you've got the place to yourself. Have your dating freaks over, tell Joe it's safe for him to come round – just make sure the place isn't trashed for me coming back, OK?'

I nod nervously.

'If you're going home, you're going to want to take that hat off,' I tell him, in a voice that does not sound like my own. I sound like a dork.

'What?' he asks.

'You know, like the song: "On Ilkla Moor Baht 'at". You need to take your hat off,' I continue, kicking myself a little harder with each word that leaves my mouth.

'Are you having a stroke?' he asks me, straight-faced.

'It was a joke,' I tell him.

'OK, what have you broken?' he asks. 'What kind of fast one

are you trying to pull? Are you trying to sneak someone in? Are you pranking me? The sooner you tell me what's wrong with you, the better.'

'Nothing, nothing,' I assure him. 'Doesn't matter. See you later.' Nick shakes his head and jogs the rest of the way down the stairs.

I close the flat door behind me and look at myself in the mirror that sits above the bowl where we keep the keys – the bowl Nick insists the keys must be kept in at all times. My God, what do I see in him, seriously? We have nothing in common. We hate each other. Look how horrible he was to me just now, and how judgemental he was. I'm the kind of girl who gets in and goes to bed at 6 a.m. and he's the kind of guy who gets up and heads out at 6 a.m. He's going for a run, I just ate two cheeseburgers. We couldn't be more opposite if we tried. Millsy is right, I just need to give it time and this silly crush will wear off. I just hope it happens sooner rather than later because things are starting to feel very awkward.

Chapter 12

'Mate, she was bang-on about your eyebrows.'

I shoot Millsy a filthy look.

'That customer from Friday,' he persists. 'She was right about those brows. You look like a pissed-off Cara Delevingne in an Avril Lavigne wig.'

I give my long dirty blonde and pink ombre curls a defensive fluff with my hands.

'I look pissed off because you're pissing me off,' I tell him. 'And you know it's because I'm part Italian. We're brow-rich, butt-rich, temper-rich and national-football-team-rich.'

'You can't just blame everything on you being a bit Italian,' he insists, suddenly inspired to start eating biscotti out of the jar. 'Like assaulting teenage boys by throwing muffins at them. Anyway, you're not Italian, your mum is half Italian. Your dad is as English as tea.'

'First of all, that was one time,' I protest. 'And tea is from China, dipshit.'

'Language,' I hear a woman gasp. 'And what's this about throwing food at customers?'

'When I asked him what he wanted, he said "your chebs, love" and it wasn't a full-size muffin, it was a mini muffin, which is a third the size of a regular one – and who are you?' I ask as it occurs to me I'm explaining myself to a perfect stranger.

'Rita,' Millsy beams, hopping over the counter to give her a hug. 'How are you?'

'I'm fantastic, how are you?' she asks him. 'Have your muscles grown *even more* since the last time I saw you?'

Oh, what a creep. She must know Millsy well, she clearly knows how to get around him. If I want him to do me a favour, I comment on how his biceps have grown. If I want to piss him off, I ask him if he's getting enough protein.

Millsy flexes, exhibiting a level of charm, narcissism and muscle mass you could only get from Gaston in *Beauty and the Beast*. I shake my head.

'Rubes, this is Rita. She used to be the manager, before you started working here. Best manager we ever had,' he says, safe in the knowledge Sally is off sick today.

'Well, what would you say if I told you I was back?' she asks. 'But there will be no assaulting customers and no dipshit-this and chebs-that.'

'No way! That's awesome. Ruby is sound really, she's just hungover.'

Millsy sounds genuinely delighted. I, however, remain unconvinced. I liked working for Sally. She'd let us arrive late, leave early, drink as much coffee as our nervous systems could handle and she found our silly stories funny – even the ones with swear words. Rita is probably only in her mid-thirties, but she reminds me of a teacher – from her cardigan to her Dame-Edna-esque glasses. She looks like she should be shushing people in a library, not giving me shit for swearing. Someone needs to have a word with her about her fashion sense (or lack thereof) and if she doesn't stop giving me dirty looks, it might just be me.

'Way,' she replies. 'Sally has started early maternity leave; it was all too much for her. It doesn't sound like she was getting much help.' Rita shoots me a look.

'Hey, don't look at me like that; he's here too, you know,' I protest, nodding towards Millsy who is trying to stealthily crunch what's left of his biscuit.

'Joe was always the model employee while I was working here,' Rita informs me, glancing over at him fondly.

Oh, so he shagged her then. I look my friend in the eye, giving him a look that tells him I'm onto him, and he gives me a subtle raise of his eyebrows that confirms as much.

'Well,' Rita starts, using her sleeve to wipe a fingerprint from the coffee machine. 'I'll head into the office; lots to do, I'm told.'

'No worries,' Millsy calls after her. 'We've got everything sorted out here.'

'No worries, miss,' I repeat mockingly once she's gone. 'We've got everything sorted out here, miss.'

Millsy shoots me an unimpressed look. 'Fuck off, she's a nice lady.'

'A nice lady you've definitely slept with,' I say under my breath. 'I just didn't think she'd be your type of person,' I persist. She's so stuck-up and boring and Millsy is the most fun person you could hope to meet.

'She was a good boss,' he replies. 'And I love all women.'

'I'm a woman,' I remind him.

'No way, mate. You're just a lad with tits.'

I think for a moment. 'I'm going to take that as a compliment.'

It's 3 p.m., and we've got a rush of customers suddenly, which means Millsy and I don't really get to chat much.

'Two small skinny caramel lattes and a flat white,' I tell him as I pop a teacake in the toaster behind us. 'Then we're swapping.'

Millsy and I take it in turns doing the different jobs behind the counter, so while one of us is making the drinks the other has to do everything else. Making the drinks is the fun bit, playing with the cool machine, messing around with latte art, chatting to the customers as they wait for their order. The other role involves taking the orders, preparing and cooking the food, taking the money and trying to juggle multiple people's requests at once, so really, if you're going to do either job, you want to be the barista and not the everything-else person.

'You'll have to do them; I've got to get to my audition,' Millsy tells me, whipping off his apron and throwing it to me.

'I can't do all this on my own,' I squeak. 'Tables need clearing too.'

'I'll get Rita to help, no sweat.'

Come to think of it, I'd probably rather run this place single-handedly. 'OK, sure,' I reply.

In a matter of minutes Millsy is back with his leather jacket on, ready to head out to his audition.

'Rita is on her way,' he tells me. 'Bump me luck.'

In the midst of the chaos of this unofficial rush hour, I give my friend a first bump.

'Joe said you needed my help,' Rita says, tying an apron around her waist as she joins me behind the counter.

She makes it sound like she's doing me a favour.

'Thank you,' I say, through gritted teeth. 'Well, if you want to serve the next customer, I'll crack on with this lady's coffee order.'

Rita holds her hand up in a 'stop' position, right in front of my face. 'Ruby, Ruby, Ruby,' she starts, shaking her head as she speaks. 'I'm the manager here, not you. I tell you what to do.'

'I wasn't telling you what to do,' I explain, very aware of the queue full of people spectating, all listening intently as I get ticked off. 'I was just telling you what needs doing.'

'I tell you what needs doing, OK? No one tells me what needs doing.'

'Well, unless you're psychic, someone is going to have to tell you what drinks this lady ordered at some point,' I correct her.

I fold my arms and stare at her as she thinks this one over. 'OK, tell me, then get back to serving,' she says reluctantly.

'Well, it was my turn to make drinks, I've been doing this for the past hour and—'

'Ruby, this is a business, not a playground. You'll do as you're told,' Rita snaps.

I glance at my customer who gives me a pitiful look. I might not be psychic either, but I can tell that this lady feels sorry for me. Still, I bite my tongue. This is only until Sally has her baby and then she'll be back, right? I just need to keep my cool until then because there's no way I'm letting a bitch like this mess up the sweet gig I've got going here.

Chapter 13

As I barge through my flat door, arse-first, it bangs against the cabinet that sits behind it, knocking over one of the framed pictures from on top of it.

I hear the smash of glass as it lands on the floor. 'Fuck,' I shout. 'Fuck, fuck, fuck.'

I dump my handbag on the floor, toss my keys in the direction of the key bowl (I miss, of course) and then lay my box of muffins down on the sofa.

At work, we had a whole bunch of food left at the end of the day, with a use-by date of today. Millsy and I usually bag it all up hand it out to the homeless people dotted around the city, but Rita says it's against company policy and that it all has to go in the bin. Still, I managed to smuggle four muffins out of there, but I didn't see anyone to give them to on the way home, so you better believe I'm going to eat at least two of them tonight.

It seems like such a waste, throwing all that good food in the bin, but if I'm learning anything about Rita, it's that she's a stickler for the rules, and authority matters to her more than anything.

'Oh, for fuck's sake,' Nick shouts as he walks out of his bedroom. He's looking good, in his perfectly ironed red shirt and black trousers. He's got that fresh-out-of-the-shower smell, mixed with his aftershave, which has never smelled more delicious. 'What have you done now?'

'It's this fucking stupid door,' I start ranting. 'I had to bang it to open it, and it smashed the fucking picture and I'm just having a really bad fucking day because my new boss is a fucking bitch and—'

I stop ranting as I realise that Nick is just staring at me blankly, probably terrified by my spectacular outburst.

'OK, that's a lot of "fuckings" so it must've been an actually bad day, not just your usual kind where they won't let you leave early to get drunk or murdered by a man you met on the internet.'

I glare at him.

'Sorry, couldn't resist,' he says with a chuckle.

As I soften my gaze a little, something strange happens. In fact, if I didn't know better, I'd think I was …

'Holy shit, are you crying?' he asks. 'I don't think I've ever seen you display an emotion before – other than rage.'

I wipe my eyes quickly. I rarely cry. It usually takes a lot to make me cry.

I have no idea what's going on in my head right now.

'Look, sit on the sofa. Accidents happen – you don't need to cry. I'll clean this up.'

I sit down as instructed while Nick tidies up. He takes his little dustpan and brush and sweeps up the broken glass. I can't help but snort with laughter at the sight of him with his girly little cleaning utensils.

'Well, that's better,' he says, putting the broken glass in the bin.

He wanders over to the sofa and stands for a second. His phone buzzes so he takes it from his pocket, punches a message to someone and then puts it away. I wipe my tears away with my sleeve, annoyed that there's nothing I can use to wipe my embarrassment away.

Nick looks like he's about to leave when he does something unexpected. He sits down next to me. It sounds stupid, but I literally pinch myself, just to make sure I'm not dreaming, because we all know how this usually plays out in my head.

'Is everything OK?' he asks me.

'I just feel really … unsettled at the moment. We've got a new manager at work who hates me; I'm sick of going on weird dates with even weirder people; Millsy is putting his acting first, which means he isn't around as much; my parents have gone on holiday for a month without telling me. I just feel like I have no idea what's going on anymore.'

I lean back, resting my head back on the sofa, gazing up at the ceiling as I wonder why the hell I'm spilling my guts to Nick, of all people.

'Ruby, everyone feels like that at some point in their life. We've all got shit to deal with, and for the most part we can handle it, but when we get too much shit at once it gets harder to cope with, and that's when we have to be tough and just do what it takes to get through it, tackling things one at a time.'

I sit up and look Nick in the eye.

'Really?' I ask. 'Even you feel this way sometimes?'

'Even me,' he tells me with a warm smile. 'I wish there was something I could write you a prescription for that would make you feel all better – actually, there are plenty of drugs I could give you that would make you feel better, but that wouldn't be ethical – I suppose,' he jokes.

I laugh.

'Well, if you have moments like this too, then I guess anyone can,' I reason. 'Because you are the one person I know who seems like they have it all together: a proper career, a girlfriend, a stable relationship with your family …'

'I don't have it all together,' he admits. 'Trust me, I'm a doctor.'

'You're a vagina doctor,' I tease. 'I bet you use that line to smooth-talk your way into girls' pants. Is that how you won Heather over?'

'It's how I won her sister over.' He laughs. His phone buzzes again.

'Speaking of Heather, I'm late to meet her, so if you're sure you're OK …'

'You sat talking to me when you were supposed to be meeting Heather?' I ask, unable to hide my surprise.

'I've never seen you cry,' he says with a laugh, by way of justification. 'I figured you needed someone.'

'Well, thank you,' I tell him sincerely.

'You're welcome,' he replies. 'Just because we don't get along very well, it doesn't mean we can't be friends, does it? I mean, Joe is a real dick, and you care about him regardless. For some reason.'

Nick gives my hand a little squeeze, laughing to himself as he heads for the door.

'See you later, kid.'

'Bye,' I call after him.

As Nick closes the door behind him, I smile to myself, lightly stroking my hand where he touched me. How have I had him so wrong all this time? Yes, he might be far more sensible than I am, but he's sweet, and he must care about me to make himself late just to talk to me, because I know how much lateness drives him crazy.

My phone rings snapping me from my thoughts. It's Millsy so I answer straight away.

'Hey, what's up?'

'So, the audition went terribly,' he starts, sounding dejected.

'Oh, fuck those fucking wankers,' I rant. Clearly I still have a few fucks left over from my bad mood. Millsy doesn't say anything. 'Millsy? You still there?'

'Erm, yeah. I was going to be cute and say, it went terribly for the other guys, because the director literally just offered me the part and I called you straight away to tell you so. On loudspeaker.'

'Fuck,' I say softly. Well, one more isn't going to make a difference. 'Sorry.'

'It's OK.' He laughs. 'I'm in the corridor now. You OK?'

'Congratulations,' I tell him. 'I'm actually pretty good. I have some big news too.'

'Ooh,' my friend exclaims. 'What? What?'

'Well, I had a super shitty day at work – Rita is horrible, I don't know how you had sex with her, even for the short amount of time I imagine you last.'

'Ha ha,' he replies sarcastically.

'Anyway I came home and Nick was here, and he was so sweet to me. He basically told me that he cared about me. He was late to meet Heather because he wanted to cheer me up. And, he said something to me about how we're still friends, even though we don't always get along, which is pretty much exactly what he said to me in my dream.'

'I'm going to be honest, you sound like a crazy person, but I'm interested to see where this is going,' Millsy says cautiously. 'Continue.'

'I'm going to make him mine,' I tell him, excitedly. 'We're supposed to be together, I just need to make it happen.'

'Rubes, he kind of hates you. He hates both of us. He makes your life miserable and – vital fact – he has a girlfriend, and just because you have a couple of sex dreams and you watch him grab an old lady from behind, suddenly you're going to try and steal him? You're crazy.'

'Maybe,' I admit. 'But I'll kick myself if I don't even try.'

'Well, I'm happy to stick around to watch you fuck up your situation even more than it already is; it sounds amusing.' He laughs. 'All I ask in exchange is that you help me learn my lines. I don't have much time at all.'

'Dude, you don't need my help. We did *Macbeth* at the end of year 11.'

'Exactly, which makes you more than qualified to help me learn my lines. I can't bullshit my way through this one. And stop saying the name of the play.'

'OK, fine,' I give in. 'But if I need any help with Nick, will you help me?'

'Oh, what are friends for, if not to help steal a boring guy from an even more boring girl so you can have awkward sex with him once and then struggle to look him in the eye ever again?'

'Thanks, babe. You're a star,' I reply sarcastically. 'See you at work tomorrow.

'Sure thing, bunny boiler.'

I hang up the phone before removing a double chocolate muffin from the box, peeling off the paper, eating the bottom bit first, because everyone knows the top bit is the best part, and I think. I know my crush on Nick has come out of nowhere, but maybe this is why I've never been able to properly fancy anyone else, because I've always had feelings for him and I never realised. They say that dreams are a window to our subconscious, which means that I'm having these dreams about Nick because deep down that's how I feel.

OK, so he's with Heather, but she's not a very nice person. She's bossy, she's selfish, she doesn't let him eat meat, for crying out loud. I've never seen her be nice to him, or anyone for that matter. I actually feel so sorry for the kids she teaches. Yep, Nick can do better, and I think I'm the girl who can give him what he wants. Now all I need to do is work out how to get it.

Chapter 14

It's 6.30 a.m., and I'm up and dressed way earlier than I need to be to get to work on time today. I'm currently lying on my bed, waiting for Nick to get out of the shower. I heard him get up a while ago and head out for a run, so I dashed in the bathroom while he was gone to make myself look as attractive as is possible ~~at this time of morning~~ when you are me, before hurrying back to my room. I heard him get back and get in the shower, so now I'm just waiting until I hear the water shut off so I can go grab my breakfast, moments before he goes for his, so we can bump into each other.

I hear the water shut off so I hop off my bed, grabbing my phone before making my way to the kitchen. I pop the kettle on and drop a couple of slices of bread into the toaster before hopping onto the worktop where I begin aimlessly scrolling through Instagram, just to look busy and to make this seem natural.

'Good morning,' I say brightly as Nick wanders into the kitchen, running a hand through his damp hair.

'Bloody hell,' he says, jumping. 'I didn't expect you to be awake. Has someone died?'

I laugh. 'Oh, you're so funny,' I say flirtatiously, although I don't think he was joking.

'Don't take the piss, Ruby. I've got a busy day ahead of me and I had a late night.'

'Fun night with Heather?' I ask, jealously suddenly hitting me like a ton of bricks.

'Yeah, it was great, thanks. We went to this place near the station called Planet.'

As my toast pops up I realise that it's burnt, testament to how often I use the toaster. Still, I hop down and begin spreading Nutella on it – after scraping as much of the black off as possible because I'm pretty sure I read somewhere that burnt food gives you cancer.

'The only place I know with a spacey-sounding name down by the station is Saturn,' I tell him.

'Yeah, I'm not talking about the godawful nightclub where you and Joe go hunting for prey. Planet is a vegan restaurant.'

'Ergh, does she make you go to only vegan restaurants?'

'*She* doesn't make me go anywhere,' he tells me. 'I do it because I care about her.'

'Give me a double cheeseburger and a big slab of chocolate any day,' I tell him, raising my toast to my mouth. I'm not used to eating so early in the morning, and while Nutella on toast sounded like a good idea on paper, I'm not sure I can stomach it right now – I don't think the fact I ate two and a half double chocolate muffins for my dinner last night is helping matters.

'So why are you up early and eating breakfast?' he asks me as he prepares his usual bowl of cereal.

'What? I get up early sometimes,' I protest.

'Except you don't,' he interrupts.

'And breakfast is the most important meal of the day. You're always saying so, and you're pretty smart.'

I think I've done well, dropping into the conversation both the fact that I listen and a compliment, but Nick just stares at me blankly.

'Piss-taking, again. I'm going to eat this in my room.'

'I wasn't—' I call after him, but he closes his bedroom door behind him.

Shit, I really was trying to be nice to him. What I'm forgetting is that we've spent the whole time we've known each other driving each other crazy, constantly at one another's throats – it's no wonder he finds it weird that I'm suddenly trying to be nice and flirty with him. I've spent so much time taking the piss out of him, why would he expect anything else?

If I want to get anywhere with Nick, I'm going to have to seriously up my game. It's not enough to suddenly start being sweet to him, I need to show him that I'm worthy of him … Now how the hell am I going to do that?

Chapter 15

Joe Mills is not the kind of person you go to for relationship advice. How to look good while you're at the gym? Yes. Where to hide in a girl's flat when her boyfriend gets home early? Yes. How to dodge chlamydia through sheer willpower alone? OK, perhaps that one is debatable. But everyone knows he's bad at relationships and as such, no one ever so much as brings up that they've dated a person more than once around him, lest such an alien level of commitment freak him out.

On the other hand, Paul Wood is exactly the kind of guy you'd go to if you needed relationship advice, because my brother has been with his wife since he was at school. Still, as successful as his marriage is on paper, I wouldn't exactly say he was happy, but he's sustaining *something* so I guess that's an achievement.

I'm not just trying to "bang" Nick, but I'm not exactly trying to marry him and have his babies, so neither Millsy nor Woody alone is going to have the answers I need, but I figure that if I get them together at the same time, between them we'll be able to come up with a plan of action that falls somewhere between banging and babies. That's why we're all gathered at my parents' house, to try and figure out how I can make Nick fall for me. Well, that and because my brother is bored out of his mind here on his own. Since he went out with Millsy and me for the night, he's been texting me way more than usual, telling me what a good time he had. Maybe he's just bored because his wife is away, or maybe he really doesn't have any fun anymore, but either way, it's kind of nice to be closer.

I'm the last to arrive and as I enter the living room, I find Millsy and Woody reading one of my mum's magazines together, swigging beer from the bottle – possibly to try and offset the magazine aimed at middle-aged women that they're engrossed in.

'Ladies,' I say, greeting them.

'Hey,' my brother replies, but Millsy clearly has other things on his mind. 'I've left my script in the kitchen. I'll just go grab it,' he says excitedly.

'Help Woody finish this quiz.'

Millsy tosses me the magazine and dashes off into the kitchen. I pick up the biro he left on the coffee table and find the page in the magazine that's all muddled up from being flung across the room.

'"Are you in a slump?"' I read the title out loud. I look at my brother in disbelief. 'Really? You're doing quizzes in ladies' magazines?'

'Well, I may as well finish it now,' he says awkwardly. 'It's just a bit of fun. You answer questions about yourself and it tells you how to analyse your answers. It's quite clever really.'

'OK, sure,' I reply. 'Are you currently going through the menopause?' I ask him before glancing up from the page, staring at him expectantly.

My brother pauses before he answers. 'Do … does it really say that?'

I roll up the magazine and hit him over the head with it.

'Of course it doesn't,' I laugh. 'I'm just wondering why you're giving a magazine like this any credit. You're a grown-ass man.'

'Just ask me the next question,' he insists.

'OK, fine.' I find the next empty box and ask the question

before it. 'What's your greatest achievement of the past twelve months?' I ask. My brother thinks for a moment.

'I had a baby,' he answers.

'Right.' I grab the pen and say what I write in the box out loud as I jot it down: 'Nothing.'

Woody shakes his head and laughs. 'Fine, forget it.'

'Right, I have my script and I have a copy for you so you can help me rehearse,' Millsy interrupts us, tossing a script at me.

'Stop throwing paper at me,' I snap. 'And, *Macbeth* is too heavy when I'm this tired.'

Millsy pulls a face. 'Come on, when we ruled Outwood High School, we blew everyone away with our parts in the Scottish play. What did Mrs Bloom say about your Lady Macbeth?'

'She remarked on my dissimulation and my cruelty,' I recollect.

'But what about the character you played?' my brother teases.

'Ahh, fuck you,' I reply with a sarcastic laugh.

'You know the Scottish play like the back of your hand, Rubes,' Millsy reminds me.

'Loser,' my brother teases and, my God, it's a sad day when my brother finds me more tragic than I do him.

'Hey, credit where it's due,' I start, quick to Shakespeare's defence. 'It is a work of art.'

My brother shrugs.

'I don't really know what it's about.'

'Really?' I squeak.

My brother shrugs again.

'So Macbeth is a Scottish nobleman. He and his friend Banquo meet these three witches who make three predictions: that Macbeth will become Thane of Cawdor, that Macbeth will become King of Scotland, and that Banquo's descendants will become kings. Banquo thinks it's daft, but when Macbeth does become Thane of Cawdor, that's it, he thinks it's all coming true. Then he tells his wife, who believes it too, and sets about helping him become king by whatever means necessary.'

'You see, women be cray cray,' Millsy insists.

'Ah, that famous Shakespearean quote.' My brother laughs.

'It's true though,' Millsy starts. 'His wife is the one who pushes him into doing bad things to make the predictions come true. And it's like, if he hadn't heard the predictions, would he even have done anything to try and make them come true?'

My brother nods thoughtfully, but inspiration hits me like a ton of bricks, causing me to jump to my feet.

'Millsy, that's it,' I squeak. 'That's what?' he asks.

'Think about it,' I start. 'Until I had those dreams about Nick, there's no way I ever would've done anything to try and get him. But those dreams I had are my predictions. Seeing those dreams has made me realise what is going to happen. Now I know that, I just need to do whatever it takes to make it so,' I say proudly.

Millsy and Woody just stare at me for a moment.

'Shall I take this one or do you want to?' Woody asks Millsy.

'Be my guest,' Millsy replies.

Woody takes a deep breath before he speaks.

'Probably don't take inspiration regarding your love life from a Shakespearean tragedy,' he tells me, as though it were obvious.

'Why not?' I ask, furrowing my brow.

'Well, how does *Macbeth* end?' he asks.

'OK, not ideally,' I admit. 'But I'm not shooting a remake, I'm just taking a little inspiration.'

'It's not like she's going to go all Romeo and Juliet.' Millsy laughs. 'That'd be worse.'

'Thank you,' I tell him, although I suspect he was just trying to be funny.

'Or you could just be honest with Nick and tell him how you feel,' my brother reminds me. Ah, the sensible option, but the one that puts me at the greatest risk of getting hurt.

'So we get to have some fun,' Millsy says excitedly. 'OK, I'm temporarily suspending play on Ruby Would/Ruby Wouldn't in favour of a new game: Truth or Date.'

'Wait, you're on her side?' Woody asks Millsy in amazement. 'It just surprises me, not only because that's really fucking stupid, but also because you hate Nick.'

'Exactly.' Millsy laughs. 'So it'll be doubly funny to watch her mess with him.'

'I'm not messing with him,' I insist. 'I just need to do what I need to do to win him over. So any ideas are appreciated.'

'Well, I have loads,' Millsy says, rubbing his hands together. 'So, Truth or Date, you've always got two choices: you can come clean with him, tell him the truth about your feelings – stupid idea in my opinion – or you can date, keep going out with other dudes, make him jealous … that *always* works.'

'I just want to go on record and say this is a stupid idea,' my brother states.

As I glance between my brother's concerned gaze and Millsy's excited grin, I realise just how relatable *Macbeth* is right now and, no, that's probably not a healthy thought.

'It's amazing,' I chuckle. 'Woody, you're my Banquo – you're just jealous about my awesome prediction. Millsy, you're my Lady Macbeth; I know you'll help me get shit done. Date it is.'

'You know it, my king,' he replies, putting on a girly voice.

I walk into the kitchen to grab a drink, turning on the light because, even though it's early evening, it's October and the sun seems to be setting earlier and earlier.

'How does *Macbeth* end?' my brother asks me, causing me to jump because I didn't realise he'd followed me.

'Shit, you scared me,' I shriek. I consider this for a second because, despite my brother not knowing the play well, I think we all know it doesn't end amazingly. 'Look, I'm not going to do anything stupid or extreme. I was only joking about the comparison.'

'Just be careful,' he warns me. 'Because despite what you might think, I lo …'

My brother's voice trails off.

'Wait, were you going to tell me you loved me?' I say, feigning shock. 'Shut up,' he snaps.

'Oh, charming. I—'

'Seriously, shut up,' he repeats, flicking the kitchen light out. 'Millsy, get in here,' he says in what I can only describe as a loud whisper.

Millsy hurries into the dark room. 'What?' he asks.

'Out the window,' Woody whispers.

'Awesome, what's Barbie doing now?' Millsy asks, dashing for the side window.

'No, the back window,' Woody tells him.

As we all approach the window behind the sink and gaze out across our back garden and into the one behind us, we spot Weird Ian, our creepy neighbour, digging a hole under one of his trees.

'What is he doing?' I ask. It's too late, dark and cold for gardening. Not only that but his garden has always been a mess; it's driven my dad crazy for as long as I can remember. Then I realise. 'He ... he's burying something.'

'It looks big,' my brother observes.

Maybe it's just coincidence, or maybe he can feel our eyes on him, but Weird Ian jolts his head upright suddenly, staring across at our house. We all duck down quickly.

'OK, what the fuck is going on with this guy?' I ask. 'He's always been weird, but this is really weird.'

'When I came in to get the beer earlier, I glanced across there. I saw him in his dining room with a woman, but I didn't think anything of it. Actually, I did think something of it, I thought "what the fuck could any woman see in Weird Ian" but that was about it.'

We all slowly climb to our feet, peeping back outside. From where we are, we can see the back of Ian's detached house, with a clear view of the open space at each side of the property. Once Ian is back indoors we don't see anything until we notice him going out, the silhouette of a man walking down the street visible toward the left side of his house.

'He's gone out,' Millsy observes. 'Let's go look in his garden.'

'Don't be stupid.' I laugh. 'I mean, OK, it's creepy, but it's probably nothing. And we'll get in trouble, just like when we were kids.'

'But we just saw him go out – see, we're smarter than when we were kids,' he reasons.

'No,' I tell him firmly. 'Now let's get on with rehearsing.'

'Fine, you party pooper,' he replies, sounding actually disappointed.

As we head back into the living room, I hear my phone vibrating against the table.

'Ergh, it's another text from Deano Gamble,' I say out loud.

'Which one is that?' my brother asks and I shoot him a filthy look. 'Genuinely,' he insists. 'I can't keep up with your men.'

'Deano is the rugby player I went on one date with, but he's dumb as fuck.'

'He plays for my team,' Millsy reminds him.

'You mean you do a sexy dance for him when he scores?' Woody teases.

I fist-bump my brother and offer Millsy some ice for that burn.

'Come on, what did he say?' Millsy asks.

'He says "Stop playing hard to get",' I tell them.

'And your reply is going to be?' Millsy continues to question me.

'Stop playing hard to want,' I tell them. 'And, send. Right, rehearsal time.'

The first plan of action is to have a sort of table read, where Woody and I share out the other parts in the play, so that we can read through Millsy's lines with him. As I glance over the script, it occurs to me just how well I remember this play. In fact, I'm pretty sure I can remember all my lines from *Macbeth* – and yet I can't remember to turn the oven off when I'm done using it, or remember to buy toilet roll when we've run out. If only there were some way to dump useless information from your brain that you no longer need, in order to make room for other, more important stuff.

'Right, let's crack on,' I tell them. 'So—'

'Wait,' Millsy interrupts me. 'Your Lady Macbeth has a plan of action already.'

'I'm listening,' I tell him.

'Go out with Deano,' Millsy says with a big grin. 'Big, buff rugby dude, famous amongst Leeds folk, practically begging you to go out with him – so do it. Nick will see how in demand you are, the calibre of bloke you're attracting and boom, he'll wish you were his.'

'I mean, I see what you're saying,' I start. 'But I wouldn't be comfortable using a man like that.'

'This isn't a man, this is Deano Gamble. He's a dog. He only uses women – and yes, this is coming from me. I guarantee he's only texting you because it will be keeping him up at night that he didn't bang you. He never gets denied. He will persist for a while yet – you may as well use it to your advantage.'

'Really?' I ask.

'Really. He'll be like a dog with a boner.'

I think for a moment. 'Do you really think that will work?' I ask.

Millsy nods his head; Woody shakes his.

'This will end in tears, sis,' he warns me.

'Long as they're not mine,' I joke, but the more I think about it, the more Millsy might be onto something. Anyway, the least I can do is try, right? I guess I'm going on another date with Deano.

Chapter 16

The second I open my eyes I am filled with regret. I regret that I went out drinking with Millsy and Woody again. I regret that I stayed out until the early hours. I regret all the things I know I'd regret if I could remember them because I drank too much. Mostly, I just regret opening my eyes because the early morning sunlight is really doing a number on them.

I squeeze them tightly shut, wiggling and stretching my body out in an attempt to try and get more comfortable. My neck hurts. I'm not sure if it's an extension of my hangover or this rock-solid memory foam pillow that I'm not used to – that's when it hits me: I'm not in my own bed.

I open my eyes, slowly this time, giving them a fighting chance of adjusting to the harsh light of day. Nope, that is not my ceiling.

Running my hands down my body, I realise that I'm in my underwear. Oh God, what did I do? And who did I do it with? I'd be happy my dry spell was over, but I'm too freaked out.

The second I sit up, I realise where I am – I'm in Nick's room. More importantly, in Nick's *bed*.

'Morning, kid,' he says cheerily.

I snap my head to the left and see him sitting in his armchair, fully dressed, his fingers pressed together. He taps them together impatiently.

'Morning,' I reply awkwardly.

'Good night was it?' he asks.

'You tell me,' I joke – but it's neither the time nor the place.

I rub my eyes, causing my fingertips to go black with eye make-up. As I glance around the room, I notice the dress I was wearing last night is over the top of the tall lamp that stands in the corner of Nick's room. Oh God, no, please no … I'm getting flashbacks. The dress on the lamp is the only trigger I need for it all to come back. I came into Nick's room on purpose, fully intent on seducing him. I remember whipping off my dress, swinging it around in the air before tossing it and climbing into bed with Nick.

'Nick, I can explain,' I start.

'You can explain why you came in drunk, got in the wrong bed and then, when I tried to tell you that you were in the wrong bed, you started blubbing about what a mess your life is?' he asks. 'Well, by all means, go ahead.'

'My life isn't a mess,' I snap defensively.

'You're in the wrong bed, in your underwear, with eyeliner literally everywhere but your eyes – that doesn't sound like a mess to you?'

'Well, when you put it like that.' I laugh. I'm just so relieved that he hasn't realised I intended to get in his bed, even if I was drunk and it was misjudged.

'You're lucky Heather wasn't in there with me.' Finally, something we can agree on.

'Look, I'm sorry. I had too much to drink. It won't happen again.'

'You're damn right,' he replies. 'I'm getting a lock for my door.'

I begin climbing out of bed before I realise something. Crap, I've still got my control tights on. These things squish my chubby bits into weird places – hidden perfectly underneath my clothes, but without a cover, I look like a string of sausages. And while

I know that Nick has seen me in these a thousand times before – heck, I usually have him pull me into them – I suddenly feel self-conscious about him seeing me like this. I don't want him to see me looking gross, my smoke-and-mirrors tights showing their hand, giving away the illusion of my relative slimness.

'Can you give me a bit of privacy, please?' I ask, not really knowing how else to phrase it.

'Can I give you some privacy?' Nick laughs. 'Sure. I'm on my way out anyway. Thank you for making things even more awkward,' he calls back sarcastically as he heads out.

Oh my God, what the hell is wrong with me? Why am I so bad at this stuff? It's like everything I do just makes things even worse. And he's right about one thing: it's going to be really hard to look him in the eye after this.

Chapter 17

I slick on some red lipstick, fluff my curls and give my bra a meaningful jiggle to make my boobs as front and centre as possible. I am a strong, brave woman, and I am ready for war.

A knock on the front door causes me to jump out of my skin. It's not that I'm usually a jumpy person (although the Weird Ian stuff did creep me out a little), it's just that no one can actually get to our front door without being buzzed in. Well, no one except one person, our neighbour, Bev. I love Bev because she's absolutely crackers. She's in her forties and I'm not sure she got the memo that the Eighties were over and that the Madonna circa "Crazy For You" look was out.

'You locked yourself out, you daft cow?' I ask as I open the door. I do actually keep a spare key for Bev, because she's so introverted, she rarely leaves the flat, and on the rare occasions she does, she usually forgets her key. I'm happy to do it though. I really like Bev. As bizarre as she is, you can just tell that her heart is in the right place. I don't think Nick is keen on her (is he keen on anyone?) but he hardly ever sees her, whereas I'll go visit her when Nick is driving me especially crazy.

I open the door expecting to see a smiley lady wearing too many accessories but instead I am greeted by a puzzled-looking

Deano.

'Oh, hello,' I say with an awkward giggle. 'I thought you were someone else. How did you get in?'

'What do you mean?' he asks. Oh my God, I should just push him down the stairs, lock the door and swear off dating forever.

'How did you get in the building?'

'Through the door,' he replies.

'How did you get up here?' I clarify, slowly.

'The stairs.'

He has to be shitting me.

'The downstairs door shouldn't be open. Anyone could just wander inside. Drunks, murderers …' Dumb-as-dirt rugby players.

'Oh!' I see a flicker of recognition on Deano's face; for once he knows what I mean. 'Your flatmate let me in.'

I peep behind Deano, his large frame blocking my view of the staircase, and see Nick behind him, post in his hand.

'Your date was waiting outside for you, Ruby. I thought I'd let him in. He was, erm, struggling with the buzzer,' Nick tells me, the corners of his mouth being gently tugged into a smirk.

Shit, I'm supposed to be making him jealous and that is not going to happen if I'm being snippy with Deano, and Deano is just being dumb.

'Thank you,' I tell Nick, before turning my attention to Deano and turning on my charm. Time to break out those acting skills. 'It's good to see you again, babe. Come in.'

'Do you not want to get straight off?' he asks me.

'Easy, tiger,' I giggle. 'Buy me a drink first.'

'What do you mean?' Deano unsurprisingly asks me.

Nick squeezes past us, placing his keys in the key bowl before wandering into the kitchen. As far as making him jealous goes, this isn't exactly going to plan.

I grab Deano by the hand and drag him inside, pushing him back onto the sofa.

'I'll just finish getting ready,' I lie. 'But Nick will keep you company, won't you, Nick?'

'Oh, I live for keeping the steadily flowing stream of men who pass through here amused,' he replies sarcastically. I shoot him a dirty look, but it doesn't matter – Deano is oblivious.

I head for my bedroom, hovering behind my door so I can listen to their conversation.

'You're a lucky bloke, living with a fitty like Ruby,' Deano tells Nick.

'Oh, I am,' he replies, still as sarcastic as ever. 'So, what's your deal?'

'You don't recognise me?' Deano asks.

I cringe.

'I don't, mate. Sorry.'

'I'm Deano Gamble. I play for Leeds Lions.' A few seconds of silence.

'Ah, the rugby team,' Nick replies. 'More of a cricket man myself.'

'Could never take to cricket myself, pal. Too gentle.'

'You like the hands-on approach?' Nick asks him.

'I do,' Deano replies.

'You like to get down and dirty with the boys?' Nick persists.

'I do,' Deano confirms, oblivious.

Nick laughs.

'What are you laughing at, pal?' Deano asks, a degree of defensiveness creeping into his voice, but I'm not sure he knows why.

Time to defuse the situation.

'OK, I'm ready,' I say, hurrying out of my room. I grab Deano by the hand and drag him towards the front door. 'Don't wait up, Nick,' I call back.

'I never do,' he replies.

Once Deano and I are out on the street, reality hits. It's not enough to parade Deano around in front of Nick, now I have to actually go on another date with him.

'Is he going to mind if we come back here after?' Deano asks, his presumptuousness confirming that every word Millsy said about him is true. He really does just want to sleep with me to tick a box.

'Oh, he doesn't care,' I reply, and sadly I think it's true. 'So, what's the plan?'

'Let's go for a drink,' he suggests. 'Where do you go?'

'Thin Aire?' I suggest. May as well get a trip to my favourite bar out of this evening.

'OK, sure. I know a guy there.'

We wander down the hill towards Thin Aire in awkward silence. I take Deano's arm, but only so I have someone to escort me across roads and to help me stay upright in these heels trying to walk at his speed. There's no doubt about it, Deano is fit. The hand I have wrapped around his bicep confirms as much; his upper arms are thicker than my thighs, and I was definitely at the front of the line for seconds when the thighs were being handed out. In fact, it's no wonder I ladder my tights so often, I don't think it's always my fingernails or my general lack of womanly grace, I think sometimes the pressure of stretching over my thighs just gets too much for them.

As we approach the lift to head up to the bar, I see a flicker of recognition on the doorman's face. He must recognise Deano, but other than letting the corners of his mouth twitch and being more charming than I usually see him being with customers, he remains a professional. I have to admit, it's pretty cool hanging out with someone who gets recognised by adoring fans. It's just a shame it's Deano.

'Welcome to Thin Aire,' Ella, the hostess beams, on autopilot. If this were your first time here, you would find Ella warm and welcoming, but because I've seen her do this a thousand times, to me, her greeting has the cold, empty charm of a well-programmed robot. She's a lovely girl, but I can imagine you lose enthusiasm after saying it for the millionth time. I remember at work, when they tried to make us use a catchphrase. As if it isn't bad enough the place is called Has Beans, we were supposed to greet each customer by asking: "Where have you bean all my life?" I believe I uttered it once, in jest, but that was it. I don't think I could spend my day saying that to every single person I served, not without bashing my head against the coffee machine until I forgot my own name.

'Ruby,' she squeaks. 'Hello. And who is your friend?'

She kisses us both on each cheek, this greeting a much more genuine one.

'This is Deano,' I tell her. 'Deano, this is Ella. She's easily my favourite person here.'

'Aww, well you're my favourite customer,' she replies with a smile. 'And that just earned you a southeast-facing table by the window.'

I wasn't kissing her arse to get a good table, but that is pretty much the best place to sit. You can look out across Leeds, with a view of the River Aire unmatchable to anywhere in Leeds.

We take a seat and order our drinks before falling into silence again, confirming what I already knew: Deano and I have zero chemistry. We had nothing to talk about on our first date and we've got nothing to talk about now and this is probably a spectacular waste of time for both of us, because he isn't going to make Nick jealous and there's no way I'm going to sleep with him. I may as well stick around, have a drink with him, and then the night hasn't been for nothing. If I go home now, Nick will be smug as well as hurtfully indifferent and I can't handle that.

'Deano, good to see you again, mate,' I hear a man's voice say as our drinks are placed down in front of us.

'Pal, how are you?' Deano asks, jumping to his feet to hug his friend. It's only as he releases him that I realise who Deano knows here: Tom the manager.

'Hello, you,' he says to me. 'I see you in here a lot. What are the two of you up to tonight?'

I open my mouth to speak, but no words come out. Crap.

'Just a few drinks, see what happens after that,' Deano replies with a wiggle of his eyebrows.

Tom gives me a "you go, girl" kind of look. 'Well, I'll leave you to it. Have a good night.'

And with that, he's gone. That was my chance to speak to him, and I blew it.

'So you two know each other?' I ask.

'Yeah, we're old mates. We were on the same rugby team at school, but I decided I wanted to play pro, and I guess he just wanted to sell drinks to …' Deano thinks for a moment. 'What do you call those kind of people?' he asks me, pointing at a group of customers.

I glance over at the bar. As the girls giggle and struggle to stay upright in their sky-high heels, their male counterparts behave generally boisterously.

'Fetch us a bottle of Moët,' one of the men insists to a member of bar staff. 'Bet you don't sell many of those, do you?'

The girl serving them politely smiles. I know that smile from working in customer services, it means: I know you're an idiot, but I'm not allowed to tell you so.

'Pretentious?' I suggest.

'Yeah, and they think they're important,' Deano adds. I give him my customer service smile.

'I'm more into throwing, but I can roll those back to you if you want?'

'What?' I ask, confused.

'Your eyes,' he tells me. 'You keep rolling your eyes.'

I think for a moment. 'It's the altitude.'

'Oh, right,' he says, relieved. 'I thought maybe you thought I was a twat.'

A couple of hours have gone by, but it feels like an age because I am beyond bored. I wish I could leave. If there's one thing I am even less keen on than having another drink with Deano, it's going home early and giving Nick the satisfaction of witnessing another failed date. The problem is that wanting to stay out as long as possible, combined with all the free drinks my northern Tom Hardy lookalike has given us tonight, has resulted in me winding up just a little drunk. In fact, I stumble on my way to the lift, proving this fact to myself.

'Careful.' Deano laughs, his large, rugby player's body clearly unaffected by the amount we've had to drink.

Once inside the non-existent privacy of the glass lift, Deano grabs me by the hips and presses me up against the door. I feel his thumbs digging into my body as his lips meet my neck.

'My place or yours?' he asks. 'Yours is closer.'

Ah yes, I forgot it was Deano's mission to sleep with me. 'Bad news,' I start. 'Time of the month.'

Yes, I'm continuing my fictitious period. This is the kind of excuse that you can only use once, and not with anyone you plan on keeping around because men are not stupid, and they can figure out when your "time of the month" is actually every day of the month.

'You're not serious?' he asks as he stops kissing my neck, rather abruptly.

'Super-serious, sorry,' I lie. 'Sucks to be female sometimes.'

'Well, there is always that,' he tells me, raising his eyebrows. I can't help but shoot him a look. 'OK, fine. Next time?'

'Next time,' I lie. Again.

Deano, without so much as a peck on the cheek, bids me goodnight the second we step out of the lift. Amazing, how when men are trying to sleep with you that they're not even willing to pretend. Don't get me wrong, I'm not saying that I want men to manipulate me into having sex with them, but they could at least try and pretend that's not all they are doing. At least fake it, just a little bit. Just make us feel a little bit special, tell us we look pretty, even if it's the most insincere bollocks we've ever heard, it just makes us feel that little bit better, like maybe, just maybe we have something going for us other than girl parts and iffy taste.

I decide to pop into the sanctuary that is late-night McDonald's, before dragging my butt up the hill towards my flat. I don't know if it's the double cheeseburger, the tough trek (because alcohol and because heels) home or the thoughts buzzing around my head – or maybe it's a combination of all of the above that is very sobering, but I can't get Nick off my mind. OK, so it was dumb of me to think I'd be able to make a man who damn-near hates me jealous, like that's suddenly going to work?! To be fair on myself, it wasn't exactly my idea, it was Millsy's – why on earth would I listen to Millsy?! The man thinks safe sex involves making sure the door is locked in case the bird's husband gets home early.

Nope, there's no way this was ever going to work, and now I have to go home with my tail between my legs and admit that it was yet another shitty date with yet another online dating weirdo. And Nick is going to just love that, isn't he? He loves nothing more than watching me fuck up. I'll bet he's tucked up in his boring little bed with his boring little girlfriend after a night watching some lame documentary they found in the deepest, darkest corner of Netflix, while they ate his gross attempts at cooking vegan food, before an impressive ten minutes in the missionary position and then bed.

At least, that's how I imagine their nights play out. I can only confirm the first two points, because I've had to endure them snuggled up on the sofa watching things that I can't even believe exist, like that documentary I once saw them watching on the secret story of where all our sewage is going. I sat and watched it for a few minutes, spoiler alert: it's so fucking boring. I also have cold, hard proof that what they cook and eat is sad, meat-free, dairy-free junk and, incidentally, cold and hard is what I would name the one dish they once insisted I try. I'm not even sure what it was, but it made my mouth so sad, I think it cried. I know there is good vegan food out there, it's just that neither of them can make it.

As for their sex life, I'm speculating, but I am basing my assumption on how boring and unaffectionate they are in real life. Sure, I see them cuddle on the sofa when they're watching TV – whatever – but I'm talking his arm around her and that's it. I never see them being silly with one another; I never see them play-fighting. She never takes the dirty spoon out of the pan of meat-free mush and taps him on the nose with it gently, or any of the other shit I have it on pretty good authority that couples are supposed to do, based on any romcom I've ever seen, ever.

I don't blame Nick, he's so sexy he should be advertising aftershave on the back of *Cosmo*. Heather, on the other hand … I'm not saying she's not attractive (well, on the outside, on the inside she is ug-ly), but she doesn't even try to be anything but dull. She doesn't dress up, she doesn't wear make-up, she doesn't accessorise – I mean, who doesn't accessorise?! It will be her bedroom game that is weak, I'm sure of it. I bet she just lies there. I bet she doesn't dress up –

Oh my God, I'm getting mental images and the jealousy is driving me crazy. This is awful. How have I fallen for someone so hard so quickly, when this time last week I hated them more than anyone in the world – including the woman I saw last year for my brow tint, who somehow "accidentally" wound up giving me a shade intended for redheads. She said it was an accident, but I reckon it was revenge because I took Millsy with me and it turned out she'd spoken to him on Matcher, but they'd never been on a date. She seemed annoyed that he'd just stopped replying to her, but that's the name of the game on Matcher, everyone knows that. You can't go into things like this with feelings or self-respect, because you'll come out broken and hating yourself if you gave even just one little fuck about what the men on sites like that think of you.

I hover around the door outside my flat until my cheeseburger is destroyed, just like my hopes and dreams. It's late, way past Nick and Heather's bedtime, but I'm scared to go up. I don't want to see them. I don't want them to nosily ask how my date went when they don't really care, they just want to hear me say bad things about the dating game so that they can feel all smug and superior with themselves because they coupled up. Still, it is pretty late and I'm very cold – I'm sure I can sneak in undetected.

I creep up the stairs slowly, placing my key in our flat door with the steady hand of a bomb disposal expert – well, one who spent the night in a bar chain-drinking strawberry bellinis. The key is turned, but – as always – the door is stuck. Stupid door, stupid cheap flat that's all I can only just afford, that there's no way I can leave without moving back out of the city. I give it a firm push, but nothing happens. I press my foot against it and push a little harder, still nothing. Finally, I shoulder-barge it as quietly as possible, causing the door to fly open. I reach out and grab the handle, stopping it just in time before it slams into the sideboard, preventing everything from falling off like the last time I had to force it open. Phew, that was close. Holding my bunch of keys by squeezing my *Adventure Time* key ring between my index finger and my thumb, I very carefully lower them into the key bowl, taking my time, lying them in the bowl as quietly as possible. I don't make a single sound. Not even as I creep across the flat towards my bedroom.

I get to my bedroom door, and as much as I need to pee, and as much as I really want to brush my teeth, which feel super gross from all the sugary drinks and then the cheeseburger that didn't actually take me that long to eat, I'm scared that the flush of the toilet and the running water of the tap will wake them, so I don't do it. Once in the safety of my room, I pull my dress over my head and lie back on my bed quietly. I grab the packet of mints that is sitting on my bedside table and eat one – although I'd imagine eating a mint is actually the opposite of brushing my teeth, because it's essentially just sugar, right? Still, tonight I'd rather have a filling than own up to a bad date, so I'll just have to take my chances.

Another failed date. I'm surprised I ever expect anything different these days – even tonight, when I went on the date with an ulterior motive. I know that I didn't go out with Deano looking for romance, but I at least had high hopes that things were going to go my way and that never happened either. So however you look at it, it's another failure.

I guess I'll have to go back to the drawing board tomorrow, assemble the troops and think about what I can do instead of what I've been doing. Or I could just give up. It was so stupid of me to think I could win Nick over. Until I had the dreams, I hated him, and if you'd told me I'd be feeling like this today I would've asked you if you were high. So unless I can go all *Inception* on his ass and get inside his dreams and convince him that he should fall in love with me, then I imagine nothing is going to happen.

So that's that. Time to give up. I'll tell the troops that we failed tomorrow, for now I need to try and sleep, not only so that I forget about what a failure tonight was, but also so that I forget just how much I need to pee.

Chapter 18

I'm awoken by a knock on my bedroom door, which jolts me suddenly from my sleep. I think I was dreaming, although I'm not sure what about. To be honest, after my recent dreams, I could happily never dream again. I used to love my dreams, even my nightmares. For me they were like an escape from real life, an adventure where I could do anything and go anywhere and no one could hurt me. It was like living in a movie with no consequences and I loved that so much. Turns out I was wrong: my dreams could hurt me, by showing me an awesome life that I'm never going to be able to have.

'Ruby, you awake?' I hear Nick call through my bedroom door.

'Erm, just a sec,' I call back. I search around my messy room for something – anything – that I can put on over my underwear, but in a room that is messy with so many clothes, I can't find anything that will do the trick. I rummage around for what feels like forever, although I'm sure it's probably only thirty seconds, and eventually find a sarong that my mum bought me before we went on holiday to Italy when I was thirteen. No, I don't know why I've kept it either, but that's all that is to hand right now. I wrap it around my body, quickly, before replying: 'Come in.'

Nick walks into my bedroom, holding a steaming mug.

'Morning,' he says as he takes in my surroundings, his expression quickly changing. 'Oh, you're alone.'

'Of course I'm alone,' I reply. 'What were you expecting? Half the Leeds Lions team to be snuggling up with me?'

'No, but at least one thirteenth. What happened on your date? It not go well? I figured he'd be here with you, and that you'd have had a late night – that's why I brought you this cuppa – and it's real milk, not my coconut milk.'

'Good, because that tastes like—'

'I know,' he interrupts me. 'You've told me many a time as I ate my breakfast.'

Nick sets the mug down next to me with an expectant smile; he wants details. That's when it occurs to me, oh my God, he's jealous. My stupid plan actually worked. Nick never makes me tea and yet here he is this morning, barging into my bedroom when he thinks I've got a bloke in here, bringing me cups of tea, asking me loads of questions about how it went. He's never done this before.

'It went really well,' I lie. 'Really, really well, actually.' Now, now, Ruby, don't oversell it.

'If it went that well, I would've thought he'd be here with you now …'

'He wants to wait,' I tell him and, yes, it is hard to keep a straight face. 'He said he really likes me, and he wants to prove it to me by not trying to sleep with me until the third date.'

'Well, isn't he traditional,' Nick replies, sounding sceptical – as well he should, because I just said the most ridiculous thing I've ever heard. 'Although … do you think he might be playing you?'

'What?' I reply, feigning surprise. 'No, of course not. How could you think such a thing?'

'You're not naive, Ruby. You're pretty street-smart – although not very fashion-smart – what the hell are you wearing?' Nick asks, finally clocking my sarong.

'It's a sarong,' I tell him, as if that might clear things up, no explanation needed. 'I grabbed it when you wanted to come in, to protect my modesty.'

'Ruby, it's transparent. Whatever modestly you've deluded yourself into thinking you have is in no way protected.'

Normally, Nick's insulting little remarks make me cross, but not today. I can't help but grin.

'What are you smiling for?' he asks, puzzled.

'Oh, it's nothing,' I reply. But it's not nothing, it's definitely something – he's jealous. He's jealous, he's jealous, he's jealous. I do a little victory dance in my head before grabbing my cuppa and sipping it smugly. Oh, it's a perfect cuppa too, super-strong, just the right amount of *real* milk.

'Well, I need to get to work. I'm glad your date went well,' he tells me, sounding like he isn't even a little bit glad that my date went well. Yes!

'Thank you,' I call after him. 'Have fun looking at front-butts all day.'

'You're so immature it's embarrassing,' he calls back.

But I'm not immature, I'm the smartest woman on earth, and Millsy is the smartest man – I'm not sure if I should tell him, it might go to his head. Ah, I don't care, all that matters is that I'm making progress. Now I just need to figure out what my next step is, and unlucky for me, I think it's going to involve a third date with Deano.

Chapter 19

As I walk through the doors of Has Beans, even though I am about to work a gruelling shift, I couldn't be happier. There's a spring in my step. I feel like cute little animals should be running around my feet as I perform an awesome musical number that everyone in the café will join in with, all in perfect pitch. Nope, nothing can ruin my awesome mood today. Nothing except …

'Ruby, you are late,' Rita snaps.

I look at the time on my phone, that is already in my hand, because it's almost always in my hand, or at least within grabbing distance.

'Oh, come on, I'm three minutes late.' I laugh. 'That's not late. You want late, you should've been here earlier this year when I slept through pretty much my whole shift. I got here at five to six – I was over nine hours late that day. *That's* late.'

Millsy sniggers quietly.

I grab my apron from the hook and give Millsy a fist-bump, hoping that will be the end of it.

'And you're proud of that, I imagine?' Rita asks me.

'Not proud, per se,' I reply, well aware that I'm annoying her, but she's annoying me too. 'Just trying to make you smile.'

'You'll make me smile by turning up to work on time and doing your job well,' she snaps. 'Two things you find impossible, it seems.'

I look over at Millsy, expecting a little back-up, but he's constantly telling me how Rita is the best boss he's ever had. He's just watching us talk, his eyes darting backwards and forwards between us, like a kid watching his parents argue at the dinner table.

Before I get the chance to defend myself, Rita storms back into her office.

'Aw, it's sweet that she pops out to see me when I arrive, she must love me,' I say sarcastically, as I eat a croissant.

'Well, you're not exactly a model employee,' Millsy replies. Such hypocrisy, I drop my croissant for dramatic effect.

'This coming from a man who tried to argue that regular masturbation breaks were important for his mental wellbeing.'

'It makes me a productive worker,' he replies.

'It makes you a productive wanker,' I correct him. 'You'll go blind!'

'I'll stop when I need glasses,' he jokes.

I laugh, shaking my head. Only Millsy can amuse and disgust me at the same time.

'You're just as bad an employee as I am,' I remind him.

'Not this week,' he tells me. 'This week I need to kiss ass, to make sure I can get all the time off that I need for rehearsals.'

I've only just retrieved my croissant from the floor, and I drop it again. 'Nope. No way. Nuh-uh. You can't leave me here with this mo … rning,' I say, turning to the customers who have just approached the counter, saving myself from saying a word that even I know I shouldn't be saying in front of customers in the nick of time.

Standing in front of me are a couple of twenty-something girls, who order two skinny caramel lattes to go. I can see that little glimmer of something in Millsy's eye, like he's going to hit on them; he's just waiting for a pause in their conversation. As I make their drinks, I can't help but listen to their conversation, in fact, the best part of my job (other than the free coffee and food) is probably listening to other people's conversations.

'... and I thought we'd been broken up a long time, but then I realised that I'm still using the same tube of toothpaste he bought me. And I know it was a new tube, but I brush my teeth twice a day, and I still have half a tube left, so I guess it hasn't been that long.'

I look over at Millsy, wondering what he'll do.

'And I don't think I've had a period since he left,' she says quietly, but not only do Millsy and I both hear, it takes us by surprise, causing Millsy to choke on whatever he's eating and me to mis-pour the hot milk, spilling it all over the counter. It drips off all over the girl's shoes, much to her annoyance.

'I am so sorry,' I babble, grabbing a cloth to try to halt the waterfall of milk that is continuing to cascade over her heels. It's not enough though, the girl looks absolutely furious. From the conversation that I couldn't help but overhear, it sounds like she's having a pretty rough time at the moment. I can't imagine she has much patience for things like this but, seriously, she looks like her head is going to explode.

'Cheer up, love,' Millsy says, leaning over the counter to rub her shoulder tenderly. 'Your calendar might be wrong.'

With this, the girl flips. She screams a furious scream that, by all rights, should shatter the latte glasses. Everyone in the café falls silent, stopping their eating, drinking, chatting and typing to spectate.

'I want to see your manager – *now*,' she says angrily.

'Look, there's no need for that,' I start, but I'm wasting my breath. Rita has heard the noise and she's storming over.

'What's the problem?' Rita asks, cutting to the chase.

As the angry girl tells her everything, Rita's expression doesn't change. She gives the girl a sympathetic nod as she listens to her account of events before sending them to sit at a table.

'Make these girls new drinks and then see me in my office,'

Rita instructs us firmly.

'What, and leave the counter unattended?' I ask.

'No, Joe can watch the counter, you are to see me in my office. He needs to leave for his audition soon anyway, don't you, my love?'

Millsy nods.

'What, that's not fair!' I can't help but squeak. 'What I did was an accident, he was the one who made the period joke.'

'It wasn't a joke, it was a reassuring suggestion,' he insists, but I know my friend.

'Ruby,' Rita says my name slowly and quietly through gritted teeth. 'Come to my office, now.'

I exhale deeply, following her like a naughty child on her way to the head teacher's office. Once inside, I close the door behind me.

'Look, I'm just going to come out with it. Your issues with authority are not going to wash with me,' she says, taking a seat at her desk, placing both of her hands flat on the table. What does that mean? It looks unnatural. Perhaps it's something they taught her at a business management course, telling her it's some body language move that will ultimately up productivity in the workplace.

'I don't have issues with authority,' I insist, calmly. Well, I don't, I just have issues with *her*. 'I didn't do anything wrong; it was an accident.'

'You're proving my point, Ruby.'

'I mean, I'm no narc,' I start, fully prepared to grass on my mate. It's not that there's no loyalty there; we just display it differently to most people. I think it comes from being best friends since we were babies. We've developed this sort of sibling relationship where it just comes naturally to throw each other under the bus so we don't get in trouble with "Mum", we can throw the harshest insults at one another and laugh them off, and we're not above the occasional play fight where necessary, because that's what siblings do, right?

Rita massages her temples for a moment and lets out a long, deep sigh. It's clear that I'm wasting my breath; Millsy is her golden boy. I'll just have to take a deep breath and go back out there and do my job.

'I'm giving you an official warning,' Rita tells me, taking a pen from the coffee jar that sits on her desk.

'What?' I squeak. 'For spilling milk?'

I'm pretty sure there's a widely documented phrase about the spillage of milk and how it's not a big deal.

'For upsetting customers, using bad language, being late, having a problem with authority and for your attitude generally, Ruby. Is that enough reasoning for you, or would you like me to go on?'

I can officially say that Rita is a not my cup of tea. So I was a little late, so I spilled a little bit of milk. OK, I hold my hands up to those, but I don't think I've done anything that deserves a formal warning. Still, two strikes and you're out, so keeping my job is reliant on me keeping my mouth shut. I bite my tongue.

'Shall I get back to work so that Millsy can get off to his rehearsal?' I ask.

'Yes,' she replies, her pen practically smoking as she makes notes about my behaviour. 'And he's Joe when we're at work, not Millsy. We're not teenage boys on a football pitch.'

We might not be on a football pitch, but she's certainly talking balls. Still, I keep my mouth shut.

'Sure,' I reply, skulking out of the office like a ticked-off kid.

I return to my post just in time to see Millsy swapping numbers with the girl he upset ten minutes prior. She looks super-over it.

'It's not what it looks like,' he assures me.

'Really?' I ask. 'Because it looks like you just swapped numbers with the girl who landed me an official warning.'

'Oh shit!' Millsy, sorry, I mean Joe exclaims. 'Well, first of all, OK, it's exactly what it looks like, but we got talking and she's a big Scottish play fan. Also, that's rough, Rubes, you didn't deserve a warning. You did nothing wrong.'

I shrug my shoulders. 'Meh, what can you do.' I think for a second. 'Sorry, did you say that girl was a big *Macbeth* fan?'

I hate to judge a book by its cover, but I never would've had this bird pegged as someone who even knew who Shakespeare was, let alone consider herself a fan. And I'm not saying this because she's a young, blonde female – because I am too – I'm saying this because she's wearing a velour tracksuit and everyone knows they went out with the Noughties.

'Yeah,' he replies confidently, before sounding less sure of his statement. 'Well, she's a big Michael Fassbender fan, and she really wants to see the movie.'

As furious as I am, I can't help but laugh. 'Go to your audition,' I tell him.

'You're a star,' he replies, going to kiss me on the cheek before hesitating. 'I don't wanna cock-block myself by kissing you. Just pretend I did.'

I give his arm a soft(ish) punch. 'Just go,' I instruct.

Millsy doesn't need telling twice. He whips off his apron, throwing it at the hook (and missing), and jumps over the counter before dashing out of the door. I'd assume this was a showy act for his new female friends, but I've seen him jump the counter many times. This is what I'm talking about; if anyone needs a warning, it should be the person who uses this counter like a dating app/piece of gym apparatus. Not that I want him to get sacked, I just want the injustice noting.

I'm not going to let this get me down, because pretty soon Sally will have had her baby, she'll be back, and Rita will go back to stoking fires in hell, or whatever duties Satan usually hands out to his favourite child. At least things are improving with Nick. That's my priority right now. That and making it out of here today without throwing the panini press out of the window in temper.

Chapter 20

Operation get in Nick's good books and make his super-rubbish girlfriend look super-rubbish by comparison is: go!

Yes, I said operation, because this is going to take a lot of work. To understand just how much of a U-turn I need to pull here, you have to understand what happened when Nick and I first moved in together. It was eighteen months ago when I grew tired of living in the middle of nowhere, having to catch the train back and forth into Leeds, just so I could have a decent social life. The worst part of that was having to catch the last train home – well, when I had the willpower to do so; 11 p.m. is no time at all to head home from a night out. That's why you would have to make a decision: leave early to make the last train home or stay out until the first train home in the morning. When you're out having fun, the idea of calling it a night in time to make the 11 p.m. train is a sucky one, because you don't want to go home, you want to stay out with everyone, you wanna drink in rooftop bars like a civilised, sophisticated lady until closing time, before heading to Call Lane to get messy with all the other drunk people until the small hours.

The only problem with staying out is that it seems like a great idea … until the clubs kick out at 4 a.m., and you've got two hours until your first train, and those two hours will be the longest of your life, especially if the weather is cold and rainy. That's why McDonald's has a special place in my heart, because it's always been my middle-of-the-night sanctuary, my port in a storm – often literally.

So, I decided enough was enough, no more commuting to work/play; I am a city chick at heart and I need to be in the middle of it to be happy. The only problem was that I couldn't find anywhere central – that didn't look like a crack den – that was within my pitiful price range. I asked Millsy, but there was no way he could afford it, and this was months before he started crashing at his uncle's place. Enter stage right my friend Marshall, who told me about his friend Nick who was looking for someone to share a flat with in the centre. I started looking around and, even paying half of the rent on a two-bed flat was a little out of my price range, until I found our little flat that we live in now, which I could easily afford with someone chipping in half.

It did cross my mind that sharing a flat with a member of the opposite sex might not work; what if we couldn't agree on the furniture in the communal areas of the house? What if he left loads of gross hair in the plughole? What if he watched noisy action movies all night like a rugged manly man? Incidentally, I will happily admit that Nick has way more of an eye for interior design than I do, if any hair is blocking up the plughole it has usually come from my legs, and if you're likely to find anyone binge-watching *Taken 1–3* in the middle of the night, then it's me. Yes, really, and that's close to five hours I'll never be able to get back.

I figured I'd be fine living with a male roommate, because I've had a male best friend all my life. I know that platonic relationships are entirely possible. I know that *Match of the Day* is a valid way to spend a couple of hours. I know that fluffy cushions, scented candles and wall decals that read things like "Live, laugh, love" are not required to make a living room awesome.

So the day came around to view the flat and I met Nick for the first time then and there. Escorted around by the agent, we chatted politely about how this place was perfect for both of us, and we agreed to think about it and let him know ASAP. We left the flat, popped into one of the bars on Merrion Street and started talking. Nick told me that he was a junior doctor, that he had refused money from his parents to help him through university and that right now, paying his own way meant that he couldn't afford to live anywhere special. I commended him for this, because it would be the easiest thing in the world to just take money from his parents. (I wish mine would throw a bit of theirs my way, rather than blowing it on things like dolphin-shaped foliage and secret cruises – don't they know how expensive cocktails are?)

Yep, we should have got on like a house on fire, and we did … until I literally set the house on fire. It was the night of our housewarming party, and the only thing Nick and I had disagreed about so far was the fact that I was a smoker. He asked me not to do it in the flat, and in an attempt to be a good housemate, I agreed. What I will say in my defence is that an addiction is an addiction, and I think I should be cut a little slack. I had been noticing that Nick was a little OTT with the neatness.

The party was in full swing, and he was buzzing around like an attentive little bee, topping up glasses (but not without sneaking a coaster under them first). It was raining outside, and Millsy and I needed a cigarette, so we figured it wouldn't be a big deal to do it in the bathroom, with the extractor on and the window open and then we'd flush the evidence, freshen our breath, wash our hands and Nick would be none the wiser. I'd like it to go on record that we were both pretty drunk at this point. We shared a fag, like naughty teenagers, before squeezing toothpaste straight from the tube into our mouths, laughing as we spluttered it everywhere, flecking the bathroom mirror with white specs. As I hastily cleaned the mirror with a towel, Millsy got rid of the evidence. We fist-bumped, celebrating just how sneaky we'd been, and what an awesome team we made, before heading back to the party.

And it all would've been fine, if Millsy hadn't tossed the cigarette into the bathroom bin without putting it out properly. The next thing we knew, smoke was billowing out of the bathroom door and Nick was running in with his fire extinguisher to put out the flames – because of course he has a fire extinguisher. Luckily he caught it before it could do any real damage, but it didn't take him long to figure out what happened and we had our first argument.

After the not-so-great fire of Upper Briggate, things only got worse as Nick and I realised just how different we were. Complete opposites, in fact. Of course, by this point, it was too late to do anything about it, because there was no way either of us could leave. Well, Nick technically could if he'd just take the money his parents offered him, but he wouldn't and this – despite me originally commending him for it – royally pissed me off.

So, back to my master plan. I think the problem is that, after eighteen months of living with me, Nick doesn't see me as the kind of girl he could be with. In fact, I'm pretty sure he's more fond of the verruca he caught at the gym than he is of me right now. But I know how I'm going to change that, I'm going to one-up his girlfriend, and I'm going to do it with meat.

Until he started dating a vegan chick, steak was Nick's favourite thing in the world. So I stopped at the shop on the way home, flying around Tesco so that I could be home first. The second I got through the door, I went full-blown Stepford Wives, tidying up all the junk I left lying around this morning. Now that the flat is tidy, I'm cooking myself a steak. The thing is, you get two steaks in a pack (lie) and the sell-by date demands that they're eaten today (lie) so I'm going to have to cook them both and, obviously, it will be too much for me to eat (also a lie, I could easily eat two steaks). Nick will get in from a hard day of swabbing people's junk and delivering babies (OK, maybe that last one is pretty hard) and the smell of steak and chips will hit his nose and go straight to his heart. Well, maybe that's a stretch, but at the very least I'll be able to give him something his girlfriend can't, and that's got to get me in his good books, right?

There are many ways to serve a steak, but only one right one in my opinion, and that's medium rare. But if Nick doesn't get home soon, I'm going to ruin them.

Just when I think I'm done for, Nick walks through the door, and as the smell of dinner cooking hits his nostrils, I see his face light up with joy.

'What is that?' he asks, salivating like a dog with a bone dangled in front of it.

'Just making myself a bit of dinner,' I tell him. 'I've had to cook two steaks; they both needed using today. Want one?' I ask.

Nick blinks at me, confused by my niceness. As his mouth snaps into a smile he seems like he might be about to say yes, until he remembers …

'I would, except I told Heather I wouldn't eat meat anymore, so …'

I can hear the disappointment in his voice. Oh man, it's embarrassing how easy this is going to be.

As I turn the almost-perfectly cooked steak it makes a satisfying sizzle. 'Come on,' I say, encouragingly. 'What Heather doesn't know won't hurt her …'

I stare at Nick intently. He's thinking so hard about this his brow furrows, but I don't think he's battling with his conscience, I think he's trying to figure out if he can get away with it or not.

Channelling my inner Nigella, I purse my lips and twirl my fork around in my hand, stroking the handle seductively – I cannot believe I've resorted to softcore porn. I don't know if I'm impressed or ashamed of myself right now, I guess we'll wait and see if it works.

'OK, I'd love some. Thank you.'

I turn back to my pan, smiling victoriously. Impressed it is.

Nick rolls up his shirt sleeves and washes his hands, as though he were scrubbing up to perform a C-section. Hmm, think I've been watching too much *Grey's Anatomy*. Nick doesn't really talk about his job, so I'm pretty much just going on what I've seen in movies and TV shows when I think of him at work. It's hard to imagine him being a doctor, mostly because he's hot. Who wants to see a hot doctor? Especially a hot gynaecologist! When I was seventeen and I took a tumble after too many apple vodka Kapops, my mum rushed me into A&E to get checked out because I couldn't move my wrist and it had pretty much doubled in size.

The triage doctor I saw was absolutely gorgeous, so much so that, when he wiggled my wrist and asked me if it hurt, I swallowed spit, screamed internally, and said no – turns out I'd broken it, but that's what a pretty face will do to a girl. The point is, I found it hard telling a handsome doctor that my wrist hurt – just try and imagine looking one in the eye and telling him that it burns when you pee.

We sit down at the table together, our plates in front of us. I pull out a bottle of wine from my shopping bag, casually, like I'd forgotten it was there.

'Well, we may as well open this. Drink?' I ask, as I remove the cork.

'If it's open, then why not,' he replies, taking a glass from me. He takes a sip before gasping with delight. 'God, you don't know how much I needed this,' he tells me.

'Really? How come?' I ask.

I watch as Nick cuts his meat with care and accuracy, and I wonder if this is something they taught him at medical school in a roundabout way.

'It's nothing to talk about over dinner,' he tells me.

'I don't mind if you don't,' I insist. 'We never really talk about your work.'

'We never really talk.' He laughs. 'And we certainly don't cook for one another.'

I think he was joking, but now I'm worried he's suspicious.

'Well, it was only going to go in the bin,' I assure him. 'And you did make me a cup of tea this morning.'

'Well that's true,' he replies, flashing me that gorgeous smile of his – that I am very rarely the cause of. 'This is good steak; I've missed this.'

'You're welcome,' I tell him. 'It's actually one of the few things I'm good at cooking, probably because there's a whole spectrum of degrees of done – so I'm bound to nail one of them.'

'Don't sell yourself short,' Nick insists, ploughing through his dinner like he hasn't eaten in weeks. Suddenly, his face falls. 'A patient lost a baby today.'

'I'm sorry to hear that.'

'I know that it's just one of the negative parts of my job, and that it's outweighed by all the healthy babies that we bring into the world, but this was especially sad because it was so early. The mum was distraught. She wanted to hold her baby, say a proper goodbye, have a funeral – but she was so early on in her pregnancy, I had to explain to her as delicately as possible that there just wasn't really a baby there to hold. Just finding the words to explain that to a grieving mum, that's the hardest part of my job.'

Listening to Nick talk, seeing the expression on his face – that's when I realise, that's why it doesn't matter that he's a "hot doctor" because he's a good doctor.

'That's awful,' I reply, not really sure what to say. Well, what can you say? 'But she had you to talk her through it, I'm sure that helped. You're very easy to talk to.'

'So are you, which is surprising.' He laughs, perking up a little. 'I don't know if it's the steak, making you seem less annoying than usual.'

I fake a laugh.

'This is nice though,' he starts, but suddenly we're interrupted by someone barging through the front door. We both look over to see who it is, only to see Heather checking the sideboard behind the door to see if she knocked anything over.

I gesture with my hands to tell Nick to pass me his plate, which is empty, but you can tell it had meat on it. As Nick slides his plate to me, I place mine on the empty dining chair next to me and slide it under the table so that she can't see.

'Drink,' I whisper to Nick quietly. Hopefully the wine will stop him smelling like he just ate a whole steak.

By the time Heather approaches the table the evidence is gone, but she still looks suspicious.

'You're here. Drinking. With Ruby.'

'Yeah, well she opened the bottle, couldn't have her drinking it alone – you know what she's like.' He laughs awkwardly, jumping to his feet to kiss his girlfriend. 'She was celebrating something that happened at work today, couldn't let her do it alone, could I?'

'Aw, you are too sweet,' she tells him patronisingly, before turning to me. 'So, what happened at work?'

'I got an official warning,' I beam. 'One more and I'm fired.'

I raise my glass and smile my biggest, most menacing-looking grin, visibly freaking her out.

'And I suppose you also celebrated being a bad employee by eating a defenceless baby animal?'

'I don't think it was a baby,' I reply, tilting my head thoughtfully. 'But yeah, it's the only way to celebrate.'

Heather literally turns her nose up at me. 'Well, we disagree, don't we, Nick?'

'We do,' he replies, a little quicker than seems natural. He's not great at this lying thing, whereas I excel at it, it seems.

'Someone has to be the bad guy,' I tell them, pulling myself to my feet, heading for my room. I think my work here is done …

'I think you're out of line,' Heather calls after me. I stop suddenly and turn around to face her. 'Excuse me?' I ask.

Heather, who is a good four inches shorter than me, takes a step towards me, as if to show me that she's not scared.

'You're out of order,' she repeats herself. 'I think it's really unfair that you cook and eat meat in front of us.'

I glance over at Nick, but he's keeping quiet. The old me would have sung like a bird, but it wouldn't serve me well to get him in trouble, it would only make him hate me. So I keep quiet about Nick being my partner in meat-eating crime, but I don't keep quiet generally.

'You walk into *my flat* and tell me how to live *my life* and you think *I'm* out of line?' I ask her. 'Wait a minute, how did you get into my flat exactly?'

'It's Nick's flat too, he gave me a key, obviously,' she replies.

My business is no longer with this horrible little woman. I turn my attention to Nick.

'You gave her a key,' I tell him, as though he may not be aware. 'Of course you did. Maybe I'll give Millsy a key. Maybe I'll give the homeless guy with the cute dog who is sitting outside a key. Maybe I'll give my boyfriend a key – I don't need to consult you, do I? We just dish out keys like we're the Holiday-fucking-Inn.'

'So he's your boyfriend, is he?' Nick asks. Interesting that he picked up on that detail above all others. 'Two dates and suddenly he's your boyfriend?'

'When you know, you know,' I tell him confidently.

'Don't you think you're rushing into things?' he persists, much to Heather's disgust.

'What do you care?' she asks. 'Let her move in with the sap, then I can move in here with you like we talked about.'

My eyes widen. I glare at Nick who seems to wince. I know he hates awkward conversations, and I know he hates confrontation, but I hope he's prepared for a fuck-load of both because …

'What the actual fuck?' I squeak. 'You want me out so you can move her in? And you have conversations about this behind my back?'

Nick runs his hands through his hair and sighs.

'It's just something we spoke about, once. It's not a big deal.'

'It's a big deal to me when you're talking about moving her in – giving her a key seems like the first logical step. Are the wheels already in motion?'

'Ruby, I can give my girlfriend a key without asking your permission,' he replies.

'Yes you can, babe,' Heather assures him.

Maybe it's the fact I'm having a bad day, maybe it's because Heather isn't very nice or maybe it's because I'm actually really jealous that she has what I want, but I snap.

'Shut up, please, this is none of your business.'

'Hey, don't talk to her like that,' Nick warns me and suddenly things are back to normal. We're falling out and the fact I smuggled him perfectly cooked meat is a distant memory.

'Leave her, Nick, she's not worth it,' Heather insists, ushering him towards his bedroom. Once they're inside, they close the door behind them.

Oh my God, how am I supposed to get through to Nick with that creature around? We were getting on just fine this evening until she showed up. At first I thought that perhaps Heather and I were just too different to get on, but the more I get to know her and the more run-ins I have with her, I realise she's actually just a horrible person. I pour myself another glass of wine. Perhaps it's time to try and make Nick realise that.

Chapter 21

When I found out that my brother was housesitting for my parents for two weeks, all on his own, I did wonder what he would do to amuse himself. I know from spending a few of days there over Christmas that I get very bored, very quickly, and my brother has it way worse rattling around in there on his own for a couple of weeks. That's why Millsy and I have been dropping in on him, to keep him company. What we walked in on today, however, I was not at all prepared for.

If I thought it was weird when I caught him hiding behind the curtain, ogling the woman next door, nothing could've prepared me for what I've just walked in on.

'What the fuck are you doing?' I ask, confused by the sight of my brother planking across the kitchen sink.

'Shh! Get down,' he insists. 'And turn that light back off.'

I do as instructed, flicking off the light before crouching down on the floor. Millsy follows my lead.

'So, to repeat my question: what the fuck are you doing?' I whisper.

My brother shifts his weight a little, clearly finding his post uncomfortable, but not about to leave it unmanned.

'It's Weird Ian,' he tells us. 'I've been spying on him.'

'Oh my God, you must be bored.' I laugh. 'So what's he been up to?'

My brother stares at me for a moment, and there's this look in his eye, like he's not joking.

'So every night he has these different women in his house with him. I see them moving around the different rooms, through different windows—'

'Fucking hell, pal. You *are* bored.' Millsy laughs. 'Granted it's hard to comprehend: Weird Ian with even one woman, let alone multiple birds, but watching them at it is kind of grim.'

'You didn't let me finish,' Woody snaps. 'They never leave.'

'Wait, what do you mean?' I ask, puzzled.

'I mean that I see these different women in his house, and then suddenly there's no sign of them moving around. But then I notice Ian hurry out, but no women ever leave.'

'You've lost me, mate,' Millsy says.

'Look, see that window there?'

We glance where Woody is pointing and notice the silhouette of a woman. She looks tall and her hair is piled up in a big beehive, which only makes her appear taller. Ian is standing next to her, and seems short by comparison. I'm not actually sure if Ian is tall or short because I haven't really seen him since I was younger. It always seemed like a good idea to keep out of his way. I mean, we call him Weird Ian, for crying out loud. We know what we're dealing with.

'So what?' I ask.

'Just watch,' Woody insists.

I am willing to humour my brother, so I do as he asks and watch out of the window. Soon enough the two figures disappear, and then …

'See, look, Ian leaves the house straight after,' Woody observes.

I glance at the gap between Ian's house and his neighbour's, only to see Ian dashing off in a hurry. That is weird.

'So, wait, what about the women?' I ask. 'When do they leave?'

'They don't,' he tells me. 'Not ever.'

'They must do,' Millsy insists.

'Nope,' Woody insists. 'I watched all night yesterday.'

I feel my eyes widen. 'OK, intervention,' I insist, grabbing him by the arm, pulling him down from the worktop. 'You need some social interaction. You're going mad here on your own. This is why people throw parties when they housesit, because it's boring and weird and lonely.'

'I tried to tell him,' Millsy insists. 'He was having none of it.'

'Actually, I think that's a very good idea,' Woody says, shocking us both. 'I've really enjoyed spending time with you both, like the good old days. Plus, Millsy said he'd bring some babes.'

I narrow my eyes at my brother.

'Erm, do I need to remind you that you're married?' I ask rhetorically, although it kind of sounds like he does need reminding. 'Who are you, and what have you done with my brother?'

Woody laughs. 'My life is boring, and going out with you guys gave me a glimpse of what a fun life is like. This is my last chance to throw a big stupid party while my parents are away, and while my wife and son are away, so I think we should go for it.'

'Yes!' Millsy booms, looking up from his script for a moment. He spends pretty much every free second he has rehearsing, but opening night is very soon, and he hasn't had as much time as the other actors. That's why I've agreed to help him, because he's my friend and he needs me. And luckily we both remember the play quite well from school, even if we did only initially join the drama club because we knew you got to skip lessons for rehearsals before big productions.

I think for a moment. Yes, OK, I would love to throw a party, and if they'd left me housesitting I would've done just that, but that's not exactly my brother's scene. Then again, it's nice to see him happy.

'OK, sure, let's do it,' I give in, a huge grin spreading across my face. 'How about Halloween?'

'Yes!' Millsy booms, twice as loud as his previous boom. 'I love to dress up!'

'That does sound like fun. Let's do it,' Woody says, clapping his hands. 'And it just so happens Halloween is on a Saturday this year, so that's perfect.'

The three of us exchange knowing glances. My brother might not be that much of a party animal, but he knows that I am, and he knows that Millsy is. When we were younger and always getting into trouble, Woody – the little goody two-shoes that he was – would hide at the top of the stairs and watch as my parents yelled at me for getting home past my curfew. So even though he's never really let his hair down, he knows that Millsy and I have this covered.

'So, what's the first rule of house-party planning?' he asks.

'Don't have it at your own house,' I tell him honestly. 'But we're beyond that. The second rule is to get loads of booze.'

'That's my job,' Millsy chirps, raising his hand.

'Then we need lots of cool people to come – I can get on that. Finally, someone needs to hide/bubble-wrap all the valuable/breakable stuff. Bro, that's your job.'

Woody frowns at the lame task he has been given, but it only lasts a second, because I don't think I've ever seen him so psyched for anything.

'Anyway, how are things going with Nick?' my brother enquires. I think he worries about me, and he makes no secret that he thinks this plan is dumb.

I puff air from my cheeks.

'It's like I take one step forward and sixteen steps back! Just when I start making progress, something happens that puts us right back to square one.'

'Here's an idea,' Woody starts. 'Just tell him how you feel, like a normal person.'

'Can't do that,' I reply, very matter-of-factly. 'First up, it's too much of a one-eighty. I can't be like: "You know how we hate each other? Well I actually quite like you now" can I? Also, he has a girlfriend. And she might be horrible, but I can't just take her out of the picture. I need Nick to realise that he has feelings for me. I'm not going to trick him into liking me.'

'You don't need to trick him,' Millsy chimes in, 'but he does need a little gentle persuasion. The Scottish play has served us well so far, right?'

'Debatable,' I reply. 'But go on.'

'You need to do a Lady Macbeth. Emasculate him.' Woody and I chuckle.

'I'm serious,' Millsy insists. 'Question his manhood.'

'I don't think I'll get much sense from that either.' I giggle, causing Millsy to toss a cushion at me.

'I'm telling you, you make him feel like less of a man, he'll jump through hoops to prove he is. Try it.'

I look over at my brother, who is laughing with his head in his hands.

'Oh my God,' he blurts, sitting upright. 'I mean, as your ridiculous plan goes, why not, but it's all stupid.'

I think.

'You're like my Lady Macbeth,' I tell Millsy affectionately.

'And don't you forget it,' he replies.

Chapter 22

I'm back in Leeds and all I want to do is curl up on the sofa and watch Netflix – preferably with the flat to myself – but it seems like Nick has something similar in mind.

'Evening,' Nick says to me as I barge through the door.

'Yo,' I reply casually. Too casually? Who even says "yo" anymore?

Nick just laughs. He's clicking through Netflix, as though he's browsing for something to watch. I stand behind the sofa and look over his shoulder.

'Oh my God, "because you watched *The Spice Movie*",' I read out loud. Nick clicks away, embarrassed.

'It was Heather's turn to pick the film,' he explains. 'She's a big fan.'

'She must be – I watched that film when I was nine and I didn't exactly regard it as a masterpiece then. I thought you guys just watched documentaries and shit.'

'You've got me all wrong.' He laughs. 'I've got excellent taste in movies.'

'Sure you do,' I reply. 'Just like I'm excellent at removing babies from people.'

Nick laughs. 'What, like snatching them? "Removing babies" is a new and fascinating way to refer to what I do – like they're an inflamed appendix.'

'You know what I mean,' I reply. 'Go on then, tell me which classics you've been choosing when it's your turn.'

Abandoning the remote to talk to me, he turns sideways to look me in the eye.

'Hmm,' he says thoughtfully. 'Well the last film we watched was *Rope*.'

'You did not,' I reply.

'We did – my choice. I love Hitchcock films.'

I walk around the sofa and sit down next to him.

'*I* love Hitchcock films,' I tell him. 'To the point where … oh my God, this is going to sound really sad.'

'Go on,' he prompts, making himself more comfortable.

'Well, as much as I'd love to, I can't bring myself to watch all of his movies. It's going to sound stupid, but I know that as soon as I watch all of his films – that's it, no more Hitchcock. I don't want to run out.'

'I can appreciate that,' he replies. 'I haven't seen them all either. I'd like to, just never got around to it. We could do it together,' he suggests.

I think for a moment. 'We could, but this could be a fluke. What was the film you chose before that?'

Nick runs a hand through his hair like he always does when he's feeling awkward, laughing to himself.

'I'm not sure how you'll feel about this one,' he starts cautiously. 'It's not so much a classic, more a personal favourite and I can't really explain why.'

I pull my legs up on the sofa, shifting my body to face his before crossing my legs.

'OK, now I'm really listening,' I say excitedly.

He takes a deep breath before quickly blurting it out, before he can think better of his confession.

'*Step Brothers.*'

'What?' I reply theatrically. 'That's even more unbelievable than *Rope*.'

'I know, I don't fit the profile.' He laughs. 'I know it's dumb, I just love it.'

'You know,' I start, 'if we were to maybe turn our two beds into bunk beds …'

Nick springs to life.

'Oh my God, we really would have so much extra room for *so many* activities.'

I feel a rush of something as he references my favourite movie to me.

'I can't believe we've been living together all this time and we've never spoken about what movies we like,' I say.

'We never talk about anything,' he reminds me.

'We don't,' I agree. 'We just argue about stupid things, like whose turn it is to have custody of the sofa and the TV, or whether or not eggs should be kept in the fridge.'

'*Of course* they should be kept in the fridge,' he exclaims in horror. 'You're a barbarian.'

I smile at him. It's a shame it has taken us until now to realise we have things in common. I guess we've always just focused on the things that make us different.

Nick's phone springs to life, interrupting our moment. He answers it, using short blunt sentences before hanging up.

'That's Heather,' he tells me. 'She needs me to go give her a hand. She can't open the door with the takeaway in her hands.'

'You guys are having a takeaway?' I gasp. Nick pulls a face.

'Don't get excited, it's from that vegan place.'

'More of a "please take this away" than a "takeaway",' I correct him, making gagging noises as I pretend to stick my fingers down my throat.

Nick laughs to himself as he heads downstairs. God, why do I have to find him so dreamy? And why does he have to be such a good guy? He's watching crap movies and eating rubbish food just for Heather. Ergh, my conscience is getting to me again. I should probably try and be nicer to Heather, get to know her a little better. That might stop me lusting after her boyfriend a bit, right?

'Oh, Ruby, hello, someone told me you'd be out,' Heather says disappointedly the second she claps eyes on me.

'Yeah, erm, I assumed you would've been,' Nick replies awkwardly. 'No big deal.'

Time to be mature.

'I'm in for the evening, but I'll be out of your way in five minutes. Just let me grab something to eat and I'll go to my room,' I assure them.

'I'd offer you some of this, but we didn't order much,' Heather tells me.

'That smells ...' I soften and refrain from one of my usual jibes '... delicious. But don't worry, I'll get myself something.'

The pair of them look confused by my reply. I just smile.

'Erm, OK,' Heather replies. 'Nick, babe, get some plates please?'

'Sure,' he replies dutifully.

He really is so devoted to her, it blows me away. Nine times out of ten I can't even get a text back, and here is a man who will do anything for his girlfriend.

Heather sits down on the sofa. I sit next to her – another move that perplexes her. She's got a look on her face, like she truly believes I might be about to attack her at close quarters.

'What are you going to watch?' I ask her.

'I'm not sure,' she replies slowly. 'You seem very ... mellow.'

'That's me.' I smile.

'It's just ... you're being nice.'

'I *am* nice,' I insist. 'Can't we all just be friends?'

Nick creeps up on us. 'What, you want to start going on double dates?' He laughs.

'OK, sure,' I reply. 'Heather, what do you say?'

Heather eyeballs me cautiously, like she's still trying to figure out what my game is.

'What, me and Nick, go out with you and ...?'

'I'm dating one of the Leeds Lions,' I tell her. 'You'd love him!'

'No she wouldn't,' Nick insists.

'Actually, I'd love that,' Heather says with a smile. 'Make the arrangements and we'll be there, won't we, babe?'

'Sure,' Nick replies, again in his usual dutiful way, but there's a reluctance he just can't hide.

'Nick, cutlery,' Heather tuts.

With Nick back in the kitchen, Heather leans closer to me.

'I've always had a thing for rugby players. Does he have any friends?' I stare at her blankly for a second.

'I'm kidding.' She laughs. 'Your face. But, you know, if he does happen to bring any of his friends …'

I frown as I climb to my feet. 'I'm going to grab some Frosties and go watch TV in my room,' I tell them. 'Have fun. I'll hit you with the details when I have it sorted.'

As I walk to my room, shovelling cereal into my face on the way before the milk gets the chance to make it soggy, I think over my exchange with Heather. That's a weird joke to make, but it kind of sounded like she was serious.

Cereal devoured, I sit down on my bed and text Millsy an update.

Millsy: She wants some rugby action, mate.
Ruby: That's what it sounded like to me. Was just trying to be her mate. Don't know why I suggested a bloody double date. Now I'm stuck with it. Help?

I'm not always sure Millsy is the best person to ask advice of, but he is certainly the person I know who gets in the most romantic scrapes, so maybe he'll have something helpful under his belt. So to speak.

Millsy: Truth or date, Rubes. I keep telling you. Either confess your feelings or play the game. Use the date to show him

> *what a catch you are, and like I keep saying, LADY MACBETH HIM!*

I laugh quietly to myself as I read his message. I suppose it wouldn't hurt to try and show Nick what a dazzling date I am, and if I can make him jealous with Deano, that's a result too. It doesn't necessarily have to be to an end, right? I just want to change his opinion of me for the better. All I need now is a plan of attack. Oh, and to try and convince Deano that a double date is a good idea.

Chapter 23

Another day, another date. My God, dating is soul-destroying. Getting all dressed up, time and time again, going out with people in the hope you'll find one another tolerable enough to stick with, just so you don't have to go on any more damn dates. I imagine it gets to a point where you start to compromise, so when you don't find love, maybe you'll settle for compatible, and when you don't get compatible, maybe you'll just settle for the person off Matcher who seems the least likely to try and strangle you while you're sleeping. Because if you can't have true love, you can at least have someone to take to family parties so that your auntie gets off your back about why you're still single.

The only difference with tonight's date is that it's a double date, with Nick and Heather. So this one should be interesting, at least.

So I thought more about Millsy's idea, to emasculate Nick, and it sounds ridiculous. So what I figured I'd do, rather than make him seem less manly, is make me seem more womanly. For too long, I have cared way too little about what Nick thinks of me, and as such, he's seen me at my worst. And when I say worst, I mean *worst*. He's seen me walking around in face masks. He checked out my semi-waxed armpits for me that one time the wax irritated my skin so badly I couldn't put my arms by my sides for a week. Worst of all, on multiple occasions, he has been the person I have called upon to yank me into my control tights. Well, not tonight.

I quickly slick on a second layer of my bright red nail polish.

'Nick,' I call out from my bedroom. 'Can I borrow you for a moment?'

Soon enough, Nick wanders through my bedroom door, looking down at his phone, almost completely distracted by whatever he's reading.

'Let me guess,' he says, without looking up. 'You need me to pull up your weird tights.'

'Not quite,' I reply.

Nick glances up from his phone, and his jaw hits the floor. A split second later, his phone does too.

I'm standing in front of him, in my dress, with it lifted up at the back just enough for him to catch a glimpse of the stockings and suspenders I'm wearing instead of my usual ugly tights and, would you believe it, one has come unclipped.

'Can you clip this back on for me, please?' I ask. 'I'm running so late, and I've just painted my nails. If I chip one, I'll have to start all over again.'

Nick blinks at me before finally finding some words. 'Erm, OK, sure.'

He fiddles around at the back of my thigh, trying to fasten the fiddly suspender to the back of my stocking. I actually find these hard enough to do and I'm supposed to be a woman. Still it doesn't stop me teasing him though.

'I thought doctors were supposed to be good with their hands,' I say softly. 'And you're a downstairs doctor – shouldn't this be your speciality?'

'Undressing patients doesn't fall under my job description.' He laughs, but he sounds nervous.

I shift my weight from one leg to the other, ever so subtly wiggling my bum inches from his face.

'You're supposed to be dressing me, not undressing me.' I giggle. Nick hastily jumps back up to eye level.

'There. Done,' he says. 'Going all out for date number three then?'

I grab a red lipstick and pucker up in front of the mirror.

'Well, you've got to, haven't you?' I give my shoulders an aloof shrug.

Nick runs a hand through his hair before spotting his phone on the floor and picking it up.

'Looking forward to our double date tonight?' I ask him.

'Not really, and I have work in the morning. I'm going to jump in the shower in a minute – if there's any hot water left. You going to be out late or are you coming back here or …'

Nick's voice trails off. I can tell what kind of information he's angling for.

'Don't worry, I won't wake you. I'll probably be back tomorrow.'

An absolute lie, but it won't hurt to let him think that. All it means is that when I creep in after he's gone to bed, he'll assume I've been out all night when, in fact, I am tucked up safely in my bed, with no plans to get up until long after he's gone to work.

'OK, cool,' he replies. 'Well—' My phone springs to life.

'That will be Deano,' I chirp, faking excitement. 'Can you answer it for me please? My nails are still wet.'

My nails are most definitely dry now. Nick pouts like a moody child.

'Do I have to?' he asks. 'He's so dumb I can't take it.'

'Oi, don't talk about my boyfriend that way,' I reply. 'I don't say bad things about Heather to you.'

'You do, actually,' he replies. 'Like, all the time.'

I shrug.

'OK, fine,' he gives in, answering my phone as he wanders into the living room.

I grab my bag and follow him. I'm not about to leave them alone to chat like last time, because the more Deano speaks, the more likely it is Nick will realise that this is nothing serious – or nothing at all, to be honest.

'Eight o'clock, yeah. So, what do you think of what's been happening in France today?' I catch Nick asking Deano.

Nope, I can't let this happen. I snatch my phone from him.

'Sorry, no time to chat about the news,' I insist, heading for the door. 'You and Heather are meeting us there, right?' I call back to him.

'Yep,' he replies unenthusiastically.

I don't want to count my chickens, but I could swear that as I closed the door behind me, I heard Nick sigh.

Chapter 24

Lights, camera, action. I am at The Bucks Head, ready to deliver the performance of a lifetime. I know what you're thinking: that double dates aren't a good idea even in normal circumstances, but in my situation, I think it's going to work.

Maybe I am clutching at straws here, but I am taking that little pang of jealousy Nick showed me this morning and I am running with it. This is my chance to show him that I am not his gross, undesirable flatmate who leaves hair in the plughole, still licks her plate when she is finished eating and frequently speaks like Lumpy Space Princess from *Adventure Time* for hours at a time. Nick just needs to see me in context, out of the flat, in the real world, on an actual date with an adult human man who actually (for some strange reason – probably because he doesn't know the aforementioned gross and annoying facts to be one hundred per cent true) wants to shag me.

The Bucks Head is not my kind of place at all, in fact, I'm instantly regretting letting Deano pick the restaurant. I had kind of hoped he'd pick somewhere nice, like where we had our first date. I figured with him being a pro sportsman, restaurants like Vici would be standard procedure, but now I'm thinking that's just his A-game for sealing the deal. Well, not with this chick. He blew his chance getting in my pants when he implied I shouldn't eat dessert because it was bad for me. I'm still trying to work out whether or not he meant "dessert is bad for you" or "dessert is bad for you specifically, Ruby, you greedy girl" – I'm trying not to lose any sleep over it.

The Bucks Head is a sort of pub-cum-restaurant, but it isn't exactly nailing either. Their first crime was not having a cocktail menu. No big deal, I guess, I just ordered a vodka and orange and the waiter who brought it to me had his finger in my glass so I suppose that's the third ingredient that makes it technically a cocktail, so what do I have to complain about really? Other than potentially catching something gross that is going to result in a trip to a clinic where I'll have some difficult questions to answer. The décor, I can only describe as, if the place were repeatedly closed down and reopened by new people who always kept one thing that their predecessor left behind. Nothing matches. Or looks at all good in any way. And everything looks like it needs a "good clean" – as opposed to a bad clean, obviously, which everything seems to have had already.

Everyone who knows me knows that I am always late for everything, so tonight I decided to make sure I was on time and, amazingly, I got here ten minutes before our booking, but it's five past the hour now, and I'm still the only one here. Wow, this must be what it feels like for everyone when I'm late to meet them – I suddenly feel like a spectacular bastard. I'd love to say that this will make me more careful with my time in the future, but all it's made me realise is that it's better to be the person who is late than the person stuck sitting all alone at the table like a Billy-no-mates, just waiting for someone to show up.

'Hello, sorry we're late,' Heather says, taking me by surprise – not only because she snuck up behind me, but because for some strange reason she's greeting me with a hug. 'So do they have a vegan menu here?'

Cutting to the chase, I see. Honestly, I swear she takes more enjoyment from people "persecuting" her for being a vegan than she does from those who embrace it.

'Erm, they don't even have loo roll in the lavs – they're not going to have a vegan menu,' I tell her.

'Are you saying those two things are similar?' she snaps.

'Ladies, are you fighting already?' Nick asks, finally joining us.

In the spirit of playing nice, he gives my shoulder a squeeze as he greets me.

I exhale deeply as I let Heather's hysteria wash over me, glancing up in Nick's direction.

'Hey, kid,' he says.

'Hey, you …' I reply, my voice trailing off as I catch a glimpse of him in date mode. I've spent so much time worrying about him seeing me "in context" that I totally forgot I'm going to have to watch him on a date with Heather.

Normally I see Nick when he's on his way to or from work, or when he's just knocking around the flat with Heather, cooking whatever no-meat, no-dairy, no-fun crap she wants before watching *A Day in the Life of the Earthworm* on Netflix. Tonight, however, I'm getting the dressed-up, relaxed, charming Nick, and it takes every fibre of my being not to bite my lip and let out a little sigh at the sight of him.

He's smart, but not too smart. Too smart for here, sure, but he's made just the right amount of effort to look good, but still come across as kind of aloof, like he doesn't care if he looks good or not, even though I can tell he's made an effort because he's got product in his hair and his delicious aftershave on. I often see Nick dressed "smart" for work, but something about his attire tonight is driving me crazy, causing my mind to stray from vegan menus and what that red stuff crusted to my fork is, to thinking about his "bedside manner" if you know what I mean. He's wearing a tight-fitting black shirt – not that I think it's intended to be tight-fitting, but his arms, knotted with muscle, underneath look ready to Hulk their way out of the confines of his sleeves, and I for one will cheer with delight when they do. His hair is the kind of effortless mess that takes a lot of product and a generous twenty minutes in front of the mirror to achieve, and he's even carrying his leather jacket – an item from his wardrobe he rarely wears because he once told me he felt intimidated by how cool it was, which probably explains why he's carrying it and not wearing it.

'So, where's Deano?' he asks as they take their seats at the table.

'He's running late,' I tell them. 'Training – they've got a big game coming up.'

Lie, lie, lie. I don't know that he's running late, I'm only guessing that he's had training and don't pro sportsmen always have a big game coming up?

I let a few seconds go by before I grab my phone to text him, to see where he is, but I don't get a reply.

After twenty minutes of awkward small talk – largely dominated by Heather telling me exactly what a cow has to go through so that "selfish people" like me can eat a burger – Deano appears.

'You're late,' I say through gritted teeth, which I am trying to disguise with a big, moronic grin.

'I am,' he tells us. 'Training.'

We all give him understanding gestures – a smile, a shrug of the shoulders, a bat of the hand. It happens. He's got a job to do. He's only twenty-five minutes late, right?

'We finished on time,' he starts. I will him to shut up before he says another word because I know that he's going to say something that will piss me off and make himself look bad, and that's not the aim of the game tonight. 'But then we had this wrestling tournament in the changing rooms. And now I could kill for some fucking meat.'

'Hello,' Heather says brightly to Deano.

That's weird. She should be annoyed that he's late, disgusted by his changing room story, and ready to defenestrate him for that meat remark. Instead, she seems quite charmed.

I make the necessary introductions, cautiously.

'Heather, this is Deano. Deano, this is Heather – Nick's girlfriend.' I feel the words catch in my throat.

'Ruby, move up a seat,' Heather insists. The four of us are sitting at a round table, and currently I am next to Heather, Nick is to her right and then there's a space for Deano between Nick and me.

'You want me to move up to Nick?' I ask, confused.

'Yeah, I just think it will make for a better environment if we're sat boy-girl,' she explains.

'Ever the school teacher.' I laugh, although I do move up, because I do really want to sit next to Nick.

A waiter is straight over to take our order now that everyone is here, clearly annoyed at us for holding up proceedings.

After ordering our drinks (their strongest white wine in the biggest glass they can find for me) a waiter comes by to give us our menus.

I cast an eye over the sticky pages, but nothing jumps out at me. It's your usual pub food, nothing special, and I don't imagine any of it is going to knock my socks off.

'Chicken salad, easy,' Deano announces, slapping his menu closed before sitting back in his chair.

'I'm a vegan,' Heather starts, to which I roll my eyes. Five minutes before she mentioned it, that's got to be some kind of record. 'But I appreciate that you need meat, given that you're a professional athlete.'

Nick and I exchange a surprised glance, because that's not like Heather at all.

'And I suppose you'll be having a steak,' Nick says to me quietly, as Heather and Deano chat. And while that would be my first choice usually, in the interest of making Nick jealous, I'm going to take a stand of healthy solidarity with my man.

'Actually, I think I'm going to have a salad too,' I inform him. 'We like to eat healthy, don't we, babe?' I say in Deano's direction, but he's too busy talking about himself and Heather is too busy giggling.

Nick takes a second to acknowledge Heather's bizarre behaviour, pulling a face before turning back to me.

'What are you doing?' he asks me.

'What do you mean?' I reply.

'You love steak. And you love upsetting Heather. So why are you ordering a salad? You've always told me that salad was grazing for your rare steak if it got hungry,' Nick reminds me. 'So what gives?'

I shrug my shoulders.

'Mate, you're always telling me to make better choices and to be healthier. So what's the problem?'

'You've always ignored me,' he says, speaking softly enough so that only I can hear him. 'You don't have to pretend to be something you're not to impress anyone – especially not this clown.'

We both glance over at Deano, who is downing his pint in one go as Heather watches on, impressed.

'You're not jealous are you, Nick?' I can't help but ask as the corners of my mouth pull into a slight smile.

'No,' he replies quickly, defensively even. 'I just …' his voice softens again '… I see you do this time and time again, tailor your personality to suit whichever guy you're dating, and you don't need to. You just need to be you. I don't want to see you get hurt. Just don't put all your eggs in this guy's basket.'

I smile a huge, genuine grin.

'Well, thank you,' I tell him. 'But I know what I'm doing.'

We place our orders and make small talk – well, it's mostly Heather telling us about her students. As dull as this is to listen to, it's stopping Deano saying stupid stuff, and it's disguising the fact that Nick is just sitting there, silent, with a face like thunder.

'I had to cover this Key Stage 2 science class today,' she starts. 'So I handed out the books and wrote the questions about the universe on the board as instructed. When you cover lessons you just do what you're asked and then sit back and make sure the kids don't harm themselves or each other, but this inquisitive-looking eleven-year-old got up from his desk, walked up to me and asked: "Miss, do you believe in aliens?"'

'What did you tell him?' Deano asks, curiously.

'I told him that they certainly do exist, as there is no way we can possibly know everything about outside our own universe, so why wouldn't there be life elsewhere?'

In the interest of trying to befriend Heather, I don't say what I would like to say, which is: *good work, Heather, telling a bunch of kids during a biology lesson that aliens definitely exist – they'll probably write that in an exam.* I keep my mouth shut.

'And do you know what he told me?' she asks us. We all shake our heads.

'He told me that he thinks aliens do exist, and that some live amongst us. That they're here to film a reality TV shows about our species. He thinks that they're using special technology to make themselves invisible to us and then filming what they do to us. And do you know what he thinks they do for this reality TV?'

'What?' I ask.

'He thinks that when we can't find things, like our phones where we left them, that the aliens have moved them just to toy with us. Or that when we fall over seemingly nothing, it's the aliens tripping us up. He thinks their technology is so advanced, that all we're good for is making fun of for laughs. He's *eleven years old*.'

Her eyes widen as she reminds us of this fact.

'Wow,' I can't help but say. 'That's … wow.'

Deano just laughs. 'Well, I find it hard to believe there's anyone out there smarter than us,' he claims.

'Really?' Nick pipes up. 'You find it hard to believe there is anyone smarter? You?'

'What do you mean?' Deano asks. Oh, for God's sake.

'Food is here,' I say brightly, eyeballing the waiter on his way over to us. He places our dishes in front of us, so we all tuck in and silence falls upon the table. Well, almost silence. The sound of Deano chomping on his chicken salad is so loud – probably because noises are echoing around his open mouth as he chews.

We all take it in turns to glance up and smile awkwardly as we eat, but the conversation just isn't flowing. This is kind of a disaster. I'm supposed to be showing Nick what an awesome date I am, and how much fun I have with Deano, but the only person who is jealous at this table is me, of other people's food, because I fucking hate salad.

The waiter clears our plates away so I take that as my cue to try and get the conversation going again, and to try and actually achieve something, anything, that I set out to do tonight.

'So, Deano has a big game coming up,' I tell them as I squeeze his hand with faux-pride. 'Don't you?'

'Yeah,' he replies. 'Some French team, we'll crush them.'

I give his hand another squeeze, but it's like holding hands with a mannequin. He's just not giving me anything back, nothing at all I can work with, and nothing at all that's going to make Nick jealous. Deano, seemingly unaware of the physical affection I'm trying to give him, pulls his hand out from under mine, causing my wrist to hit the table. I watch anger fill Nick's eyes, so I think fast to distract him.

'Nick is a bit of sportsman, aren't you?' I say.

'Cricket,' Nick replies. 'Played a bit at uni, don't get much time these days.'

'That's your fault, pal,' Deano tells him, shrugging his big, strong shoulders casually. 'I always make time for rugby.'

'It's your job,' Nick reminds him. 'My job is being a doctor. We might not be "crushing" any teams, but we give plenty of diseases and illnesses a run for their money.'

'More exciting than cricket then.' He laughs. 'Hardly what you'd call a sport.'

'No,' Nick replies. 'I should be playing rugby, getting my head kicked in so that I can be an absolute moron.'

'What do you mean?' Deano asks.

'Oh my God.' Nick laughs. 'You're so dumb, you don't even know when people are telling you that you're dumb.'

'OK, calm down,' Heather insists, placing a hand on Nick's bicep.

Deano might be dumb, but not so much that he doesn't realise Nick just offended him.

'Come on then, Doc, let's take this outside,' he shouts, pushing his chair out suddenly, standing up, beating a fist on his own chest like a gorilla.

'Because that's how civilised adults behave,' Nick replies sarcastically.

'That's how I show you who is the dumb one,' Deano shouts back.

That doesn't even make any sense. My God, he really is so dumb.

I look over at Heather, to exchange a glance with her, to ask her with my eyes what we're supposed to do, but she's too busy watching Deano getting angry, gazing up at him in what seems like adoration, biting her lip. I don't think she'll be happy when he punches her boyfriend's face in, which seems very likely at this particular moment.

'Heather,' I say, but it falls on deaf ears. 'Heather,' I try again a little louder. She looks at me. 'We can take care of the bill, just take Nick home to bed before this escalates. I'll calm Deano down, don't worry.'

'OK,' she replies, grabbing her things. 'Come on, babe.'

Nick reluctantly stands up and tucks his chair under the table, all the while maintaining eye contact with Deano, who looks so ready for a fight he's done everything but smash a bottle on the table, ready to stab him.

Once the two of them have left, and the audience we seem to have attracted go back to their meals, Deano sits back down. He looks at me, expectantly. I'm not sure if he's expecting an apology or a thank you or what, but he isn't getting anything of the sort.

'Just so you know,' I tell him, grabbing a menu from a passing waiter. 'I'm definitely having dessert.'

Chapter 25

Dear diary, last night I had my third date with Deano and it was awful. I've always had it on pretty good authority that date three was when the magic happened, but the only thing magical about my dates with Deano is the fact I manage to endure them.

I could feel bad, using Deano like this, but when he does things that reminds me he's using me too (and with arguably worse intentions: I'm doing this for love, he's doing this to sleep with me so he can move on to the next chick), I don't feel quite so bad anymore.

Tonight was a fine example. I've noticed something: Deano hasn't tried to kiss me. I mean, don't get me wrong, I don't want him to kiss me and it is a relief that he isn't trying to because that would be harder to get out of, but I think it says it all that he has no desire to do it. He really does just want to sleep with me, and he's not even trying to pretend otherwise – so I had to be ready with another excuse tonight.

It was only 10.30 p.m. as we strolled along Park Row. The street was still busy, the bars were still full, but I'd insisted I wanted an early night. Yes, OK, maybe that wasn't the best turn of phrase, but I did mean it literally.

'We going back to yours?' Deano asked.

I bit my lip and pulled a bit of a face. 'About that …' I started.

I had a feeling this might happen. I also figured that even Deano would realise I was having a never-ending period, so I looked up different excuses to get out of sex. Some of them were hilarious, like: "the dog is watching" or "I've eaten too much dairy" but, sadly, Deano knows I don't have a dog, and he's seen that I haven't eaten anything all night. It's unpleasant, and it's awkward, but I had to go with the only excuse I figured would work.

'I have thrush,' I told him.

'What do you mean?' he inevitably asked.

'It's a fungal infection,' I told him. 'Downstairs.'

Deano recoiled in horror.

'Who have you caught that off?' he asked accusingly.

'You don't catch it from anyone,' I told him. 'It's when the natural balance of your vagina is … off.' I'm pretty sure, I can't remember what I read on the NHS website word for word, despite trying to memorise it earlier.

'So I can't catch it, we're fine,' he said with a shrug.

I can't help but be amazed, and a little impressed, at just how much Deano will put up with for a shag. The fact I told him I have a "fungal infection" – and I used those exact words – and it didn't put him off. Never mind the fact it would probably mean I didn't feel up to sex at all, that's a non-issue.

'Well, there's a chance I could pass it on to you,' I told him, because I did read that, even though it was uncommon, it could still happen. 'I wouldn't wish this on you.' Much. 'It's horrible. Itching, burning – discharge.'

If that isn't a boner-killer of a statement, nothing is.

'Fuck,' he replied. 'No way do I want that. When will it be gone?'

'Few days, tops.'

I smiled sweetly and we parted ways, as usual.

I've just relayed this story to Millsy, who finds it absolutely hilarious. 'Ruby, I told you he was an absolute animal,' he cackles. 'That's grim.'

'I know, right?'

I've been rehearsing lines with Millsy all morning, but I couldn't keep this story in a second longer so we've taken a coffee break. Even though Uncle Mills is never here, his flat has all the bells and whistles you could imagine – including an epic coffee machine that might intimidate most people, but can be easily navigated by a couple of trained baristas. We made our drinks and took them outside. Even though it's late October, there's something so relaxing about getting wrapped up and sitting on the benches outside, looking over the river, people-watching, sipping good coffee and chatting rubbish with your best friend.

'Anyway, we need to get back to rehearsing,' Millsy insists, jumping to his feet before pulling me up with his free hand.

'But you haven't sorted my problem for me,' I tell him.

'I think you get a cream from the doctor for it – Nick might get you some, mates' rates,' he tells me. 'In fact, getting him to give you the once-over might be the best way to seduce him.'

'You know I don't mean my faux-thrush, and that's a disgusting joke, even for you,' I reply.

We head back inside and sit down on the sofa, grabbing our scripts and opening them on the page where we left off.

I sigh deeply.

'Mate, come on, he's not worth it,' Millsy tells me, giving my shoulder a gentle, semi-patronising bump with his fist.

I pull a face. 'Maybe,' I reply.

Millsy screams theatrically. 'I hate seeing you like this,' he tells me, exasperated. 'Look, I'm telling you, Lady Macbeth his ass. Emasculate him.'

I roll my eyes. 'And how do you propose I do that?' I ask. 'Because there isn't a jar in the world that I'll be able to get into quicker and easier than he can, not even Nutella. And I fucking love Nutella.'

'I know you do,' he replies. 'I'm still not over that sweet lasagne you made. But I'm not talking about out-macho-ing him. If I were, I'd just out-macho him for you.'

I think for a moment.

'He already has a girlfriend who wears the ethically made trousers, she's doing a pretty good job of emasculating him all on her own.'

'That's it,' Millsy says victoriously, clapping his hands. 'Have her do it.'

'How?' I ask.

Millsy thinks so hard it looks like it physically hurts him.

'I don't know,' he says slowly. 'Yet. But you'll think of something. You've always been good at improvisation.'

'Well, sticking to the script certainly isn't doing me any good,' I reply.

A message comes through on my phone, snapping me from my thoughts.

'Oh, for fuck's sake,' I complain. 'It's Deano. He keeps trying to sext me.'

'Oh man, he *is* desperate.' Millsy laughs. 'He sent you any dick pics yet?'

'Not yet,' I tell him, just as another message comes through. And there it is. '*Now* he has.'

Why do men think it's a good idea to send unsolicited dick pics? Seriously, what thought process takes place that ends with: I know, I'll send her a picture of my junk? And, I'm not saying I would appreciate them if they had some artistic merit, but they're always so awful. Bad angles, poor personal hygiene and, arguably one of the weirdest moves I see so often, using something like the TV remote control for perspective – something that doesn't make me think: "my, what big junk you have", it just makes me less likely to want to change the channel at your house.

Nope, I'll never understand dick pics. It's the photographic equivalent of when a cat brings you a dead mouse as a gift. Like, I appreciate the gesture, I guess, but what the fuck do you actually expect me to do with that?

'You going to send him something back?' Millsy asks curiously.

'What, like sext him back out of duty? Like it's admin work?'

'Exactly.' He laughs. 'Sexting is a mere formality of modern dating.'

As Millsy continues to deliver his lines, I wonder just how happily I could drive a rift between Nick and Heather. I mean obviously I could happily do it just because I don't like her, but I'm talking about morally. Yes, I have morals too. No matter how much I want him for myself, I'm not sure I could comfortably use underhand tactics to steal a man from a fellow female. I don't struggle to understand why she likes him, but even though I'm unsure what he sees in her, he must see something, and if that's what he wants, I should let him have it, right? I'll just have to try and get over this stupid crush.

Chapter 26

After the long walk up the hill from Millsy's – not made easier by all the coffee I drank and the biscuits I ate during rehearsals – I am positively knackered. I must be so unfit, to feel so shocking after walking up a hill. Then again, I did rush a little, because it's freezing out there tonight, and also because I really need to pee. I don't like to use the bathroom at Chez Mills, mostly because it doesn't get cleaned ever, but also because with the number of different girls who sit on it, it'll be like an STD hotbed. Like my friend's face, probably.

Just when I think I couldn't be happier to be home, I walk into the living room to see Heather sitting on the sofa.

'Where's Nick?' I ask.

'He's in the shower,' she tells me, as she flicks through a magazine.

'Fuck,' I can't help but exclaim. 'I really need the lav.'

'You should've gone at break time,' she tells me.

I shoot her a look.

'Sorry, just a little teacher humour.'

'Hilarious,' I reply, sitting down in the armchair. 'Why are you reading a bridal magazine?'

'Because it came free with my usual mag, and because it doesn't hurt to be prepared,' she informs me.

'Yes, of course,' I reply sarcastically. 'One must always be ready to tie the knot. Just in case.'

Heather raises her eyebrows and gets back to her magazine.

'Well, Nick and I certainly are serious about one another,' she tells me, despite me not asking. 'I'd make a good wife for him. And, of course, his family are loaded, so I wouldn't say no, would I?'

'Sorry, what did you just say?' I ask.

'Don't get me wrong, I'm not saying I'm with Nick for his money. I know he doesn't like to take it from his family. But he is due a large inheritance at some point, given that his parents only have him and his sister to leave everything to. But even on his future doctor's wage, I imagine we'll be more than comfortable. And I know he's got his grandma's ring ready to give to someone, and that thing is worth a fortune.'

'Funny,' I reply. 'Because it sounds exactly like you're saying you're with him for his money.'

'Now, now, Ruby. Don't be jealous,' Heather ticks me off. It's weird. It's like since I tried to befriend her, I guess she thinks she can open up to me a little more. 'It sounds like you've found yourself a rich sap in Deano. Don't try and pretend you're with him for his personality.' She laughs. 'At least he's hot like Nick. I could certainly go there too.'

I might not be "dating" Deano for his personality, but I'm certainly not seeing him for his money; in fact, that's never crossed my mind. On every date I've been on with him so far, I have insisted on splitting the bill, just because I don't feel comfortable taking money from men. I know that many of my female friends – even if it's just because they're traditional – are more than happy to let men pay for everything, but I'm not happy doing that. Heather, on the other hand, doesn't seem to feel any shame at all in targeting well-off men.

Finally, things click into place. Whether I end up with Nick or not, there's no way he should be with this chick. She wants to bleed him dry and I care about him way too much to let that happen. I know exactly what I need to do, and exactly how I can go about doing it.

'I'm not being jealous,' I tell her. 'It's just that I don't want to ruin the surprise.'

Heather's ears prick up. She puts her magazine down. 'Oh?' she says.

'Yeah, well, I mean maybe I should tell you. It sounds like it might help things along.'

Help me to help you show Nick your true colours, more like.

'Go on,' she insists. 'And hurry up about it, he'll be out of the shower any minute.'

'OK, sure.' I lean in and switch to a hushed voice. 'I overheard him on the phone, saying that he wanted to propose to you. In fact, he mentioned giving you his gran's ring.'

'No way,' Heather squeaks. 'Do you know how much that thing is worth?!'

'Way,' I tell her. 'Thing is, he's scared to ask you, in case it freaks you out because it's so soon in your relationship.'

'Who cares?' she says excitedly. 'Nothing would make me happier.' Oh, I'll bet it wouldn't.

'Here's the thing: if he knows that you know, he'll be upset that the surprise has been spoiled – it won't be special.'

'So what do I do?' she asks, anxiety consuming every last muscle in her face. She's terrified she's going to lose him and therefore his money.

'Oh, I don't know,' I tell her. 'Unless you take the initiative? I mean, it's a sure-thing, right?'

Heather considers this for a moment and I can practically see the pound signs rolling around in her eyes.

'OK, can you give us some privacy?' she asks. 'This shouldn't take long.'

'Of course,' I say with a smile. 'Take all the time you need.'

I pull myself up from my chair and head into my bedroom.

All I need to do is wait in here for a few minutes, and then I can go back out there and enjoy the fireworks. And I do love a good firework display. Any feelings of guilt I had before evaporated the second Heather showed herself for the gold-digger she really is.

I make the decision to get changed, hopping out of the Victoria's Secret tracksuit I've been wearing all day and slipping on a dress. Because if I'm going to be the first female Nick clocks eyes on after Heather blindsides him with a premature, emasculating, blatantly gold-digging proposal, then I want to look my best. I slip on a dress and run my straighteners over my hair. Twenty minutes go by.

'Ruby, get in here,' Heather yells. Uh-oh, has it not gone well? This is so surprising to me.

'What's up?' I ask, poking my head around the door.

'Come in here,' Heather repeats herself. 'And sit down.'

I do as instructed.

'What's up, guys?'

'Let me ask you a question,' Heather starts. Uh-oh, it's all going to kick off …

Nick emerges from the kitchen area with a bottle of prosecco in his hand.

'We just wondered if we could have a bottle of your prosecco. We're celebrating … because we're getting married,' she squeals joyfully, flashing me her ring finger.

My eyes dart from granny's ring on Heather's finger to Nick, popping the cork on one of *my* bottles.

I blink for a moment. This is not what was supposed to happen. What the fuck is he thinking?

'Congratulations,' I gush, giving Heather a hug because I really don't know what else to do. And the Oscar goes to …

Heather snatches the open bottle from Nick and begins pouring it into glasses, leaving Nick and me just standing there, looking at each other. His expression is blank, I can't quite figure it out. I feel my own smile slip from my face.

'Congratulations,' I tell him, grabbing him for a hug, stretching up onto my tiptoes to give him a kiss on the cheek.

'Thanks,' he says awkwardly.

Heather thrusts a glass into my hand, before examining the ring on her own.

'It's a bit big, babe. We'll have to get it resized,' she tells Nick.

'Yeah, sure,' he replies.

I knock back my drink in one big gulp and head back towards my room. 'I'll replace this bottle for you,' Nick calls after me.

'Don't be daft,' I reply, using all my strength and acting abilities to make sure that I don't let slip how upset I really am. 'Consider it an engagement gift.'

'Well, we'd better ring and tell our parents,' Heather insists. 'And Ruby, looks like one of you is going to have to move out of here after all.'

'Yeah, I guess so,' I reply. Because there's no way I can stick around to watch them play happy families.

Chapter 27

So far my day off has been entirely out of character for me. I got up early, tidied up my room (hoping my life would follow suit and fall neatly into place) before heading into Boots to buy a few things ... things I never thought I'd buy.

So Nick must be in love with Heather if he's marrying her – no matter what her intentions are – and there's no way I can stand in the way of that. All this time I've been motivated by two things: how amazing life would be if it were just like in my dream, and that Nick maybe did have feelings for me after all. But there's no way he'd agree to get married if he felt anything for me, so that's that.

It has got me thinking about the kind of guys I attract though. Girls like Heather get guys like Nick and chicks like me are stuck with the likes of Deano Gamble trying to hump and dump us. It isn't because her personality is better, because we've established she's a gold-digging bore – it must be because she looks like a doctor's wife, whereas I look like more like the kind of girl who has a repeat prescription for lice lotion.

OK, I'm being hard on myself, but maybe a more demure look would help me attract nicer guys. Maybe blokes take one look at my pink and blonde 'do, and my daring clothes and think: this bird just wants a good time. That's why I've picked up a warm mocha brown hair dye. Well, I knew brown would be sensible, and there were hundreds of different shades so obviously I went for the coffee option.

Standing in front of the bathroom mirror, the bottle in my hand, I look myself in the eye.

'Are you sure you want to do this?' I ask myself. I feel like my funky hair and my Cara Delevingne-esque eyebrows are what make me who I am.

I nod to myself. I need to do this.

I carefully apply the colour all over, closing the lid on the toilet so I can sit down while it develops. There's no turning back now.

When the time is up, I rise and towel-dry my hair before grabbing my hairdryer, blowing my hair straight and leaving it that way, rather than opting for my big, silly curls. I look in the mirror again.

'You don't look like you any more,' I tell myself. Truth is, though, I don't really feel like myself at the moment anyway. I slip on my underwear and stroll into the living room, safe in the knowledge I have the flat to myself this morning.

I walk up to the fridge and grab a Flake, because I'm one of those people who likes their chocolate refrigerated, but as I go to open it, I pause. No, I'm going to make better choices. I put it back and look in the cupboards until I find Nick's healthy snacks. I guess I'll have a cereal bar instead.

I turn around too quickly and walk into the drying rack Nick puts his clothes on. Ergh, it's started already, Heather's stuff is all over it. First she has a key, now she's doing her washing here – I'm going to be out on my arse in no time.

As I pick up items of clothing and pop them back on the rack, curiosity gets the better of me. Heather is definitely what you'd call petite, whereas I am what you'd refer to as all those buzzwords that are just euphemisms for a little bit too close to chubby. Still, I select a few of the baggier items of clothing – a brown jumper and a long black skirt – and slip them on, before looking in the full-length mirror that hangs in the living room – something I insisted we have, so that I could give myself the once-over as I dashed out the door late, just in case my dress was ever tucked into my knickers or something like that.

I look drab, boring and miserable, and I'm not even sure it's the new hair or the outfit, it's probably just my face.

I'm just about to slip off the jumper when I notice something sparkly catch my eye: Nick's grandma's ring. Heather did say it was too big, I guess she decided it best to not wear it until she's had it adjusted.

I eyeball it, biting my lip thoughtfully. I'm ripping off her hair, wearing her clothes … I could slip her ring on, just for a second. Just to see what it looks like.

Before I've had the chance to really think it through, I'm wearing Nick's grandma's ring. I only get a split second to check it out before the door buzzer snaps me from my thoughts. Shit! The first thing I do is try to take the ring off, but it won't budge, it's stuck. Fuck, fuck, fuck. The more I try, the more stuck it seems. OK, I just need to calm down and it'll pop right off.

The door buzzes again. Shit. It's probably one of Nick's stupid food deliveries where they send him fifty pieces of frozen chicken, because: protein. I'll answer the door, get that sorted and then the pressure is off.

I hit the button that opens the downstairs door before opening the front door, ready to sign for whatever it is. It isn't a deliveryman who walks up the stairs, though. It's a woman.

'Hello,' I say cheerily to the stranger.

'Hello,' she replies. 'Oh, the ring looks divine!' I nibble a fingernail, nervously.

'Oh, thank you,' I reply. 'Erm …'

I don't really know what to say, I think I'm supposed to know who this woman is, but I have no idea. She's got to be in her fifties, she's dressed smartly, with her brown hair cut short and she's wearing minimal make-up. Although distinctly Yorkshire, I can't help but notice how well-spoken she is.

'I'm so sorry, allow me to introduce myself. I'm Deborah, Nick's mum. He said he'd told you I was coming to meet you – did he forget?'

'I guess he must have,' I reply. I shake the hand Deborah is offering me. 'Well, come in. Can I get you a drink?'

'Tea would be lovely,' she replies, taking off her coat and scarf, hooking them on the rack behind the door. Yep, she's Nick's mum. OK.

As I make the tea, I wonder why on earth he's sent his mum to meet me.

Is she here to kick me out or something?

'Milk and sugar?' I ask.

'Just milk, please,' she calls back. 'I'm sweet enough.'

Deborah joins me in the kitchen. She spies the cereal bar crumbs I left on the worktop and scoops them into her hand, putting them in the bin before dusting her hands off by clapping them together. So *that's* where he gets it from.

'So, it's just us?' Deborah checks.

'It is,' I reply, cautiously. Is she here to kill me or something?

'Good,' she says with a smile. 'I was worried Nick's roommate might be here. I've never met her, but I can't get to know my soon-to-be daughter-in-law with her around.'

Oh shit, she thinks I'm Heather. Well, of course she does, I'm like a clone of her right now, right down to her engagement ring.

'Ruby isn't so bad,' I say, jumping to my own defence. 'I think she and Nick are just polar opposites.'

'Perhaps,' Deborah replies, before leaning in closer to me and lowering her voice. 'He told me she has pink hair. What kind of grown woman has pink hair?'

Deborah laughs at the ridiculousness. I join in.

'Not me,' I reply awkwardly. Why am I going along with this? To save her the embarrassment of mistaking me for someone else and then insulting me to my face? Or just to save myself the embarrassment of being caught with another girl's engagement ring stuck on my finger? Probably both.

'He does have some nice things to say about her though. And I don't suppose he would live with her if she were as crazy as her hair.'

I want to ask what kind of things he says more than anything, but it's going to make me seem like his jealous girlfriend.

'So Nick told me you had the day off, I thought we could talk arrangements.'

'Oh, that man,' I giggle sweetly. 'I'm only off this morning, I have to head to work very soon unfortunately.'

'Oh, well that is a shame,' she tells me. 'Well, I'll finish this and then leave you to it. But it really was so nice to meet you. You'll have to come over for dinner with Nick, meet his dad too.'

'I would love that,' I tell her. I actually would love that, but she thinks I'm Heather, so that won't be happening. I may be able to act the part for Deborah, but I'm pretty sure Nick would realise I wasn't his fiancée – you know, when I was actually nice and ate a cheeseburger in two bites.

Deborah makes her way to the door, kissing both my cheeks before she leaves.

'It was nice to meet you, my love,' she tells me, warmly. 'You have a great day.'

'You too,' I reply, watching as she heads down the stairs and out of the door. Just as I'm about to head back inside, I see Bev, my neighbour, letting herself out of her flat.

'Ruby, hello,' she beams. 'How are things?'

'Not bad,' I tell her. 'I haven't seen you in ages. What's new?'

'No, it's been a while since I went outside – I've just been so caught up in the book I'm writing.'

'What's this one about?' I enquire.

'It's a little bit like the story of the *Titanic*. It's set in space, and all the characters are sloths.'

That sounds the least like *Titanic* of anything I've ever heard in my life. 'That sounds awesome,' I say with a chuckle. Bev is just the best kind of barmy.

'What's new with you?' she asks. 'Other than your hair. That's very … different for you.'

Bev wears whatever she wants, regardless of what people think. Today she's wearing a floor-length black maxi dress and a black fur coat. She looks absolutely badass; it's a shame she doesn't go out more.

'Nick is getting married,' I tell her. That's when I remember the ring stuck on my finger. 'Are you in a rush?'

'Not at all, what can I do for you?' she asks.

'I tried on Nick's fiancée's ring and I got it stuck,' I confess.

Bev laughs. 'Oh, love, come here.' She gives me a hug. 'Let's go inside, I'll get this off for you.'

Bev runs my hand under the cold tap to try and reduce the swelling of my puffy fingers.

'So, what's his fiancée like?' Bev asks.

'Erm, she's … I don't know. I'm not a fan.'

Bev squirts a liberal amount of washing-up liquid onto my finger. As she pulls on the ring, it pops straight off.

'There you go,' she tells me, rinsing the soap off of it before placing it in the palm of my hand. 'So you don't think she's right for him?'

'Not really … but it's not my place, is it?'

'Maybe not,' she tells me as she heads for the door. 'But if there's one message I'm trying to make clear in my sloths in space novel, it's that if you love someone, you should always tell them what you think.'

'You've given me a lot to think about,' I say. 'Have a nice day.'

As soon as Bev has left, I hurry off Heather's clothes and return them to the drying rack. Seconds later, Heather walks through the door.

'Ruby, I think it's really inappropriate that you walk around like that.' I gasp dramatically.

'In my underwear, in my own home, when I know my flatmate will be at work all day – yes, that is shocking, isn't it?'

I grab one of my dirty T-shirts from the washing I was sorting on the kitchen floor and pop it on.

'Well, I'm here,' she tells me. 'And what have you done to your hair?'

'Well, I forget that you have a key because I wasn't consulted,' I remind her. 'And I dyed it. What are you doing here?'

'I approve,' she tells me. 'It's more sensible. Pink was silly. I came to collect my ring, to take it to be adjusted. Thought I might make myself some lunch in the meantime – Nick's mum is supposed to be popping in to meet me.'

I panic about two things: the first is whether or not I dried the ring before putting it back on the sideboard. As Heather picks it up to examine it, I assume that because she isn't freaking out over how wet it is, that it's fine. My other problem is that Nick's mum thinks she met Heather, and when she mentions it to Nick, and he mentions it to Heather, and she says that she didn't meet her – oh, I'm in a whole mess of trouble. I just need to buy myself some time while I figure out what to do.

'You just missed her,' I tell Heather.

'I did?'

'Yes, she left just before you got here.'

Heather's eyes widen. 'Not that woman in the fur coat?'

Oh, this is brilliant. Deborah thinks that I am Heather, and Heather thinks that Bev is Deborah – this really is like something fresh out of a Shakespeare play.

'That was her,' I lie. 'Did you speak to her?'

'We passed in the doorway, she said hello to me, asked me if I was having a glorious day – I thought she was a bit weird. Ah, well, that's rich people for you, right?'

'Totes,' I say sarcastically. 'So I guess you don't have to stick around now …'

Heather's phone rings, causing her to instantly ignore me and answer. 'Nick, sweetheart,' she squeaks. 'One sec, let me put you on speaker. OK, you can talk now. I'm just making lunch.'

'No worries, I just got off the phone with my mum ... She really likes you!' he says, proudly.

'She does?' Heather asks. 'I wouldn't have thought she'd seen me for long enough.'

'She did mention that it was a brief encounter, but she approves,' he tells her.

'Oh, well that's great.' Heather sounds unenthusiastic. 'What did you think of her?'

'Erm, yeah, she seemed nice. Fashion-forward,' Heather adds.

'*My* mum? Really?'

Heather looks at me and rolls her eyes, laughing silently. 'Oh yeah, totally.'

'Well, I'm so pleased the two of you got on,' Nick tells her. 'Anyway, I'd better go. Just thought I'd let you know that.'

'OK, honey. Bye.'

Heather hangs up.

'His mum likes me? Ha! She hardly even met me. How daft is she?'

I shrug my shoulders. Now I'm even more annoyed at my situation, because that means that Nick's mum actually likes *me*. I might not have looked myself, but I acted myself, and she liked me. She thought I was good enough for her son.

If only I'd gone about this better, Nick and I could've been perfect for each other. It's just a shame it took me so long to realise I had feelings for him, instead of realising after months of annoying him to the point where he can't wait to kick me out. Still, nothing I can do now. I guess I should find somewhere else to live, oh, and I should probably reply to that dick pic Deano sent me and tell him that I don't think we should see each other anymore. He's just going to have to make peace with the fact that there's at least one girl in the world who doesn't want to sleep with him, just like I need to make myself OK with the fact that there is one person in the world who doesn't want to be with me – and, annoyingly, he's the only one I want.

Chapter 28

This afternoon, I am in a foul mood. The sky is dark, thunder is clapping, my eyes are glowing red – the works.

When you work in customer services, keeping in a good mood can be a real struggle, but today in particular, I feel like a bomb that's ready to go boom.

After the morning I've had, I don't have time for any more bullshit; that's why I'm going to clear up all these messy loose ends today, and try to drag myself out of this slump.

Rita isn't here this afternoon, she's in meetings or something, which I'm grateful for, given my current mood. This means that work feels much more like it used to today, and that's nice.

I've been thinking about how to call things off with Deano, and as much as I know he doesn't give a shit about me, I want to do this with as little drama as possible. And as soon as possible, so with the boss not expected back in until tomorrow, I've asked Deano to come here so we can talk.

I know (unfortunately, first hand) that there are a multitude of ways for people to break up with other people. "It's not you, it's me" is a good one. It's kind enough in that it reinforces that there is nothing wrong with the other person, while at the same time making it clear that it's over and it's final. Ghosting is another option, just going silent, cutting contact, nailing that fine line between missing that first message and faking your own death. Then there's the friendzone. My friendzone is so populated they're going to open up a Nando's there.

I joke, but I strongly believe that there is no such thing as the friendzone, I think it's just something that people say to try and make themselves feel better when someone has absolutely no romantic feelings for them. It is absolutely fine to just not fancy someone for whatever reason and, usually, if they're not an absolute dick, you'll want to be friends with them, because not being a dick is usually pretty good grounds for friendship. Sometimes we go off people, sometimes we don't develop feelings for them for a while – women don't meet people and file them away in boxes. Still, if people can make themselves feel better by claiming they've been put in a special zone for the under-appreciated, then good for them. Usually, if I find someone so completely undateable, I don't even want to be friends with them. If I have anything, it's a "I'm going to pretend you died" zone.

There are so many good options for breaking it off with Deano, but when he finally arrives and sits down opposite me, none of the above feels like it's going to do the trick. I need something he can't dispute, something he can't talk me out of, something solid, like …

'I just … don't want to be with men anymore,' I blurt.

Deano nearly chokes on his cinnamon latte.

'*You're* a lesbian?'

I mean, that's not exactly what I meant, but he can't argue with that, right?

'I am,' I tell him. 'I realise this may come as a surprise …'

'Yeah, I mean, not really. You talk and act a bit blokey sometimes. Your best mate is a bloke—'

Wow. Did he really just say that?

'OK, thanks,' I interrupt. 'Well, there you go. I'm out the closet.' I exhale with faux relief. 'So I think it's best we don't see each other anymore. I'll always be wanting more – or less? I don't know. You've got, like, the opposite of what I want.'

Oh God, I'm floundering. I just need to stop talking.

'Wait,' Deano starts, his brow furrowing with a thought – possibly his first this year. 'Your phone wallpaper is a photo of Zac Efron with his shirt off.'

'Body goals,' I tell him. 'I want to buff up.'

Deano laughs to himself.

'I suppose it makes sense,' he starts. 'I've never met a girl who didn't want to fuck me before. And the bigger girls are usually happy to take what they can get.'

'Exactly,' I agree, glad he's catching on. 'Wait, what?'

'No offence,' he insists. 'It's just that curvier girls like you are usually more grateful for the opportunity.'

'To sleep with you?'

'Exactly,' he agrees. 'But if you're into birds, it makes sense.'

I pop the lid off my latte, dipping my finger in to test the milk. It's not too hot, so I climb to my feet, sucking the coffee off my fingertip as I do so, before walking over to Deano.

'The only thing that makes perfect sense …' I pour my cup of coffee all over his crotch '… is what an absolute dick you are.'

Deano jumps to his feet. Not because it's hot, just because it's wet and, I'd imagine, because he's wearing a pair of ill-advised pale blue skinny jeans.

'You fucking crazy bitch,' he snaps at me before storming out, embarrassed.

I give myself a mental pat on the (apparently fat) back until I realise that everyone in the coffee shop is looking at me.

'Ladies and gentlemen, I'd like to apologise for that,' I start. 'Men are crazy, am I right?'

Hmm, that probably wasn't the best way to explain what happened, but soon enough everyone gets back to their drinks and their lunch.

Well, this is what happens when I'm left on my own. Millsy

is supposed to be on shift too, but he's had to pop to the theatre for something for this bloody play that I am absolutely sick of hearing about.

I go back behind the counter and hover, waiting for a customer. Soon enough a couple of little old ladies wander in with their shopping bags and ask for two cups of tea. I tell them to take a seat and that I'll bring them over for them. Just as I've finished putting everything on the tray, Millsy gets back.

'Perfect timing,' I tell him. 'Can you take this to those two lovely ladies over there?'

'Ooh, lovely ladies,' he says with a wiggle of his eyebrows. 'Oh, old ladies. No worries, they love me too.'

Millsy takes them their drinks and hangs around for a quick chat – he really does have the ability to charm any woman he wants.

'So, anything eventful happen while I was out?' he asks. 'Sorry for abandoning you, but I've got a job tonight and I needed to get measured up for my pants.'

'Nah, nothing much,' I tell him. 'Although I did break up with Deano.'

'Oh shit, how did he take it?'

'Erm, he basically called me fat.'

'I told you he was a cock,' my friend reminds me, with a shake of his head. 'And you're not fat.'

'I know. And I know,' I say with a smile. 'I guess I can see why he was pissed off though. Kind of. I've made such a mess of things.'

My friend grabs me a triple chocolate muffin.

'Eat that, fatty, and tell me what's up. It's quiet now, we can talk. You haven't seemed yourself today. And you still haven't explained that hair.'

'The hair was a mistake, end of story. Anyway, I thought of the perfect way to break up Nick and Heather. I managed to convince her that he was thinking about proposing, but that he was too scared to do it and that he liked bold women who made the first move.'

'She didn't fall for it?' he asks.

'Oh, no, she did. And now they're engaged. That pretty much sums the situation up.'

'What the fuck?! He said yes?'

'Yep,' I reply. 'And it kind of sounds like they're expecting me to move out. And I can't even try to be happy for him because before this happened, Heather made it pretty clear that his money was a major factor in their relationship.'

'She sounds like a bad person,' he concludes.

'And that's coming from you,' I tell him with a smile.

'You need distracting,' he insists. 'We need another man for this job tonight, why don't you do it? It's easy money, it will distract you.'

'You need another man?' I laugh. 'Will a woman do?'

'No,' he says with a grin. 'But we'll make it work.'

Chapter 29

During my life-long friendship with Millsy, I have done many, many things for him. When we were ten years old, Millsy smashed his mum's favourite ornament – a china swan – by playing football in the house, even though his mum had already told him not to a million times. Not only did he knock it over, breaking its neck, but he made things worse by trying to glue it back together. He applied the superglue that he stole from his dad's shed before wrapping his hand around the bird's neck tightly to hold it in place – sticking his hand to it tightly. When his mum found out, I took the blame, because I knew I'd be in much less trouble than Millsy would.

Flash-forward a few more years when we were sixteen, and I had to take his then girlfriend for the morning after pill because they'd got "caught up in the moment" and neglected to use a condom. Or what about just last year, he got caught kissing some guy's girlfriend at a party, and I had to convince him that Millsy was gay and that we'd been playing truth or dare – something I'm not sure he believed until I kissed his girlfriend too. He seemed fine with that.

Yes, I've done lots of things for Millsy over the years, but tonight takes the cake. Millsy has all these random not-quite-acting acting jobs that he fills his time and his CV with when he isn't working at the coffee shop, like being the Leeds Lions' mascot. One of his other gigs is for an agency who supply in-character waitstaff for parties and events, and tonight they were a man down – literally a man down.

We arrived at the large house in Ilkley and were shown to a room where we could get into character – at this point, I still didn't know what that character would be. The house was stunning, though. An absolute mansion, up a leafy, floodlit driveway that looked like something fresh out of a romance movie. We passed through the main room where the party is being held, just as the finishing touches were being made on the decor. Despite the house having quite a traditional look and feel, the party looks positively modern, with colourful disco lights, crazy cocktails complete with umbrellas and Eighties pop music booming from the speakers. As I watched Millsy unpacking the costumes, I got quite excited. Maybe it would be disco-themed attire? Maybe the theme is the Eighties and I'd be dressing up like Cyndi Lauper or someone equally as awesome and stylish. Then I found out our dress code: men in drag. So when Millsy said they were a man down, they were literally a man down.

'You'll pull it off,' Millsy insisted. 'So don't even worry about it.'

So I slipped on my sparkly purple dress, my big blue wig and the most make-up I have ever worn in my life. As Millsy and I stood side by side, looking in the mirror, I realised something.

'You look more feminine than I do,' I told him, unimpressed.

'I do, don't I?' He laughed.

So here I am, in yet another Shakespeare twist, a woman, pretending to be a man, pretending to be a woman. I'm working the room, handing out peach bellinis to all the beautiful people having a beautiful time. Millsy was right: this is easy money, and it's definitely taking my mind off things. It's quite nice, even though I'm not technically a guest, blending in, circulating and chatting to different people – most of whom tell me they'd never have known I was a man, which I'm very happy with. Best of all, there's nothing here to remind me of Nick.

'Thank you very much,' a lady says as she takes the last full glass from my tray.

'You're very welcome,' I reply, heading back towards the bar to get some more. As I hover while the barman fills up glasses, I glance at all the cool stuff behind the bar: ornaments, holiday mementos, family photographs – that's when Nick catches my eye, staring back at me from one of the photos, sitting atop an elephant across a river.

'Lovely party, Deborah,' I hear someone call out. I look over and see Nick's mum, sauntering around the room, warmly greeting guests, sipping from her glass with a grace and elegance I'll never manage.

'Thank you,' she calls back. A couple walk up to her, exchanging air kisses as I look on, paralysed by fear. With the rate she's moving around the room, it's a miracle I haven't crossed paths with her already. I know I'm in costume, but I'm in drag, not a ski mask. 'I'm just going to grab another drink.'

As the words leave her lips, panic washes over me. She's coming over here. She's coming over here and she's going to see me and this whole stupid series of events is going to unravel and there's nothing I can do to stop it. Unless …

I grab my empty drinks tray and hold it up, to shield my face, eyeballing the nearest exit. I make it into the kitchen and look around for an escape route. I notice that the back door is open – perfect – but as I dash through it I don't realise that there's a step and I go flying, landing on the cold, hard flags outside. Just in case that was too subtle, the metal tray that I was using as a shield hits the floor and spins a few times before settling, causing a loud clatter.

'Oh, shit,' I hear a man's voice shout. I hear him rush over before he helps me to my feet. 'You OK, mate?' he asks. 'This is why men should never wear heels.'

I'd know that voice anywhere.

'Hello,' I say awkwardly, finally looking Nick in the eye. Oh, this is so embarrassing.

'I have so many questions, I don't know which one to ask first – for starters, my mum is going to want a refund. She wanted men, and I know you're not one of those – your skirts are too short.' He laughs.

I laugh too, and playfully bat him with my hand, but it hurts. 'Ouch,' I blurt, holding my hand to my body.

'Are you hurt?' he asks.

I nod my head. 'I think I must've landed on my hand.'

'Come over here, let's take a look at you.'

Nick leads me back over to where he was sitting and it's gorgeous. It's like a mini secret garden within their garden, a cute little area secluded by the privacy of fairy-lit bushes. Nick sits me down on a comfy garden chair.

'OK, let's take a look at this wrist first,' he insists. 'Then we'll work out why you're at my parents' house in sort-of drag.'

'OK, sure.' I laugh through the pain.

Nick takes my hand gently in his and examines it. I follow his instructions and answer his questions.

'Well, it's not broken,' he tells me. 'We need to put something cold on it, bring the swelling down.'

'Can we just sit here for a moment?' I ask, and it's not just because I need to hide from his mum, it's because it's peaceful and quiet, and in this secret garden, in this costume I feel a million miles from my real self and my real life.

'Sure,' Nick replies.

'Heather not here tonight?' I ask.

'No, she's out with her friends. Well, I say "out" but that makes it sound like she's gone to a bar or something – she's protesting for animal rights.'

'That's commendable,' I reply.

'Not really.' He laughs. 'It's that new hotdog restaurant. She takes issue with the fact everything is named after a real dog. Like a Chilli Chihuahua dog.'

'Dude, that sounds delicious.'

'I know.' He laughs again, but then his face falls into a more serious expression. 'Look, tell me if I'm being out of line by asking, but are you OK? Because you haven't seemed yourself for a little while now.'

'I'm fine,' I tell him. 'And what about you, huh? I can't believe you're getting married.'

'Neither can I,' he replies solemnly, a little too quickly. 'Sorry, ignore me,' he adds, probably after seeing my reaction to what he just said.

It's chilly out here now, but I'm enjoying Nick's company.

'You know you can talk to me, right?' I remind him. 'Like you said to me before, we might not always get on, but we're friends.'

'Well … I'm not sure I even want to marry Heather. We've been getting on well, but this just feels way too soon. And she hit me out of nowhere – with my own grandma's ring – and I just panicked. I figured I was supposed to say yes – I didn't want to upset her by saying no. But I don't think she's right for me … Do you think she's right for me, Ruby?'

This is it. This is my chance to say something. But what do I say? Obviously I think Heather is wrong for him, but how do I tell him without seeming like I'm just trying to get her out of the picture? I have to do it, I have to tell him that she's wrong for him and I'm right.

'Well, it's like with me and Deano,' I start, ready to tell him all about just how wrong we were for each other.

'About that,' Nick interrupts. 'Look, I think it deserves mentioning how well you're doing with him. I'm impressed. The old Ruby would've thrown a drink in his face by now and moved on to the next Matcher bloke, with some silly game or other in mind. You seem to be embracing a proper relationship and that makes me so happy for you.'

'Thanks,' I say, faking a smile. Well, I can't tell him now, can I? Because he's not really that far off the mark.

'Sorry, what were you going to say?' he prompts me.

'Oh, I can't remember,' I lie. 'I'm too cold to think straight.'

I glance down at my hands. The one that Nick hasn't been holding is absolutely freezing.

'Why do I go purple when it's cold?' I ask, changing the subject completely. 'Am I going to be OK? Will I live?' I joke.

'I know you – you're a hypochondriac. Whatever you do, don't google "Raynaud's disease".'

'Definitely going to do that,' I reply.

Nick laughs and squeezes my hand. Actually, wait a second ... 'Bro, are you taking my pulse?' I ask.

At first I thought he was just giving my hand a reassuring squeeze, but then I felt his thumb press into my wrist.

Nick pauses before he answers, a look of concentration plastered across his face – he's counting.

'It's weak,' he tells me. 'I'm disappointed.'

'Why?' I ask quickly. 'Is there something wrong with me?'

'It just means that me holding your hand is having absolutely zero effect on you.' He chuckles. 'Oh, wait, now it's quickening.'

I feel my cheeks flush.

'You look so funny dressed up,' he tells me with a smile. 'You don't look like you.'

'Well, that's the beauty of dressing up,' I explain. 'You get to be someone else.'

Nick shrugs his shoulders. 'Never dressed up before,' he confesses.

'Ever?' I double-check.

'Nope.'

'Not even at school?' I persist.

'Nope.'

'What did you do on World Book Day at your school?' I ask, gobsmacked.

'Read books.' Nick laughs. 'What? I'm sorry, we can't all be scantily dressed, sparkly versions of Mr Benn.'

I pull an obviously jokey angry face at him.

'I'll give you one chance to redeem yourself,' I start. 'We're having a fancy-dress party at my parents' house while they're away on holiday. Come – you have to dress up though.'

Nick smiles widely. 'I'd love to,' he replies. 'I was only going to spend the evening watching Netflix with Heather anyway.'

We both have a moment where we remember that Heather is a person who exists, who we have to take into consideration. I can see Nick coming to the realisation that he has plans, as I come to a similar one.

'Bring Heather too,' I insist. 'I mean, this is the last time Halloween will fall on a Saturday while we're in our twenties. We should make the most of it.'

'That's a good point. I'll see if she's up for it.'

'Great,' I lie, secretly hoping she can't make it, but that Nick still comes. 'Thanks for looking out for me, by the way.'

'You're welcome, kid. It all falls under the Hippocratic Oath anyway, don't think you're getting special treatment.'

I laugh. 'Get back to your family's party,' I insist.

'I suppose I should,' he starts, although he isn't making much of a move. 'Look, I might be late here, and I know you're working … but could we talk in the morning, maybe? I'll check your wrist out, and maybe I'll ask you again if you think I'm doing the right thing, because I'm not sure you answered me tonight …'

'I didn't,' I tell him. 'Sure thing. We can grab some breakfast.'

'I might even have a cheat day – I might even have some meat,' he tells me, widening his eyes for effect.

'Oh wow, well I look forward to leading you astray,' I tell him with a smile.

For a brief moment, we just look into each other's eyes. My God, I love it when he makes eye contact with me. There's something about those deep, dark brown eyes – when they're on you, you feel like the most important person in the world. I blink to break the intensity of my stare, but when I open my eyes again I realise that Nick's face is much closer to mine, his mouth inches from my own. He's so close that, if I were to so much as pout gently, our lips would be touching. He moves the last few centimetres until our lips touch, but just as we make contact, we're interrupted.

'Nick? Are you out here?' a woman's voice calls.

'I am,' he calls back. 'On my way.'

We go back to looking at each other for a second before he heads back towards the house.

'See you around, kid.'

'Have a good night,' I call after him.

Am I actually getting somewhere with Nick? He definitely sounds like he's having doubts about Heather, and I really feel like we're getting on. And, OK, we didn't really kiss, but that was the start of one, for sure. Maybe there is some hope for us.

As I stroll back towards the house I spot Millsy, sitting on the edge of the fountain, swigging champagne from the bottle. His make-up is smudged, his dress is hanging off and his wig needs some major adjusting.

'Not one element of what I can see right now surprises me,' I tell him. 'But what the fuck are you doing?'

'I got fired,' he tells me, holding his arms out, laughing wildly.

'You don't seem too bothered.'

'I'm not,' he informs me. 'I'm going to be a huge movie star. Why are you out here?'

'I fell over, hurt my hand, it's not exciting – go on, why did you get fired?'

I take a seat next to my friend, who hands me the bottle of champagne. I take a nice, long, medicinal swig.

'I was hitting on the birthday girl,' he tells me. 'But then her husband showed up – what can you do, eh? I was only trying to give her a present.'

'That's Nick's sister, by the way,' I tell him.

'What? No way. So this is Nick's mum and dad's house?'

I nod my head.

'Wow. This dicks all over where we grew up.' He laughs. 'No wonder Heather is marrying him for his money – I'm surprised you're not trying harder.'

'Hilarious,' I tell him, splashing him with fountain water.

'So, I'm not allowed back in there,' Millsy informs me. 'But one of the others said they'd bring my bag for me. Shall I ask him to grab your stuff too, and we'll hit the town in our pretty frocks?'

If there's one thing I love about Millsy, it's the very small number of fucks he gives about anything. He won't bat an eyelid about going out in town dressed as a woman; in fact, he'll enjoy the attention.

'I'd love that,' I reply. 'I'll book us a taxi to the station.'

'Woop!' Millsy booms. 'Does my lipstick need touching up first or …?'

'No way, you're all good, babe,' I reply.

I'll have a girly night out with Miss Mills, make sure I get home at a reasonable time and then I'll have breakfast and a chat with Nick, and finally lay my cards on the table. No more games, no more manipulating – no more Macbeth-ing.

Chapter 30

Not a hangover, sleeping on an uncomfortable sofa, nor the pitiful amount of shut-eye I actually managed can affect my awesome mood today; I woke up feeling so positive.

OK, so I didn't get an early night last night; I stayed out into the crazy hours with Millsy, but we were just having so much fun that we didn't want to call it a night. Also, Millsy left his flat keys at the party with the rest of his stuff, so he had nowhere to go. Adamant he couldn't enter my flat while Nick was there, he refused to stay the night – until it got cold, and I promised him that if we just left it late enough that Nick would go to bed, and we'd be able to sneak him in. Somehow, we managed it. I hid Millsy safely away in my bedroom and slept on the sofa, making sure to wake up super early to head out and grab Nick's favourite breakfast stuff (I know he loves croissants with cream cheese and bacon on his rare cheat days).

Now I just need to smuggle Millsy out before Nick is any the wiser. You literally have to get up pretty early in the day to get up before Nick, but I think I've managed it – that is until I climb the stairs to the flat and bump into Nick as he's walking from the bathroom to his bedroom.

'Morning, you,' I say brightly.

'Morning,' he replies quietly. 'Late night last night, huh?'

'A little.' I laugh, awkwardly. He seems mad. I wrack my brains for what I might have done wrong. 'My wrist was hurting so I didn't think I'd be much use at the party. It feels better now.'

'Yeah, I heard,' he replies, heading off towards his room.

'So shall I start breakfast?' I call after him.

'Not hungry,' he calls back, closing his door behind him.

Well, that was weird. Last night he couldn't be sweeter with me, now he's back to hating my guts again. OK, I need to make sure I don't make things worse, I need to get Millsy out of here ASAP.

I creep into my bedroom to find Millsy already wide awake, painting a clear coat of nail polish on his toes.

'Mate, you drag-up once and suddenly you want to be more girly?' I ask.

'I just want shiny toes,' he tells me. 'Girls always tell me I have Hobbit feet.'

I pull a face. 'No way have you ever slept with a girl who knows what a Hobbit is.'

'Fine, I'm paraphrasing,' he admits. 'But they tell me that they're gross and it's hard to get girls into certain positions if they're gagging over your toes.'

'Anyway … so we need to a) get you out of here and b) make sure you never tell me anything like that ever again,' I start, grabbing his things before realising that he arrived here in a dress. I grab my largest pair of joggers and an oversized hoodie, hoping he'll be able to fit into them, but also hoping he can't, because if a big, muscular dude can fit into my clothes, then maybe I am a little bigger than I should be.

Millsy slowly pulls himself to his feet.

'You're actually about to realise you owe me a huge thank you,' he tells me.

'For getting toe hair in my nail polish? I doubt that, babe. Now hurry up.'

'I'm awake because Nick woke me up,' he informs me. Oh, so

that's why he's mad? Just because Millsy is here? That's extreme. But I didn't want him to know I was here, and I know you're trying to make him jealous ...'

I stop dead in my tracks. 'Oh, fuck. What did you do?'

'You don't seem happy yet, which is confusing, but OK. So I figured he'd assume if you had a bloke in here, it'd be Deano, so I made sex noises. Loud, grunty, epic banging sounds – you were phenomenal, by the way. And that's why I'm an actor,' he announces proudly, until he sees my face. 'Why are you looking at me like you want to kick me in the dick?'

'Millsy ... you have no idea what you've done ...'

'Saved the day?' he asks. 'Is it saved the day? I've fucked up, haven't I? I thought you were trying to make him jealous.'

'Yeah, until last night. I told you all about it last night. That I had a really good talk with him, we nearly kissed, and that we were going to talk this morning.'

'Did you tell me post getting off the train in Leeds?'

'Yes.'

'Well, there you go. I'd had a fuck-load of champers by then, and then I drank even more. Come on, Rubes. You know me.'

'I know I want to "kick you in the dick",' I tell him. 'Right, let's just get you out of here. Maybe I can fix this.'

'He's not even worth it,' Millsy insists as I usher him towards the door.

I peep out of my bedroom. The coast is clear. Nick's bedroom door sits exactly opposite from mine, in fact, they're less than two metres apart. His door is still closed, so as long as we're quiet, we're fine.

'OK, let's ...' My voice trails off. As an example of my exceptionally bad luck, Nick walks out of his room, just as I am dragging Millsy out of my bedroom – Millsy who is still pulling my hoodie over his head.

'About me snapping before,' Nick starts, but then he glances over my shoulder, spotting Millsy just as his head pops out of the hoodie. I watch Nick's eyes widen with horror.

'Wait, that was Joe I heard you having sex with earlier?' he asks, visibly disgusted. 'I knew there was something going on between you. Men and women are never such good friends without *something* ... and then there's Deano. You know, when you were upset the other day, I felt so sorry for you – I also saw this whole other side to you, and I liked it. And then last night ... but now this ... What the fuck is wrong with you, Ruby? Exactly how many men are you juggling?'

Oh, shit. I don't know what to say. What words are going to make all of this OK? Because his very wrong version of events is awful, but is the truth going to sound much better?

'Nick, wait, there's nothing going on between Millsy and me,' I start, but he's not listening.

'Save it,' he replies. 'I don't want to know.'

'But if you let me explain,' I start.

'Mate, I wouldn't touch her with yours,' Millsy jokes, but this only makes Nick even angrier. He grabs his coat and storms out of the flat. Millsy and I stare at each other for a moment.

'So you were right,' he says eventually. 'I did fuck up. But, I will do anything to make it up to you. *Anything*.'

'Yes you will,' I reply. 'And I've got just the thing in mind.'

Chapter 31

Another day, another costume, except this time it's Halloween, and this time I'm picking what I get to wear – Millsy too. I can't be mad at him about this morning; it's not his fault that Nick got upset, not really. Everything is such a mess with all the lying and the manipulating, and Millsy was only trying to help.

He has promised me, no questions asked, that he will help me fix things with Nick – to whatever degree is possible, just as soon as I think of something. Things felt a little fraught between us earlier and he's my best friend, I don't want that. So we agreed that we would forget about it for the rest of the day, and just enjoy the big Halloween party at my parents' house. I did get him to agree to a double-act Halloween costume though, so tonight, we are Khal Drogo and Daenerys Targaryen from *Game of Thrones*, and we've nailed it.

It's 5 p.m. and we've arrived back in Outwood, ready to help Woody get ready for the party later. It's cold and dark out, and weirdly, all the lights are off at home.

Millsy and I stare at each other, exchanging a "what the fuck" glance, no words needed.

'Hello?' I call out as we walk in through the unlocked door. 'Woody?'

'I'm in here,' he calls out, from the kitchen, I think.

We head into the kitchen and find Woody sitting on the floor, in the dark.

'Every time I come over, you're doing something proper weird,' I tell him.

Millsy flicks the light on.

'No, don't,' Woody insists, but it's too late.

I can't help but notice that my brother is in his usual clothes.

'You're dressed as a …' I pretend to think about it. 'Middle-aged bore,' I conclude.

'Oi, I didn't spend ages helping you find a Spider-Man onesie so that you could chicken out of wearing a costume – not after last year's cringe-fest,' Millsy insists. He's referring to photos on Facebook from last Halloween, that show the "family" costume my brother, his wife and my nephew dressed in. 'I guess not dressing up is preferable to the old man from *Up*, but only just.'

Yes, my brother did dress as the old man from *Up*. His tiny wife, Dani, dressed as the little boy and Robbie, my nephew, was the dog. It was as awful as it sounds. Spider-Man is a much cooler choice, and Millsy has spent the best part of the last week trying to find this onesie for Woody.

'Fuck you,' Woody says to me. 'And fuck you,' he tells Millsy. 'Guys, listen, I messed up.'

'Yeah, you've been banging on all week about how you shouldn't have got married so young, you want to be more like Millsy, blah blah,' I state.

'I'm pretty good hashtag: life goals,' Millsy insists.

'Yeah, if the life goal is to collect STDs like they're Pokémon,' I quip.

'At least people will have sex with me because I'm not a big fucking Pokémon nerd.' Millsy laughs.

'Guys, listen,' Woody snaps, seriously. 'I really messed up.'

We both sit down on the floor next to him, me being careful not to pop a boob out of my Daenerys dress.

'What's up, bro?' I ask. 'You're scaring me.' He exhales deeply before he starts talking.

'So I've been keeping an eye on Weird Ian,' he starts. 'I'm obsessed with what's going on over there. I saw him go in there with a woman earlier ... this keeps happening. A woman goes into the house with him, I see them moving around and then suddenly he leaves, and the woman is never seen again.'

'You've still never seen a woman leave?' I ask. 'Ever?'

'Nope. And I've been watching.'

I can tell from his tired eyes and nervous disposition that he really has been keeping an eye on things, and that what he's saying, he is sure is true. 'So how did you fuck up?' Millsy asks.

'Well, tonight I decided enough was enough. I needed to know what was going on ... so I waited until it was dark and snuck over there. I climbed the fence into his back garden and I tried to look in the window.'

'So what happened?' I ask.

'I knocked a plant off his garden table and the pot smashed. He heard and headed for the back door, so I ran back to our garden – I just made it in time.'

'Well, there you go, no harm done,' I reassure him. My brother shakes his head solemnly.

'OK, what harm did you do?'

'I'd been using my phone for the torch,' he tells us. 'I must've dropped it in his back garden.'

'You idiot,' Millsy tells him. 'Everyone knows: make sure you never leave any evidence at the scene of the crime.'

'Like your DNA, or your name written in Sharpie on the bathroom wall,' I remind him.

'I still have no idea why I did that.' He laughs.

I turn back to my brother. 'What happened next?' I ask.

'He went back inside, and then he left not long after – no sign of the woman.'

'So, just go get it.'

'No way,' my brother insists. 'He's up to something, I'm not getting strangled.'

'Millsy?'

'Fuck that,' he says.

'You two are supposed to be men,' I remind them, but not even a swipe at their masculinity is going to talk them into it. 'You're both pathetic,' I tell them. '*I'll* go, because *I'm* not scared. And anyway, if you said he was out, then it's no big deal.'

'Go on then.' Millsy laughs again. 'Reverse psychology won't work on me, dude.'

I shake my head as I pull myself to my feet. The two main men in my life would sooner see me trespass in a potential serial killer's garden, rather than risk it themselves.

I leave via the back door and make my way down to the end of the garden. I glance back and see that not only is the kitchen light off again, but I can just about make out my brother and Millsy peeping up from above the worktop. Pathetic.

I reach the fence at the bottom of the garden, the one that backs onto Ian's garden, and wonder how the fuck I'm supposed to get over it. Not only am I at least seven inches shorter than my brother, but I'm wearing a long cream dress. Definitely not climbing attire.

What would Daenerys do? She'd be strong and resourceful. Or maybe she'd just have a dragon fly her over. The only pet we have back at home is a nameless fairground fish that just refuses to die – that's not going to be much use to me.

I glance around the garden, spotting the toddler-sized F1 car that my dad prematurely and excitedly bought for Robbie. I push it up towards the fence and climb on top, using it as a boost to get over the wall. Just as I manage to get one leg over the top of the fence, my foot slips, sending the car flying. I manage to keep balanced on the top of the fence, but there's no turning back now. I swing my other leg over and drop down on the other side into Ian's garden.

I blow air out of my cheeks. Here we go. I creep in an almost crouched position across his garden, towards his house, carefully checking in the long unkempt grass for Woody's iPhone. He said he was looking in the window, so my best bet is to look there.

There it is! I grab it, ready to turn on my heels and run, when curiosity gets the better of me and I peep in the window. My heart bangs hard against my chest the moment I realise that Ian is in the window, looking out, right into my eyes. Fuck, I thought Woody said he had gone out. And what's that in his hand? No way. Is that … a woman's head? I step back from the window in horror, but Ian is straight outside.

'What are you doing on my property?' he asks me, his stony face giving nothing away.

'I, erm, well I came to tell you that we were having a Halloween party. Just to let you know we might be a bit loud, but that you could tell us to turn the music down or whatever if it's disturbing you,' I babble. 'I tried the front door but you didn't answer. I thought maybe you were back door people. You know how some people insist on everyone using the back door? My mum tried it once; it didn't last. So yeah, I thought I'd try the back door, in case your mum is the same, and then I dropped my phone and …' My voice trails off. I can't help but stare at the "head" in his hands. He's holding it by a fistful of hair but he's in the shadows, so I can't quite make it out. I don't know what else it could be, all I need to know is that I need to get out of here.

'My mum doesn't live here anymore,' he tells me.

'Oh, OK. Well, bye,' I blurt.

'Wait,' Ian insists. 'Stop right there. I know you've all been spying on me.'

'Spying? What do you mean?' I ask innocently.

'Cut the crap,' he snaps. 'I can see your minions watching us right now.'

I glance back at my house just in time to see Millsy and Woody bob down. Those fucking idiots.

'Look, it's nothing to do with me,' I tell him. 'I just came to tell you about the party and now I'm going to go home.'

I make my way around the side of the house to leave out of the front garden – because I've no idea how I'm going to get back over that fence and also because the front garden isn't secluded enough to murder me in.

I hear Ian follow me.

'Stop,' he calls after me. 'Or I'll call the police.'

We're out of sight of my house now, and no one can see us.

'Fine, call the police, I'm sure they'll be interested in all the women who come over to your house and never leave,' I say boldly, except I can't hide how terrified I am and my voice wavers and cracks.

Ian laughs manically.

'What's so funny?' I ask as Ian approaches me slowly. As he reaches me he raises the severed head to my eye level.

'That's a wig,' I tell him.

'I know it's a wig,' he replies. 'What did you think it was, a head or something?'

Yes, but I'm not going to vocalise that.

'It's for my latest photography project,' he tells me. 'I'm photographing men in authoritative positions dressed as women.'

My brain spends a few seconds processing this. That's why we see women in his house who never leave – we're not seeing Ian make a hasty exit, we're seeing the models leave in their normal clothes. That's why we see him with his hands all over them, he's making adjustments. That's why he's got a wig in his hand – not a human head.

'Well, we saw you digging a hole in your back garden, and …'

'I wasn't digging a hole,' he explains, 'I was filling in a hole next door's dog dug up.'

'So, where's your mum?' I ask him.

'In a home,' he replies. 'What on earth has been going through your heads?'

I laugh to myself. 'Look, we are having a Halloween party if you'd like to come?'

'I'd like that,' he replies. 'I've never been to a Halloween party. Do I have to dress up?'

'It's not a big deal if you don't, but feel free,' I tell him, suddenly feeling bad. It's like the neighbourhood sex offender all over again – when will the three of us learn to stop judging books by their covers? Just because Ian is introverted, we just went nought-to-serial killer.

'Can I bring anything?' he asks. 'Anything to eat or drink?'

'If you like,' I tell him.

'OK, I'll bring soup,' he replies.

'OK,' I say with a laugh. 'See you in a couple of hours.'

Having left via the front of Ian's house, it takes me at least five minutes to get back to my parents' place. As I walk up the driveway, Millsy and Woody come rushing out. Woody is armed with a baseball bat, Millsy with a lighter and can of deodorant.

'Ruby, you're OK,' Woody gasps happily.

'I'm fine. It was all a big misunderstanding,' I assure them. 'But, before I tell you all about it, were you just coming to save me with a baseball bat and a DIY flame-thrower?'

The boys nod sheepishly.

I smile, touched, until I realise Woody is wearing his Spider-Man onesie. 'I see you found time to put your costume on.' I raise my eyebrows in disbelief.

'Rubes, I spent hours tracking that onesie down – you know that,' Millsy reminds me. 'Plus, it would've looked badass – and if we'd made the news …'

I shake my head in despair.

'Let's just get ready for the party,' I say. 'And I'll tell you what happened with Ian while we do – I invited him to the party, by the way.'

'So Weird Ian isn't weird?' Woody asks.

'Oh, he's definitely weird,' I tell them. 'He's bringing soup.'

Chapter 32

The party is in full swing, and it's going amazingly. Everyone is eating, drinking and being merry. Millsy invited one of his cool DJ friends, Woody did an awesome job making the house look all spooky and, as promised, Weird Ian brought soup.

'It's tomato,' he told me, waggling the ladle around in the big pot of red gunge as he hovered on our doorstep. 'Like blood.'

'What are the white balls?' I asked, a little grossed out.

'Pickled onions,' he told me. 'I thought they looked like eyeballs.'

So far, everyone is having a lovely time – although Ian is the only one I've seen eating the soup.

'Ruby, come here,' Woody calls my name as I walk across the living room.

'This is—'

'Elsa, nice to meet you,' I interrupt, greeting the blonde girl in front of me who is absolutely nailing the *Frozen* character.

Ah, I really miss my blonde hair. Now more than ever. It would have been perfect for my costume tonight; I'm having to wear a cheap, nasty wig instead. Because my change in hair colour was so last-minute, so was my trip to the fancy-dress shop. When I got there, people were queuing around the corner. They had a rope system, letting people in a few at a time – like a nightclub. Or Hollister when there's a sale on. So by the time I got in there, there wasn't much left. The wig I'm wearing is more Donald Trump than Daenerys Targaryen.

Woody laughs. He sounds pretty drunk.

'Hello,' she says enthusiastically. My God, she's absolutely hammered.

'She's a dancer,' he tells me. 'Millsy introduced us.'

'Cool,' I reply, dragging the world out, slowly. 'Well, I'm going to go find Millsy and see what he was thinking.'

I laugh awkwardly as my brother and his new friend look on, confused.

As I approach Millsy he springs into his *Game of Thrones* character. 'My wife,' he says, thrusting a glass of an unidentifiable punch into my hand.

'My hubby,' I reply. 'A word please.'

'Sure.'

I drag Millsy away from the crowd he was entertaining with his Dothraki moves, swinging around the replica arakh weapon that he bought on eBay.

'What's up?' he asks.

'Why did you introduce my drunk brother to an even drunker blonde babe? You know how he's feeling at the moment.'

'Exactly, he needs cheering up – nothing cheers up a guy like a pretty lady.'

'He's married, Millsy. He's married and he's miserable and you just introduced him to a drunk, sexy, blonde temptation.'

Millsy thinks for a moment. 'Rubes, I've had a bit to drink. I apologise, but you're right – that was a fucking stupid move on my part and I'm sorry.'

'You're just full of stupid moves at the moment, aren't you?'

He nods sheepishly.

'Right, let's just go talk to him, take over the conversation, I'll take him; you take her. We separate them, crisis averted.'

He nods in agreement to the plan, but as we head back into the living room, they're nowhere to be seen.

'Crap, where have they gone?' I ask no one in particular.

'Looking for someone?' Ian asks, rocking up next to us, eating (probably) his millionth bowl of soup.

'Spider-Man,' Millsy tells him.

'Ah, he went up to one of the bedrooms,' Ian informs us with a wiggle of his eyebrows.

'What?' I shriek. I run upstairs.

'Oh shit,' I hear Millsy shout as he runs after me. 'Look, this is my fault, so just calm down.'

'I will not calm down,' I snap back. 'I will not let every relationship I'm aware of be based on lies and shit and bollocks.'

OK, so in my slightly inebriated state, I'm not the most eloquent, but I know what I mean, and I need to put a stop to this.

We burst into Woody's old room, only to find Luke Skywalker and Princess Leia in bed together – only identifiable by her hair and his lightsabre.

'Sorry, guys, as you were,' I tell them.

'You know you're related, right?' Millsy laughs. I shake my head at him.

'I don't have time for your jokes.'

'Not even the good ones?' he asks.

Next up, I try my parents' room. In there we've got someone going down on a Minion.

Millsy and I pause for a second, trying to work out what we're looking at.

'Dude, what the fuck?' the Minion complains.

'Dude, you are in my mum and dad's bed. So quit your bitching about privacy. And what are you supposed to be?' I ask his female friend.

'I'm naughty nurse,' she tells us.

'Yes you are,' Millsy replies.

I roll my eyes, grab him by the wrist and head for my old

bedroom.

'Eww, in my bed, seriously,' I moan.

Once through the door I can just about make out Spider-Man on top of a girl. I flick the light on, grabbing my brother by the scruff of his onesie, pulling him off. Except it isn't Elsa underneath him, it's the Black Swan.

'What the fuck are you doing?' I ask, releasing him.

'I thought that was obvious,' he replies. That's when I realise it's not my brother, it's someone else in a Spider-Man onesie.

'She's just reminding you that with great power comes great responsibility. So rubber up,' Millsy tells them, ushering me out of the room.

'Oh my God, I feel sick,' I confess. 'I was sure that was him.'

I hear the toilet flush before the bathroom door opens. Woody strolls out. 'Hey sis, hey Millsy. Everything OK?' he asks.

'Where's Elsa?' I demand.

'She was really drunk so I put her in a taxi home. Why?' he asks, puzzled.

I kiss my brother on the cheek.

'You're a good man – you know that? Maybe the best.'

'Hey, what about me?' Millsy asks.

'You're a cu—'

My brother places his hand over my mouth, stopping me from cracking a cheeky joke.

'My God, I hope you washed that,' I say, pulling a disgusted face. We make our way back downstairs.

'Ooh, jelly shots,' Millsy exclaims excitedly, grabbing a tray of them from the table. 'I have it on pretty good authority that whoever made these, made them really strong.'

'It was you, wasn't it?' I say, watching him knock them back.

'It was,' he replies proudly.

'And yet here you are, consuming enough to get a rugby team hammered,' I laugh.

Millsy pulls a face. 'What? I can share. Here's one for you,' he tells me, pushing one of the little, brightly coloured, ridiculously alcoholic jellies into my mouth. 'And what about you ... Hitler,' he says, turning to the person next to him. 'You'll have one, right?'

'I'll have two,' he replies. 'But I'm not Hitler, I'm Charlie Chaplin.'

'Where's your hat then?' I ask, knocking back another shot before turning to look him in the eye. 'Oh my God, Nick! You came! As Hitler!'

'I'm not Hitler, I'm Charlie Chaplin,' he insists again, angrily. 'Someone stole my hat!'

The dark suit, the slicked-down hair, the little moustache and the stern look on his face. It's amazing how a bowler hat is the only difference between Charlie Chaplin and Adolf Hitler. It's a small, but much-needed part of the costume, it turns out.

'Of course they did,' Millsy says angrily. He obviously and unashamedly shoots me a filthy look, to let me know just how annoyed he is that I've invited Nick. When he vowed to never be in the same room as him again, I promised him (with a fist-bump, no less) that I would always do everything in my power to make sure he never had to come face to face with him ever again – now it's happened twice in one week.

'Ruby invited me,' Nick tells him. 'So I'm here. It's good manners – I can explain manners to you if you like?'

'Yeah, sure, and while you're at it, explain to me how it's good manners to turn up to a party dressed as Hitler,' Millsy snaps back.

'I bloody told you, someone stole my bloody hat the second I got here,' Nick replies, raising his voice.

'OK, time for me to intervene,' I say, physically getting between them. 'Millsy, go do some more jelly shots until you don't give a shit about anything anymore, which I'd estimate at, like, three more. You're angry drunk Millsy right now; I need you somewhere between here and the Millsy who tries to have sex with furniture, ideally.'

'That was one time,' he mutters to himself as he wanders off, knocking back more shots.

I turn my attention back to Nick.

'You came,' I say brightly. A couple of people walk past and one mutters something about how insensitive Nick's costume is, causing my smile to fall. 'OK, let's find your hat before you get your head kicked in, yeah?'

'OK, sure,' he replies.

We stroll around the room that is busy with people all pretending to be something they're not, but no one is doing a better job than I am right now. I'm so crazy for Nick, so why can't I just be honest with him?

'So, what's Heather dressed as?'

'Eva Braun,' he replies.

I stop in my tracks and stare at him.

'I'm kidding, Ruby,' he says with a bit of a laugh. I'm not sure if I was surprised by the fact she might actually be dressed that way, or by just how appropriate an outfit that would be for her. 'She's not here.'

Wait, Heather hasn't come with him? I know they had plans together tonight. Could there be trouble in paradise? I feel a fleeting glimmer of hope.

'Don't worry, we'll find your hat; we've got all night. Can I get you a drink?'

'I'm not staying,' he replies quickly. 'And I'm driving. I only came because I said I would.'

'I appreciate that,' I tell him, trying to pull my mouth into a smile, but the truth is that I don't want him to go. I want to wrap my arms around his neck and tell him how much he means to me. But despite this glimmer of hope, I don't think that's what he wants me to do.

Millsy staggers over. He was drunk before, but the recent barrage of shots to his system have clearly kicked in. But he isn't angry drunk Millsy or horny drunk Millsy, he's a Millsy I've never witnessed before: emotional drunk Millsy.

'Nick, I need a word, mate,' he insists, grabbing him by the shoulders, pushing him down onto the nearest sofa before taking a seat next to him.

'Millsy, maybe don't say anything at all,' I insist, suddenly worried sick about what my bestie might say while under the influence. I trust him implicitly, of course – when he's sober. But when he's drunk and he doesn't know what or who he's doing, or worse, what he's saying, that's when I need to be worried. This man knows all my secrets.

'I need to ret the secord straight,' he slurs insistently, muddling up his words.

'What?' Nick asks, clearly annoyed that he's having to deal with Millsy at all – never mind when he's smashed and even more of an acquired taste than when he's sober.

'What?' Millsy repeats back to him. Millsy thinks for a moment.

'I need to set the record straight,' he says – somehow managing to nail each of the seven words this time. 'When you knocked on Ruby's bedroom door, and you heard sex noises, that wasn't Ruby. No one wants to have sex with Ruby,' he explains.

'Wow, thanks,' I can't help but interrupt. I know that he's trying to help me out here, but he's not exactly painting a very alluring picture, is he?

'It's true,' he continues. 'Except Deano, obviously. He considered sleeping with her even when she had thrush.'

Oh my God, he's making this so much worse. 'I … I didn't have thrush,' I insist.

Nick just looks back and forth between us, confused.

'The thing I'm trying to say,' Millsy starts, thinking for a second, wracking his brains for what he was actually trying to say, 'it was me making those noises. Alone. You get what I'm saying?'

'You were making sex noises alone,' Nick repeats back to him. 'Yeah, I get exactly what you're saying.'

'Good, good,' Millsy replies, for some reason talking with his eyes closed now.

'So when I heard you saying, "You like it like that, bitch?" that was you, alone, talking to yourself?' Nick asks for clarification.

'Exactly,' Millsy replies. 'I was saying it to myself.'

'You're fucking weird,' Nick tells him.

While I kind of commend Millsy for doing the right thing, setting Nick straight that I wasn't in my room that morning, he probably should have done it better/sober. All he's done is made it sound like he's been jacking off in my bed, talking dirty to himself.

'*You're* fucking weird,' Millsy replies. 'God knows why you've got women fighting over you.'

Nick's eyebrows shoot up.

'OK, Mr Mills. Time to get you to bed.'

'I'm not going anywhere. Make him go. He's the fucking loser we're always talking about how much we hate. Laughing at him because he's so lame. Remember when you pretended to be him?' Millsy laughs hysterically. 'When you put on his stethoscope and did his voice and listened for your own heartbeat but said you couldn't find one because you were a robot? That shit was funny, mate.'

I'll admit, I did do that, but it was a long time ago, and it was after he yelled at me for not folding the tea towels properly. I was only venting my anger, I didn't mean it.

'I'm going,' Nick says, climbing to his feet before storming off.

'Nick, wait,' I call after him. 'I didn't mean it.'

But he's not listening. And now he's gone.

I sit down next to my so-called best friend.

'Here's another nice mess you've gotten us into, Millsy,' I say with a sigh. As sidekicks go, it's all or nothing with Millsy. He either does the absolute worst thing or the absolute best thing in all situations.

'Come on,' he insists, placing an arm around me as he springs back to life. 'Let's go drink some more.'

See what I mean? As much trouble as he causes me, sometimes he knows exactly what I need.

Chapter 33

If we're being technical, Millsy and I have just arrived at work two minutes late – impressive considering the fact that we had to get an early train back from Outwood this morning. Despite being hungover, we're super-efficient too, as we pop on our aprons and begin setting everything up for the day.

'So I've had a chance to think things through,' I start as I clear the coffee machine. 'And I know how you can repay me for fucking stuff up with Nick.'

'Go on,' Millsy sighs. 'I said I'd do anything, so I'll do it.'

'OK, so you know his girlfriend …'

'Nope. No way. I'm not shagging her. She's not hot, is she? I mean, no, absolutely not. Think of something else.'

'Millsy, calm down,' I laugh. 'I don't want you to sleep with her. I want you to get Deano to sleep with her.'

'What?' he asks, sounding both baffled and annoyed that I want someone other than him to do my bidding.

One thing I know for sure is that the main reason why Heather is so keen to marry Nick is for his money. That needs a stop putting to it, no matter what. That also means that Heather will be very easy to get around.

'So I know that every Sunday she goes to these vegan nights

at Baa Bar Black's,' I start.

'There's a vegan bar called Baa Bar Black's?' he asks in disbelief.

'Yes, it's stupid, but focus. So I want you to take Deano there—'

'Rubes, I know I said I'd help, but I'm so busy with rehearsals. The play opens tomorrow night. Plus, do you not think you're taking this too far?'

Wow, Millsy the moral compass, that's hilarious. I ignore him.

'I want you to go there and "bump" into her. During our double date, she couldn't take her eyes off him. I think because he's rich and famous, that one-ups Nick. She'll show her true colours and ditch Nick for Deano in a heartbeat.'

'OK, I still think you're taking things too far, but I'll do it if you're sure it's what you want …'

'I'm sure,' I tell him. Because I am. Because even if Nick doesn't want me, he can't wind up with her.

'OK then. I'll do it. Because I know I made stuff worse for you – I just hope this won't make things *even* worse.'

'At this stage, I don't think anything could get worse,' I tell him.

'That's her,' I hear Rita say. I look over and she's pointing at me. Two PCSOs are standing either side of her.

'Hello, boys, are you here to put me in handcuffs?' I joke.

Millsy sniggers.

'No, Ruby, they're here to escort you off the premises. You're fired.' I frown at her, confused.

'Wait, what? Why am I fired? And why do I need escorting?'

'Yeah, come on, Rita, what did she do that was that bad?' Millsy asks.

'She assaulted a customer,' she tells him.

'When?' I gasp. 'No way.'

'I was told that you poured hot coffee into the lap of a customer,' she tells us. Oh shit – Deano.

'He wasn't a customer, he was my boyfriend, I was dumping him and he called me fat. I checked to make sure my drink wasn't hot first – who complained? Was it him? I bet he's just being petty.'

'Ruby, I received several complaints from customers. I told you that you were on your final warning, so now you're out. These gentlemen are here to stop you making another scene or getting violent.'

'I wasn't being violent, I was trying to fuck up his jeans,' I protest.

'Either way, I can't have you acting like that around customers. So get your things and leave.'

I stare at her for a second. She looks so pleased with herself. 'You know what, stuff your job,' I tell her.

'Ruby, wait,' Millsy starts. 'Rita, come on, don't be so hasty.'

'I'm sorry, Joe. She's done too much.'

I whip off my apron and grab a brownie from behind the counter, taking a big bite out of it before marching out of the shop.

'I'll text you details about tonight,' I call back to Millsy.

'OK, sure,' he calls after me. 'You're a badass.'

I certainly feel like one. Although we'll see how badass I'm feeling when it's time to pay my bills.

Chapter 34

I suck my straw, taking in several mouthfuls of Mai-Tai before placing my drink back down on the table in front of me. I'm out on the terrace at Thin Aire – the only one out here tonight. I suppose because it's Sunday, it's not that busy tonight.

When I ran through the plan with Millsy earlier, I decided that it would probably be best if I kept out of Nick's way for a while, because I can't face an argument and I really don't know how to explain myself.

So here I am, all on my own, drinking cocktails and admiring the night sky. I love the view from up here, surrounded by tall buildings, pretty lights, the river – it's just stunning. I could Instagram my hand off up here.

"The Power of Love" by Frankie Goes to Hollywood starts playing through the speakers. I sigh, because it's one of my favourite songs.

I feel someone place a fur throw around my shoulders. 'Thanks,' I reply as I turn around. 'It's freez …'

My voice trails off. It's the fit Tom-Hardy-looking manager.

'Freezing? Yes it is,' he says with a smile. 'I figured you'd need this. No Deano tonight?'

'We broke up,' I tell him. That's all he needs to know.

'Oh, that's a shame,' he replies. 'I'm Marco, by the way.'

Oh, he would have a sexy name, wouldn't he?

'I'm Ruby,' I shake his hand. 'Nice to officially meet you.'

It's taking all my energy not to freak out – in fact, it's a miracle I'm forming sentences right now.

Marco takes a seat next to me.

'Fancy some company for a bit?' he asks.

I try not to show how surprised I am to hear him suggest that. Or how ecstatic I am. I just need to be cool.

'OK.'

But not so cool I'm as cold as this rooftop.

'So, have you had a good day?' he asks me.

'I got fired, actually,' I tell him. 'For assaulting a customer.'

Marco's eyes widen, but he laughs.

'OK, I need to hear this story,' he insists.

I tell him all about my break-up with Deano, even though they're sort of friends. Well, why not. If my friends were telling girls they were too fat I'd want to know so I could be ashamed of them too – obviously I'm not counting that time at Leeds Fest when the girl Millsy was hooking up with wanted to sit on his shoulders. Even for a strong dude like Millsy, there's just no way. And he did tell her tactfully. Sort of. He did also tell her that she had a face like a "punched lasagne" – however, she did spend most of the weekend covered in ketchup because she refused to eat anything that wasn't a hotdog. No wonder Millsy liked her.

'That's rough,' he tells me. 'Well, I think you're perfect as you are, so don't give it a second thought.'

'That's because I spend so much money here, I probably single-handedly pay your mortgage,' I joke. 'And you're welcome.'

Marco laughs.

'You're pretty funny, you know,' he tells me, gazing into my eyes.

'You're not so bad yourself,' I reply.

My God, his eyes are gorgeous. So dark, and deep. I feel like I could get lost in them.

'You seem like a pretty cool bird,' he tells me. 'You've never been that friendly with me before, I thought maybe you were a bit stuck up.'

I choke on my drink a little, making super unsexy spluttering noises. 'God no,' I insist. 'I'm just … shy until I get to know people.'

Not technically true. I'm not shy at all. I'm just an absolute loser around people I have epic crushes on.

'I like that,' he tells me. 'Girls can be too forward these days.'

'Yeah, I guess,' I reply.

'OK, I want to ask you out on a date, but I have to confess something first.'

'Go on,' I say cautiously.

'I'm only telling you this because you do seem like a really cool girl, and I wouldn't feel right hanging out with you without coming clean.'

I stare at him expectantly.

'Your mate came in earlier. Muscular dude, longish hair—'

'Yeah, Millsy,' I interrupt. 'Go on.'

'Well, he told me you were having a hard time dealing with some stuff, and he asked me to chat you up. He said something about showing you that there were other fish in the sea. He gave me £40, so I figured I could do it, no problem. But you seem cool, I don't know why he was worried.'

I take a few minutes to process this. It all makes sense now, the warm blanket that is lovingly placed around my always cold arms, by the man I have a crush on, on the terrace of my favourite bar, as one of my favourite romantic songs plays – Millsy is trying to play *me*.

'He should be worried,' I tell him. 'Because he's going to regret setting this up.'

'I think he was just trying to match-make,' Marco says in Millsy's defence. 'And it kind of worked.'

I think about it for a second. Before I had that dream about Nick, all I've ever fantasised about was the hot manager from

Thin Aire having his wicked way with me. Now he's here, talking to me, telling me he thinks I'm cool … and all I can think about is Nick. It's Nick that I want more than anyone.

'I'm sorry,' I start. 'I need to get home. This is just a lot to take in.'

'No worries,' he assures me. 'I get it, this must be weird. I didn't expect this either. But you know where I am, right?'

'I do, thank you,' I tell him, dashing off for the lift.

If a Tom Hardy lookalike can't win me over then, I'm sorry, no one can. I just hope that Millsy has stuck to the rest of the plan, because it seems like he's meddling, like he thinks he knows what is best for me – well he doesn't. So long as he's stuck to the plan, everything will be fine.

Chapter 35

It's 8 a.m. and I'm wide awake. I came home to an empty flat last night. I guess Nick is keeping out of my way too. Weirder still, I haven't heard from Millsy at all. I texted him last night and then again this morning, but I haven't heard a peep. Millsy is like me; his phone is never more than a few feet away from his body, so I know something is up.

As I ponder why on earth he might be avoiding me, my phone springs awake. It's a text from Millsy.

Millsy: At rehearsals. Speak later.

Seriously? That's all I'm getting? I'm not having that. If he thinks he can agree to plans and then go rogue, backstabbing me along the way, he can think again. It's like when Macbeth plans Banquo's murder – except worse, because now he's tainted my favourite Frankie Goes to Hollywood song *forever*.

I jump out of bed, throw on some clothes and before I know it, I'm marching up the road to the theatre. He thinks he can ignore me? No way, mate.

'Hello,' I greet the woman at the box office. 'My friend is rehearsing for *Macbeth* at the moment, but I really need to see him.'

'The director doesn't like to be disturbed,' she tells me.

'But it's an emergency,' I tell her, forging the most worried face imaginable.

'Wait here, I'll find out,' she says sympathetically.

'Take your time,' I say to myself as soon as she's gone. I glance around, taking in my surroundings. The stage is that way, so if I go through this "staff only" door … and along here …

I push open a double door and suddenly I'm in the wings of the stage, and I can see Millsy centre-stage, rehearsing. It only takes a few seconds for him to spot me before he starts fluffing his lines.

'Erm, can I just take a break, please?' he asks.

'Fine, hurry up,' the director barks.

Millsy rushes over to me.

'Rubes, what are you doing here? I'm working. Our opening night is tonight.'

'I know, but I needed to talk to you,' I insist.

'Didn't you have a good night last night?' he asks.

'Not really,' I reply. 'Not £40 worth, anyway.'

'Fuck,' he replies. 'Look, I just wanted you to see that there are plenty of men out there and that you shouldn't be so fixated on Nick.'

'We're best friends, Millsy. I can't believe you'd try to trick me like that. *Me.*'

'I'm sorry for the way I went about it, but I think it's for the best,' he assures me.

'What's for the best is if you tell me what happened last night,' I demand.

'Oh, Mr Mills, in your own time,' I hear the director call.

'Rubes, I've got to go, please,' he pleads.

I give him my best resting bitch face. 'You owe me.'

'OK, look, I did as you asked, I took Deano out, we "bumped" into Heather, we had a few drinks and, you're right, she was all over him. But then it seemed like they were getting on really well, like they really liked each other. We wound up going to a club – Saturn – until 3 a.m., so forgive me for not feeling on top form today, OK?'

'She was in a nightclub with you and Deano until 3 a.m.?' I ask in disbelief.

'Yes, but, look, we've got a problem: they kissed. Not only did they kiss, but the club photographer took a picture.'

'Holy shit,' I cackle. 'He led her astray. This is amazing. How do I get a copy of this photo?'

'You can't,' he tells me. 'The photographer puts them live on their Facebook page at midday. You can request them taking down, but only once they're live. So Heather is at home, waiting for it to go up so she can get it down ASAP.'

'Millsy, she's cheated on Nick. He has to know about this. I have to save this photo before it gets taken down.'

'Ruby, you can't. Look, if you just storm Nick with a photo of his girlfriend cheating on him, you're going to crush him. And he's going to go from loving her to hating her – but he's going to hate you too, because you couldn't wait to stick the knife in and twist it the second you had dirt on her.'

'Fair is foul and foul is fair,' I remind him.

'Stop quoting the Scottish play,' he snaps. 'Look, I know I was on board with this at the beginning when I thought we were just messing with him, but I'm worried about how obsessed with Nick you are. You're only going to hurt him too. It's wrong.'

'Wrong?' I echo. 'Wrong? What's wrong is you paying someone a measly £40 to hit on me. Wrong is Deano kissing Nick's fiancée. And wrong is you insisting on calling it the Scottish play when it's called fucking *Macbeth*.'

As I fling my arms out wildly for dramatic effect, I lose my grip on my iPhone. I feel it fly from my hand, and watch as it travels through the air in super-slow motion. Before I have the chance to warn him, it hits a stagehand in the face. He instinctively lets go of the rope he's holding and grabs his nose in pain. Suddenly, there's a deathly scream.

'What the fuck is going on?' the director shouts. As I peep

out onto the stage to see what all the commotion is, I realise that something has fallen from the ceiling and landed on Lady Macbeth's head.

'And that's why we call it the Scottish play,' Millsy tells me. 'Quick, get out of here,' he insists. 'Before you get in trouble.'

I hover for a second, holding eye contact. I don't know what to say to him.

'Ruby, seriously, go. You're going to be in big trouble if you don't.'

I dash from the theatre as quickly as possible, running all the way home because, about thirty seconds after I left the theatre, I realised I'd left my phone in there. If I'm going to have any chance of saving this photo before Heather has it removed, I'm going to need to get on my laptop and wait for it.

I get inside, switch on my laptop, load up Saturn's Facebook page and wait. Just fifteen minutes to go and the evidence of what a bad person Heather is will be all mine.

Alone with my thoughts, I think about what Millsy just said. Am I obsessed? OK, so I do want Nick for my own, but if Heather has cheated on him then surely he deserves to know. I know it's not going to feel good for him, when I just present him with a photo, but seriously, what else can I do? I can't turn a blind eye.

The door buzzes. Crap. Whoever this is, I need to get rid of them ASAP so I can get back to my post. I only have five minutes to spare now.

Whoever it is, I buzz them in, and hover at the flat door waiting for them. 'Deborah, hi,' I babble, surprised. 'What are you doing here?'

'Oh, Heather, it's such a mess,' she tells me, tears in her eyes. 'Arthur, Nick's dad, they think he's had some kind of heart attack. Is Nick not here?'

'I'm so sorry to hear that,' I tell her. 'He isn't, he's out somewhere.'

'I got the call while I was shopping in Harvey Nics. I'm headed straight back there. But I've got to pick up my grandkids on the way, and I've no one to leave them with, and I can't have them running around the hospital unattended – oh, it's such a mess.'

I place an arm around her, giving her shoulder a reassuring rub.

'Look, it's going to be fine. Your husband is in the right place, you're on your way over there, you'll be with him soon enough,' I reassure her. And then it hits me – exactly what I need to do. Well, I have two options: sit at my laptop and wait for the incriminating photos of Heather and Deano to go online, or help Deborah out when she really needs it. There's only one option really.

'I'll come with you,' I tell her. 'I can watch the kids while you figure out what's going on.'

'Are you sure?' she asks. 'He's at a hospital not too far from Ilkley. I'm driving over anyway.'

'Of course I'm sure,' I tell her. 'Just let me grab my coat.'

I close the lid of my laptop, grab a jacket and head for the door with Deborah.

OK, so I'm not going to get the smoking gun I needed to break up Nick and Heather, but some things are just more important.

Chapter 36

'I can't believe you've never seen *Button Moon* – it's a classic,' I insist. I'm sitting in a hospital waiting room with Megan and Sam, Nick's sister's kids. They're twins, aged nine, and they're beyond smart for their age. What they are lacking, however, is knowledge of decent kids' TV.

'I liked *Dora the Explorer* when I was little,' Megan tells me. 'But I'm too old for that now.'

'I'll never be too old for *Button Moon*,' I insist. And I still have the VHS to prove it – not that I have anything I can play it on.

'Is granddad going to be OK?' Sam asks.

'The doctors are taking care of him,' I assure him. 'You know how your Uncle Nick can fix anything? Well, the doctors here are just as good.'

'Once I fell off our slide and Uncle Nick glued my head back together. It was so cool, and my mum says I have a scar,' Sam brags.

'That's so awesome, can I see?' I ask.

Sam offers me his head, but I can't really spot anything. Still, I get excited.

'Whoa, that's so cool,' I tell him.

'You're good with them, aren't you?' Deborah observes. I'd no idea she'd crept up on us.

'Must be having the same mental age,' I muse.

'Oh, I assumed it was because you were a primary school teacher,' she replies.

'And there's that.'

'Anyway, Nick will be here soon. He can take over babysitting duties. You're welcome to stick around – you're family now after all. And I don't know what I would've done without you watching these two.'

'It was nothing,' I assure her. 'How's your husband?'

'He's going to be OK,' she assures me. 'They're just running a few tests.'

'I am so pleased to hear that,' I tell her sincerely. 'You get back to him; I'll watch the kids until Nick gets here.'

Deborah gives me a warm smile before heading back out into the corridor. As she passes the window around the corner, I notice her bump into Nick. She's telling him everything that's going on, which means I only have a few minutes to get out of here without him seeing me.

'OK, kids, your Uncle Nick is here, so I'm going to go. But it was so nice to meet you both.'

'See you soon,' Sam tells me.

'Yes,' Megan agrees. 'And I can't wait until you're my auntie. You're cool.'

I give them both a smile and pull them in for a group hug. 'Take care of each other,' I tell them.

I quickly dash for the door, hovering there for a second while I make sure the coast is clear.

'Heather has been amazing,' I hear Deborah telling Nick. 'Honestly, I couldn't have coped without her. You've got yourself a good one there.'

I make my exit from the hospital as swiftly as possible. Once outside, I flag down a taxi that's just dropped someone off.

'Any chance I can get a lift to the train station ASAP?' I ask.

'Sure, hop in,' the guy agrees. Within minutes, I'm on my way home.

I get out of the taxi and straight onto the train. As I get closer to Leeds, I notice how dark it's getting.

There's a couple sitting opposite me on the train, they've got to be in their late fifties/early sixties, and yet they're kissing like teenagers.

'We're celebrating our wedding anniversary,' the man tells me, his sentence interrupted with enough hiccups to confirm that they have celebrated well.

'Congratulations,' I reply.

'Eight years we've been married,' the lady tells me. 'But we actually first met when we were at uni.'

'Really?' I reply, too polite to seem uninterested in their story. Although that is quite a long gap before they actually got together.

'Our first year, I tried to chat her up – she rejected me.' The man laughs. 'And even during our second year, I saved her from a mugger – a proper Mills & Boon moment where I swept in and saved the day – still, she didn't want to know.'

His wife laughs and squeezes his hand.

'Your persistence paid off in the end, dear,' she reminds him.

'It certainly did.' He smiles.

'That's lovely,' I tell them, sincerely. 'What have you done to celebrate?'

'We've been out for dinner, maybe had a little too much to drink,' she giggles. 'Now we're just heading back into Leeds, few more drinks and then home. Do you live in Leeds?'

'I do,' I tell her.

'No work for me tomorrow,' she tells me. 'I'm a registrar. Births and deaths.'

'I bet that's interesting,' I reply.

'It is,' she replies, her face falling slightly. 'It can be a sad job, hearing everyone's stories, but a joyous one too. Watching life. People coming into the world, people going out – it's very humbling.'

I nod thoughtfully.

'What do you do?' she asks curiously.

'I, erm … I work in a coffee shop,' I lie. No point telling them I got fired this week. Telling them I work in coffee shop is less embarrassing than telling them I'm unemployed now … although that's the first time I've actually been embarrassed to admit what I do. Or did. Not because there's anything wrong with working in a coffee shop, but because I don't love it. Because I can't talk passionately about it like she does about her job. I do it because it's the absolutely bare minimum I need to do to survive. Not once have I ever hoped for better for myself, up until now.

'Well, everyone loves coffee,' her husband replies cheerily.

The conductor makes an announcement over the train speakers: 'We will shortly be arriving at Leeds Station, your final destination. Please remember to talk all belongings with you and thank you for travelling with us this evening.'

'Well, it was nice to meet you,' I tell them both as the train pulls in.

'You too, dear. Take care,' the lady tells me.

'Yes, you take care of yourself,' the man chimes in, struggling to his feet and heading for the door.

'Have a great night,' I call after them.

I step off the train and stroll towards the ticket barrier, the drunk couple still on my mind. They had to be in their mid-fifties at least, say they were eighteen when they met – that means it was nearly thirty years from when they met to when they finally got married. Thirty years! That's such a long time, so much of their lives that they've wasted apart when they could've been together and as happy as they are now.

I suppose you can't look at it like that, can you? If I were in a good mood, I suppose the lesson to learn here would be patience. Because I don't know what happened in the years between them being at uni and finally getting married, but his patience did pay off. They were meant to be together and they are now, even if it took a long time. Maybe that's just the way things are supposed to go sometimes, *que sera sera*, whatever will be will be and all that.

One thing that won't be, without a bit of help and a lot of apologising on my part, is my friendship with Millsy. He was right: I was getting too obsessed with this Nick thing, and showing him that photo really would've crushed him. He doesn't deserve that at all. And Millsy has been my friend my entire life, no man is worth falling out with him over.

I stand outside the theatre for a second, scared to go in. I know that the show is supposed to start within the next two hours, but hopefully there's time for me to have a conversation with my best friend.

Once inside the theatre, I overhear two members of box office staff talking.

'So Emma has concussion, she's still in hospital under observation,' the girl says.

'That's awful,' the boy adds. 'But wasn't she the understudy?'

'Yeah,' the girl replies. 'So basically the show can't go on.'

We have a saying in theatre, and that's that the show *must* go on, so if that means stepping up to the mark, so be it.

'Excuse me,' I address them both. 'I couldn't help but overhear your problem and I think I can help,' I tell them.

'Well, unless you know all the lines to this play, then I don't think you can,' the boy says.

'Not only did I play Lady Macbeth in high school, but my best friend is playing Banquo, and I've been helping him rehearse every day for the past couple of weeks, so, yeah, I think I can help you.'

'Oh really?' The boy laughs in disbelief. 'You don't look like a Shakespeare nut.'

'How now, my lord! Why do you keep alone,' I start. 'Of sorriest fancies your companions making …'

As I deliver my lines perfectly, I watch as the boy and girl just stare at me, stunned, then impressed.

'Let me get a message to the director,' the boy says excitedly.

'You do that,' I call after him.

Chapter 37

The last few hours have been a whirlwind of events, with more unexpected twists and turns than a Shakespearean tragedy.

The play must've been in big trouble because, before I knew it, I was plonked in front of the director with the promise that I could save the play. With literally no other option – and after a brief audition – he agreed to let me fill in as Lady Macbeth for tonight's show, and I have to admit, I've enjoyed every second of it.

After my dramatic exit scene, I dashed back to my dressing room to slip on my red dress, ready to step out on stage and take a bow.

The opening night was a triumph, if I do say so myself, with the audience loving it. I have to admit, it's really reignited my love for acting. Proper acting. Not lying to the librarian about why my books were returned late, not convincing bad Matcher dates that I had weird nipples so they'd give up on trying to see me naked, and not messing with girls in the street, telling them tall stories, simply because I was bored.

Finally back in my dressing room, I sit back in my chair and exhale deeply.

There's a knock on my door. 'Come in,' I call out.

'Hey you,' Millsy says cautiously. 'You're not going to give me a concussion like you did those two other people, are you?' he teases.

'Don't,' I insist. 'I feel bad enough as it is. Are they OK?'

'They're both going to be fine,' he assures me. 'But Emma has quit the play. Just a heads-up, the director is looking for a replacement as soon as possible. I suggested he might want to keep you on in the meantime – if not for the whole run. Nothing to do with you being my best friend, or newly unemployed – you earned it, Rubes. You were phenomenal out there. This is what you were born to do.'

'Thank you,' I tell him, climbing to my feet. 'I know it's going to seem sudden, but it's just reminded me that acting is my passion, and that this is something I want to pursue. I don't know why I was convincing myself otherwise.' I offer him my fist to bump. He hesitates for a second before doing it, but then he grabs me and he hugs me so tightly.

'Let's never fall out again,' he insists.

'Never,' I tell him. 'Unless it's over what to watch on Netflix or what topping to have on a pizza.'

'No chance of that.' He laughs. '*House of Cards* and pepperoni. That's the way it's always been, that's the way it's always going to be.'

'Amen to that,' I tell him.

'Right, well, I need to go outside and check out the groupie situation, so I'll see you in the bar later?'

'You will,' I reply. 'Enjoy your groupies.'

Millsy has no sooner left when there's a knock at my door again. 'What's the matter?' I ask. 'You need lube or something?'

I open the door expecting to see Millsy. Instead it's Nick. 'Lube?' he asks, stifling a laugh.

'Don't ask. Just come in,' I insist. 'What's up?'

'I called your phone looking for you. Millsy answered it, said you'd left it here. He also told me you were about to go on stage and perform. I was already back in Leeds, so he hooked me up with a seat.'

'So your dad is OK?' I ask.

'Now how did you know about my dad?' he asks with a smile.
'I … you mentioned it?'
'Give it up, Ruby,' he says. 'I know it was you at the hospital. First of all, because when my mum described Heather to me, it sounded nothing like her in any way. Not looks, not personality – and when she said good with kids, well I definitely knew it wasn't her. Her class hate her because she makes them eat vegan cookies and she tells them that sausages are evil.'

I laugh.

'I also knew that it wasn't her because when my mum finally got through to me and told me that "Heather" had stepped up to look after the kids, I was actually already with Heather, talking about our future.'

'Oh, well that's good,' I tell him, my heart breaking. 'Good to have a plan.'

'It is,' he replies, slowly making his way towards me. 'Because we realised that we weren't right for each other. I don't love her and, anyway, she's met someone who she reckons she's crazy about – who am I to stand in the way of that?'

'Yeah, I reckon she deserves him,' I reply, safe in the knowledge Heather is finally going to get her comeuppance now that she's saddled with dumb Deano the womaniser.

'Look, I can't really explain it,' Nick starts, seemingly wracking his brain for the right words. 'You've always annoyed the shit out of me.'

'Oh, thanks,' I say sarcastically.

'I mean, you're messy – so messy, you don't have a wardrobe, you have a mountain. You eat nothing but junk food, somehow managing to leave Coco Pops everywhere, even when you haven't eaten them. You swear even more than I do, you need a dating app intervention, but, more than anything else, you need to realise just how amazing you are. Without the scary tights. Without the hair colour that just isn't you. Without pretending to be whatever you think you need to be to impress people. Whether you're eating cake with your hands or setting our bathroom on fire, what I'm trying to say … it's not that something has changed, I think I've just finally realised what I knew all along. That when we met that first day and we hung out and we had a blast – that was us, and that was real. There is something between us. Other than piles of washing and Coco Pops,' he adds, defusing a little of the awkwardness.

I can't believe it. Ever since I had that first dream, I've tried so hard and been through so much to try and get Nick to like me, and yet everything I did just pushed him further and further away. As soon as I stopped trying to force the issue, things have fallen into place. It's like that couple on the train who finally got together after all those years – what will be, *will* be.

I place my arms around his neck as he wraps his around my waist.

'Well, seeing as though we're assassinating each other's character,' I start. 'Sometimes it seems like all you care about is the gym, and protein, and how the tea towels are folded before they're draped over the oven handle. You go to bed way too early, you get up way too early, you don't know what you've been missing these past few months because there are so many cool new bars and restaurants with things like steaks and burgers that you've been avoiding … but when I was upset, you took care of me, and when I need you, you're there. And when you got engaged to Heather, it broke my heart,' I confess.

'I just panicked,' he tells me. 'I didn't want to hurt her. Silly really, considering how easy she found it telling me she'd got off with some guy in a club. When I said I couldn't believe it, she offered to show me a picture. Can you believe that?'

'Shocking,' I reply. 'So what now?'

Nick runs his hands up and down my back before releasing me. The second he breaks contact with me, all I want is for him to touch me again.

'Now this,' he tells me, taking my face gently in his hands, kissing me. It's a long, lingering kiss and it makes the ones in my dream seem like the kind of peck you'd give your elderly auntie on the cheek.

'Then what?' I ask cheekily.

'Well, as much as I want to pick you up and lay you down on that sofa, I've heard you've got a three-date rule,' he teases. 'So I guess I'd better take you out on a date.'

I giggle.

'You heard right,' I tell him. 'Just let me get this Lady Macbeth dress off, and we'll head out.'

'Don't worry about it,' he assures me. 'You look good in red.'

Acknowledgements

I'd like to say a massive thank you to Sophia, George and the team at HQ for doing such a fantastic job with my books.

Huge thanks to my readers for taking the time to read and review my books. It means so much to me.

Finally, thank you to my wonderful family, and my amazing fella, for all the love and support. Couldn't do it without you.

The biggest shout-out of all has to go to every bad date I have ever been on – I cannot believe I shaved my legs for you, but thanks for all the inspiration.

Fallen in love with *Truth or Date*?

Discover *Drive Me Crazy*!

Another uplifting and laugh-out-loud romantic comedy from Portia MacIntosh.

Continue reading for a sneak preview of *Drive Me Crazy* …

Chapter 1

'We should get up.'

'Just five more minutes,' I plead as I snuggle closer.

'Two more minutes,' he negotiates. 'Someone will be round with the post any minute. Do you want them to see us like this?'

'Let them see,' I gasp. 'I'm too happy to care.' Of course I'm joking, and Will knows this.

For two peaceful minutes we just cuddle up, naked, in perfect silence. I have my head resting on Will's chest, gazing down at his bare stomach. He's starting to get a bit of a belly, the one a lot of men seem to develop as they approach the big 4-0. Will can't be blamed for "letting himself go" a little, though. As the managing director of his family's massive haulage company, he works tirelessly to keep the business running smoothly.

I use a finger to trace lines on his body, of where his six-pack used to be. His heart is pounding, but the gentle rise and fall of his chest relaxes me, quickly returning my own heart rate to normal.

I wonder what he's thinking right now. I often wonder what's going through his mind, and how often he thinks about me when we're not together.

'I'm starving,' I say out loud, although I'm pretty sure I only meant to think it.

'You're always starving.' He laughs. 'Sticking to the diet though?'

'Of course,' I lie. I mean, I am sticking to it for the most part, but it's so hard when you have to pass a branch of Millie's Cookies on the way home from work – that temptress still manages to seduce me every now and then.

Conscious of the tummy he's developing, Will is on a health kick at the moment, and knowing how much I love my junk food, he suggested I might like to join him. I suppose I was a few pounds overweight – and maybe this was his tactful way of telling me – so I agreed to do the same. Oh, how I wish I hadn't now.

'OK, fine, I'm getting up,' I say, although I make no attempt to move whatsoever. 'Can I get you a coffee?'

'Please,' he replies, also remaining in position. 'This thing wreaks havoc on my back. It's not very comfortable, is it?'

'Well, it's a desk, not a bed,' I say as I pull myself upright. 'It's not supposed to be comfortable.'

'Maybe we should get a bed for in here. Well, not a bed, that would seem odd.' He laughs as he glances around his office, as though trying to figure out where one could go. 'Maybe a sofa bed?'

'Yeah, maybe,' I reply, unable to fake even a little enthusiasm. He makes it sound like we're a married couple, picking out furniture for our home.

A few more seconds of silence together, me alone with my thoughts and him with his – that is until a knock on the door breaks us from our thoughts. We know the drill.

'Damn,' Will says quietly as he wrestles on his trousers before calling to whoever is behind the door: 'One minute, please.'

'It's locked, right?' I ask as I hurry on my underwear, then my dress. 'Yes, it's locked, but that still makes us look bad.'

This isn't our first moment like this; you think we'd be better at it by now.

'No rush, Mr Starr.' It's Caroline, his secretary. 'Except I've got the post for you, and it's quite heavy.'

'She's not going anywhere,' he whispers to me, panic in his voice.

I exhale deeply. Being romantically involved with your boss is not all it's cracked up to be, especially when you have to keep your relationship a secret.

Will and his wife, Stephanie, were in love, once upon a time. They got married, had a couple of kids but then, as Will moved through the ranks of the company, eventually reaching the top spot when his dad retired, they just fell out of love and decided to call it a day. The thing is, Will is very much the face of the family business, and despite the company being huge, they really play up the family angle. Now that Will is in charge, they paint him as a good guy, a family man, so leaving his wife and two young kids simply because he didn't want to be with his wife anymore would not have painted a pretty picture. And in a way Will was lucky that Stephanie agreed to pretend they were still together, to keep up appearances, and to keep Will's/the firm's wholesome reputation intact. So, despite Will and Stephanie's understanding, divorce isn't on the cards any time soon, and if Will were to be caught sleeping with his assistant, it would ruin him. So it isn't exactly unusual for us to sneak around and keep our relationship a secret.

'You're going to have to hide,' he snaps at me in a whisper – like this is *my* fault.

'Hide?' I ask in disbelief. I've never had to hide before. 'Where?'

'Under the desk,' he instructs, pushing me under the large, oak desk in the centre of his office.

'You're effing kidding me?' I ask, and Will shoots me a look – I know that he doesn't approve of swearing, but I thought that might be OK given the circumstances. I can tell from the look in his eyes that he is dead serious. 'Fine.'

Down I go, underneath his desk. I watch as Will straightens up his tie before bushing his suit down, exhaling deeply as he heads for the door. I am just about to tuck myself away when I realise that I forgot to put my stockings back on. I spy one of them on the floor, and it's within arm's reach so I grab it. No sign of the other one, but there's nothing I can do. Will is opening the door.

'Good morning, Caroline,' he says breathlessly. 'I thought you were at the doctor's this morning?'

'I was,' she replies. 'I've been, all is well. I know I took the morning off, but I thought there's no sense in waiting until the afternoon to come in – may as well make myself useful. I see Candice is running late.' Caroline sighs. 'Ah well, best she has a lie-in. I think that one is getting a lot of late nights at the moment.'

I can only see Caroline's feet, but I feel my eyes narrow as I shoot them a death stare.

Sweet Caroline (that's what I call her – because she isn't) may just be an evil genius, and were I not the target of her evil master plan to oust me from the company, I might actually be impressed by the way she operates. You see, Sweet Caroline is nothing but sweetness and light to me – in front of other people. Sometimes, I even hear her saying nice things about me to other people, making caring excuses for any mistakes I might make, or excusing my lateness for me like she did today (by making it sound like I'm out partying every night). This means that, to everyone else at the firm, Caroline *is* Sweet Caroline, but when it's just me and her she is horrible to me, and because I know her niceness is an act I cannot be nice back to her, or be nice about her to others. This leaves everyone else wondering why I don't like Caroline, because she's just *so* nice to everyone, and speaks *so* highly of me … I'm telling you, she's an evil genius.

There aren't too many female employees here, but Caroline is certainly the queen bee. As female employees come and go, she takes them all under her wing (everyone but me, who she took an instant dislike to) and I'm guessing she drips poison in the ears of them all, because none of the women seem to like me. Thankfully, I always have Will on my side.

'You look warm,' she observes, not suspiciously as far as I can tell, just curiously.

'Yeah, I was just getting a bit of exercise in,' he tells her, before laughing it off. 'Getting a bit portly in my old age.'

Oh, that was fast thinking. I'd probably be impressed were I not so incredibly mortified right now.

'I just bumped into Stephanie,' I hear Caroline say.

'What, she's here?' Will replies.

'No, no. I saw her at the doctor's – how is she doing? She looked a little peaky.'

'She's fine, she's fine,' Will babbles, instantly arousing my curiosity. I get that Will is sticking around for his kids, and because it's a smart business move, but it never occurred to me that he might be staying around for other reasons – is his wife ill? I mentally pinch myself as Will and Caroline chat about work stuff. It's this silly situation; it makes me paranoid and needy and feel just plain bad about myself. I know that we're not doing anything wrong and that it's only a matter of time before we can be together properly – Will assures me every day – but on days like today, when I'm hiding underneath a desk clutching one of my stockings, it doesn't feel like I'm not doing anything wrong. I feel very much like the "other woman" that I am most certainly not.

As Will and Sweet Caroline chat, I watch them from my hiding place – well, I watch them from the knees down, like the opening sequence of *The Bill* circa 1985. That's when I notice my other stocking, caught on the heel of Caroline's shoe.

I slowly peep out from under the desk, in an attempt to quickly grab the offending hosiery before it can be spotted. I pull it, but it's not budging. It's well and truly caught on her heel. I give it a hard yank and it finally comes loose, but Will spots me out of the corner of his eye.

'Come here,' Will instructs Caroline, pulling her close for a hug. 'I'm glad you got on OK at the doctor's.'

'Oh, thank you,' Caroline replies brightly. I quickly crawl back underneath the desk and Will finally releases her and she leaves.

With the door closed, Will locks it before leaning back against the wall and breathing a sigh of relief so huge, I practically feel my hair blow in the breeze.

'That was a close one,' Will says.

'Yep,' I reply, scooching out from underneath the desk. I feel deflated at having to hide, but I do my best to remain positive.

'You want to be careful hugging Caroline like that.' I laugh brightly. 'She'll have you for sexual harassment.'

'Candice, that's not funny,' my lover ticks me off. 'That was too close. Way too close. And when she mentioned Steph, I thought she might be here.'

'Is Stephanie OK?' I ask, curiosity getting the better of me.

'Yes,' Will replies quickly, 'why do you ask?'

'Just that Caroline said she'd seen her at the doctor's … I was just checking.'

I smile sweetly, hoping that if my face looks happy then my mood will follow. The truth is, I'm starting to grow tired of our situation. I mentioned this to Will recently and he promised to do something about it.

'Your stomach is looking a little … full today,' Will observes, changing the subject.

'What?' I run my hands over my tummy self-consciously. 'Oh, I ate a bagel yesterday – wheat makes me a bit bloated,' I explain.

'Wheat isn't great for the body,' he reminds me. I know that he's just trying to help me keep healthy and in good shape, but sometimes it feels like criticism and it makes me feel self-conscious.

Will walks over to me and helps me up from the floor.

'Don't be grumpy,' he says, pinching my cheek between two of his fingers as he flashes me a smile. I am weak for him; I wish I wasn't, but I am. 'Everything will be better next week, when we have our little holiday from the world.'

I feel myself defrost almost immediately and my forced smile blends seamlessly into a real one. I cannot wait for my holiday with Will. It's going to be an entire week, just the two of us. We won't need to sneak around or hide, no sex on uncomfortable desks, we can hold hands in public and go out for dinner together – all the little things that couples take for granted. It's going to be pure bliss, and the mere mention of it appeases any doubts I may be having about our relationship. I just want things to be normal, and this holiday is going to be a glimpse of that. Depending on how it goes, I think this will be make or break for us, which just makes me all the more determined to make sure things are perfect.

I examine my stockings before I put them on and realise that the one I yanked from Caroline's shoe is laddered. I toss them in the bin. It'll have to be bare legs today. Thankfully I keep on top of waxing them, or I'd have been in big trouble.

'So, how about that coffee?' he reminds me as he starts tapping away on his laptop. 'And, Candice, maybe put those in a bin somewhere else. And make sure no one sees you leave.'

'Sure,' I reply, grabbing them from the bin before heading for the door. He isn't exactly in my good books after making me hide under his desk, but that combined with the fact he now expects me to reach into the bin …! If we were a normal couple I'd be able to tell him to get his own fucking coffee. I've no choice today, though. He is my boss, after all.

Dear Reader,

We hope you enjoyed reading this book. If you did, we'd be so appreciative if you left a review. It really helps us and the author to bring more books like this to you.

Here at HQ Digital we are dedicated to publishing fiction that will keep you turning the pages into the early hours. Don't want to miss a thing? To find out more about our books, promotions, discover exclusive content and enter competitions you can keep in touch in the following ways:

JOIN OUR COMMUNITY:

Sign up to our new email newsletter: http://smarturl.it/SignUpHQ

Read our new blog www.hqstories.co.uk

𝕏 https://twitter.com/HQStories

f www.facebook.com/HQStories

BUDDING WRITER?

We're also looking for authors to join the HQ Digital family! Find out more here:

https://www.hqstories.co.uk/want-to-write-for-us/

Thanks for reading, from the HQ Digital team

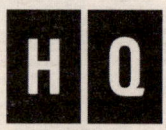